A BETTER LIFE

A Better Life

A Novel

Norma Murphy

Go Diane,
With joy and gratitude—
Enjoy the story!
Norma
10-26-19

Cover photograph by Matthew Blodgett

Cover design by Jason Blodgett

ISBN No. 9781727602296

For

Ava

Madyson

A.J.

Leah

and Savannah

Chapter 1

They are silent for most of the drive home, the volume of their day finally, thankfully turned down. Jenny crosses her arms and hugs herself, not sure what she should be feeling. She tries to be hopeful, that she did the right thing, that Gene isn't mad at her, that they don't get caught. As she rocks a little she stares straight ahead at the uneven road with its patches and swirls of black tar, takes a deep breath that releases in jagged pieces.

Cars parked along the street are mostly gray or faded blue-green. Clouds the color of concrete press down, everything forming the beginning of a black and white movie, everything in slow motion except Jenny and her thoughts.

Jenny takes a quick glance at Gene, focused on driving, thinking his own thoughts, then she turns around towards the back of the van. The little girl sleeps on her side, behind Gene, covered by the flag he keeps draped over the back of the driver's seat. The girl's mouth is open like she is surprised. Sleeping kids should look more peaceful than that. Jenny tries to imagine what it will be like when the girl wakes up. It will probably be hard for her, being born into a whole new world.

Jenny hasn't told Gene yet about seeing the face of Jesus last night and how she knew it was a sign. It scared her at first, but Jesus has always scared her. He is supposed to. Jenny learned young about the fear of God from her mother and from the old women in the neighborhood who sat on the green benches in the shade and talked about sin, and of course from the nuns in first and second grade. Not in public school, though. Kids there hardly ever mentioned Jesus or God or church, and if they did it was just to say his name like it didn't mean anything but a swear. *Jesus Christ.* Or to repeat jokes about priests and altar boys. As if that was funny. But listening to them helped her get a new perspective so she wasn't so scared all the time, though it still takes a conscious effort not to completely open herself up to Jesus and let the fear take over because even the fear feels like ultimate and unconditional love.

She loves watching Gene, so calm behind the wheel, always in control of his emotions and sometimes hers. Jenny would give anything to know what he is thinking right now, but she asked him so many times when he got back from Kuwait, whenever he got quiet for too long, he finally said not to ask him anymore and he meant it. He doesn't like it when she tries to get into his head.

When he turns to her for a second, he raises his eyebrows and gives her a serious smile. He is thinking of something good. Jenny takes a deep breath and gives him a hint of a smile back so he will think she has good thoughts, too. She wants them to be one of those couples who know each other so well they don't need words, and she hopes it happens soon.

Sometimes Gene makes her think of Jesus, the way he gets into her thoughts any time, the way he knows everything she's thinking. She tries to be in control of her thoughts, keep them as pure and simple as she can. But she can't help the shadows crowding in when she lets her guard down, the vague accusation that she is living her life all wrong. She reminds herself and whoever is listening that Gene is all she ever wanted and here they are living together, as happy as anyone.

There is no way of knowing for sure whether seeing the face of Jesus was a sign of a blessing to come or a warning, but it surely means something. Right now it seems like it might be a blessing, but Jenny knows as well as anyone how fast life can take a turn.

They pass a bright yellow house, square and neat, with a *For Sale by Owner* sign out front. The phone number is too small and they go by it too fast anyway. Jenny wonders how much a house like that would cost.

They pass a gas station, $3.85 a gallon for regular. Gene used to get upset whenever they passed a gas station. Just before he went in the service and for a while after he came home, he talked about the Middle East and the oil and the politicians and all the boys getting killed so the rich bastards can get richer, but now she just notices how his eyes get dark as his memories try to move him to another time, another place. But when Jenny puts her hand on his leg or strokes the back of his neck, he returns to her.

She has saved him. She is the reason he is getting over everything. Even if he doesn't say it. His family gave him zero support when he got back, when he didn't know what to do because his whole world changed by him being over there, seeing how the people lived like animals and all the kids in the service trying to make a difference, for what? He needed time to try and make sense of it, figure out what his place was and all they wanted was for him to forget about it, as if giving up two years of his life was nothing. All they had were empty words. *Put it behind you. Get on with your life. Find a job.* As if it were that easy. Turn off the memories and turn off the noise in your head.

Jenny is thankful he came back after two years, mostly in one piece. He acts calmer now than he was in high school. Jenny knows his wild ways are still there, but he keeps them below the surface. In control. Most of him has come back. He is still her Gene but now there is also a part that wasn't there before, this dark part of him she can't quite reach and isn't sure she wants to.

They pass another house for sale on Gene's side, a brown house with a red door and a big yellow dog out front, just lying there in the shade. He looks up at them as they go by but doesn't bark. She always wanted a dog like that. The house isn't big or fancy. It would be perfect. That could be their house and their dog. That could be their life.

Jenny isn't in a hurry to get back to their apartment. It feels good to ride around and look at houses. "Can you slow down just a little?" she asks.

He stays focused on the road, even though there is no one else around. "We're fine."

The last time they were stopped for speeding he told the cop he was a vet, just back from his second tour. A small lie. He would have done a second tour if they had let him. The cop nodded then studied Gene for a second, glanced at Jenny then let them go. Just a nod, like a secret code. No questions, no license or registration, not even a warning, as if he knew it would do no good to tell a vet to be

4

careful. They lucked out that time and now Gene thinks he's invincible. That's one thing that hasn't changed since high school.

He takes a left at the yellow blinking light, cutting off a white SUV that had slowed down before the intersection just enough to make Gene go. He senses any hesitation and takes advantage, always ready. Jenny sees the look of surprise, then anger on the driver's face, a woman not much older than her with a cell phone pressed against her ear. Everyone has a cell phone pressed against their ear and all they think about is themselves and what they have to say. Their conversations are so important and interesting they need to have them in public. How can people have so much to talk about, so much to say? What could be so important? Jenny wants nothing to do with cell phones.

"I heard on the news the other day that cell phones cause brain cancer." She might have already told him this, or he could have told her.

Gene keeps his eyes on the road and says nothing, but Jenny knows he heard her because he frowns. Lost in thoughts. That's okay.

They are still about twenty minutes from their apartment and Gene should have turned right, but Jenny doesn't mention it. He knows where he is going. She opens her window, takes a deep breath. The rush of the wind and the sounds of the outside world fill the van. Car engines and horns, a buzz saw somewhere, a person shouting for someone to stop it.

She puts her window back up, then turns to face Gene, always amazed by how he can be so careful and reckless at the same time. He checks the mirrors, the speedometer and gauges, the mirrors again. Just a quick flick of his eyes, every detail recorded in his mind, ready to tell you exactly how things are if he needs to. He takes different routes home when he is hyped about something. Adventure mode. She can tell from his silence and the way he grips the wheel and the way his eyes scan the road that they are in this together, everything happening just as it's supposed to, without any questions or need for explanations. They pick up each other's ideas and intentions so naturally.

When Jenny glances back again the little girl is sitting up, rubbing her eyes the way kids do. She doesn't cry right away, not until Jenny climbs in back and reaches for her. As soon as she gets close and touches her arm the girl starts screaming and Jenny notices how tiny she is, how pink and delicate her lips are. The girl is only about two or three, her face so pale like she never gets outside. Kids should get to play outside. Her eyes are dark brown like Jenny's, staring into her face, waiting for Jenny to do the right thing, to say just the right thing, but Jenny doesn't know exactly what that is.

The girl looks around now as she cries and her shoulders lift with each breath like she's a little bird trying to fly away. She stares at the back of Gene's head, then beyond him to the windshield. Jenny is afraid for a second the girl will escape; maybe she is supposed to. But when the girl kicks the flag away and tries to get up, Jenny holds her down. She needs to keep her safe. That's what this is all about in the first place.

"Tony," the girl wails. "Tony."

It surprises Jenny that she doesn't ask for mommy or daddy. "Who's Tony?" she asks, but the girl just cries and cries and then Jenny isn't positive Tony is what the girl actually said. Maybe she did say mommy.

Jenny tries to scoop her up in her arms. She just wants to hold her like she used to hold her doll in the night so she wouldn't be afraid. Whatever happened to that doll? Kathy. She called her Kathy and she was her best friend for a while. The girl is scared and Jenny needs to show her there is nothing to be scared of, nothing to cry about. She puts her arms around her, pulls her close and rubs her back. She won't tell her too much right now, won't tell her yet she is going to have a new life or that today is her birthday. Or maybe she should. Kids love birthdays.

"It's okay, honey. We're here to take care of you. You're safe now." All the time she talks, she rubs the girl's back like her grandmother rubbed Jenny's back when she was upset.

The little girl pushes away as if Jenny is trying to hurt her, as if she has done something wrong. She cries louder and calls for Tony again. "My want Tony." Her face is angry and red and afraid and she definitely said Tony.

Jenny liked her better when she was asleep. "Tony's not here. We're taking care of you for him." That was true.

The girl's crying is an awful sound, coming from somewhere deeper than Jenny has ever been able to go. She doesn't like crying and neither does Gene. The sound pierces Jenny's brain, but she manages to force her mouth into a smile to hide her anger and hurt. She keeps her voice calm, holds the girl tight as she squirms and pushes away. The girl has no idea she should be thankful, that Jenny has saved her life.

"You're fine, honey. Tell you what, we can go find Tony, okay? Shhh. Tony is our friend and we'll see him soon, okay?"

"What are you telling her? Who the hell's Tony?" It is the first thing Gene has said about the girl since they drove away, the first time he has acknowledged she is even there. His angry voice surprises her.

Jenny puts her hands over the girl's ears. "I want her to trust us. I want her to feel safe. I mean she is safe but she doesn't know it. Do you think Tony could be her father? Why would she call him Tony? Maybe it's her stepfather. Or just her mother's boyfriend. That's more likely. It's a good thing we were there. We saved her." As Jenny says this she is not sure what's true, not sure at all exactly what they are doing with this screaming kid in their van, but there are too many things to figure out and keep straight, too many things to remember.

It feels like she is back in school. She just needs a little time to think and there was never enough time for her to sort through all the things she had to remember and make sense of. The time was always up before she was finished. She wouldn't be surprised if Gene pulled over and let this screaming girl out of the van. *Okay, time's up.* They could just drive back to their lives, but their lives are already changed because it's too late now to give her back even if they wanted to. He knows it's too late.

"We saved her, right?"

"We?"

Jenny is confused now. She felt so sure just a minute ago, but here she is holding onto a strange little girl who doesn't want to be there, who is actually afraid of her, and she is not at all sure what they are doing. "Do you have any more speed?"

Gene looks in the rearview mirror and slows down a little, pulls a joint and lighter out of his shirt pocket, lights it and takes a long hit before he offers

8

it to her. "We're almost home. Relax. You don't need any more speed."

Jenny takes a deep hit, holds it in and feels the smoke fill her lungs and her brain, feels it settle her nerves. Now the girl is screaming "No!"

No what? Jenny exhales a cloud around them, hoping it will calm them both. She takes another hit and passes it back to Gene.

Holding the girl close, one arm around her tiny waist and the other around her shoulders, Jenny scoots back, keeps the little girl on her lap and leans against the wall of the van. She thinks about what a morning they had, a morning that feels like forever. Cashing her last unemployment check, scoring the weed, breakfast at a diner they have never been to. Kitty's or Katie's? Three or four or five cups of coffee, blueberry pie with vanilla ice cream. Gene had a couple nips and poured them in their coffee as soon as the waitress turned away. He always knew the perfect thing to do in any situation, always knew her needs even before she did.

And now they have this little girl. It feels good to hold her now that she has stopped fighting. She's still crying, just a whimper now, like a little puppy. She shouldn't be so sad.

"I won't hurt you, honey. We're taking care of you. Why are you crying? I told you there's nothing to cry about." It's unbelievable. She has an actual child in her arms. A tiny thing, soft skin and little bird bones and all she wants is to be held and all Jenny wants right then is to hold her, keep her safe. She isn't sure where they are and doesn't care.

The speed is wearing off and Jenny closes her eyes, feels the burn behind them and tries to remember the last time she slept. What night was it? She leans her chin on top of the girl's head as she rubs her back and thinks of how nice it would be to change places with the girl, to have someone rubbing her back and loving her. She takes a deep breath and tries to relax into everything but then nerves crawl to the surface and all Jenny wants is to stop moving, get out of the van and in their apartment with the door locked and the curtains closed, in their own world. That's where they can relax and think and figure things out.

Jenny listens to the power of the engine, the humming of the tires, feels the tiniest pebble, every little bump and pothole. Just them and the road, that's all her senses hold right now. Then thoughts pour in, filling her head with images and amazement. Less than an hour ago it was just the two of them; now they have a child. Less than an hour ago it was just her and Gene and their biggest decision was what they would get for beer, if they wanted tequila or vodka. That was their only concern for the day and now they have all this responsibility. Here they are, saving this little girl's life like guardian angels.

When it started happening, when things were in motion, it was like the beginning of a movie. She expected Gene to stop it, but now he is as caught up in it as she is. And the beauty of it, the absolute beauty, is that it wasn't planned. Or maybe it was, but not by her or Gene. There was the hand of Jesus right there. It happened just the way it was supposed to, and looking back Jenny would do everything exactly the same. Bonnie and Clyde. Jenny and Gene.

The little girl squirms out of her arms and starts crying again. "My go home."

Jenny lets her go. Give her some space. Jenny is not a fighter. The girl crawls to the back corner of the van and just stares at her with wet, angry eyes and after a minute she starts wailing again, as if

Jenny is the bad guy. She gets a little closer, but doesn't touch her. "What's your name, honey? Stop crying and tell me your name. There's nothing to cry about." The girl doesn't answer and Jenny isn't doing any good right now by being in her face, so she climbs up front with Gene, puts on her seat belt and turns on the radio.

"I'm not listening to that screaming much longer." Gene's voice is even and hard and Jenny wants to ask what he will do to stop it, but she just turns up the radio, checks the side mirror. No one behind them.

"Maybe we should get her a Popsicle or something. A lollipop. That might make her feel better."

"You think that would make it all better? A lollipop?" He laughs his nasty laugh that puts her in her place. He doesn't mean anything by it; it's just his way of reminding her he is in control.

"I just mean she's scared and it might calm her down. She doesn't know we saved her. She's too little to understand what happened and why we have her."

"And why do we?"

She thinks for a minute. "So she wouldn't die."

He doesn't respond and Jenny knows he is thinking about it and coming up with a plan now. This is what he does, always planning so he can be two steps ahead of her and she doesn't have to worry about anything. She takes a deep breath and lets it out, feeling calmer when she sees St. Anne's up ahead on the right. The cross on top is so sad. "I saw the face of Jesus today." She hadn't meant to tell him about it yet, but once the words are out there it's all right. She feels lighter and holier and everything will be fine. Jesus has a plan.

Gene finally looks at her and smiles. There is something behind the smile Jenny can't quite read, but at least she got him to smile.

"Go ahead and laugh but I did. He was looking right up at me when I was scraping the plates into the trash last night. I stopped as soon as I saw it, but it was too late. There I was, watching beans and pork-chop bones fall right onto his face. I felt terrible, but it was okay. Somehow I knew it was okay. What do you think it means?"

Gene shakes his head and laughs at her. "What do I think it means? You serious?" He laughs hard, just for a few seconds, then he presses the button on the radio to a country song and turns it up. Good country. Johnny Cash. *Because you're mine. I walk the line.*

Jenny doesn't know how to feel when he laughs at her like that but it is something like shame. It makes her think of her father, the time he laughed at her like that. Until he saw she was serious and stopped laughing and everything changed.

She pushes that down and stares at the side of Gene's handsome face. He looks good when he hasn't shaved for a couple days. Maybe he is not so much laughing at her as being amused by her. She hopes he loves her enough not to really laugh at her.

She turns towards the window to take in everything they pass. The street is not familiar but they must be almost home. They have been driving for a long time. She puts her window down and feels the rush of warm air mixing with the air conditioning. He will tell her to put it up in a minute.

She likes to look at people's houses and yards. They will have a house one day, maybe that yellow house back there. The yards they pass are either open to the street or there are chain link fences low

12

enough for anyone to climb over if they wanted. There is a blue plastic slide sitting in a plastic pool full of dirty water, two white plastic chairs sitting empty on each side of the front door. Everything is made of plastic. Gene calls their credit card plastic. She can't remember if he gave it back to her after he bought the beer and cigarettes, but doesn't think so. She likes to hold onto it, likes to have one thing she is in control of.

The girl has stopped crying and is lying on her side in the corner, her legs pulled up to her chest and her fingers in her mouth. Maybe she is still crying, but at least she is quiet.

Jenny stares at the side of Gene's face, his long sideburns and the way his hair already reaches his shoulders and curls at the bottom. He hasn't cut it once in the four months he has been back.

"I still can't believe she was right there, right on the street all by herself like that, like they were just asking for someone to take her. Do you think they left her there hoping someone would take her?"

"There's a lot of stupid people out there. And there's a lot of people shouldn't have kids. Including us."

"But you don't mean forever, right? We will have kids someday, right?"

"Not today."

"But someday." She remembers the time she thought she was pregnant and how happy it made her. Even though she was only sixteen and anyone else probably would've been scared, it made her happy to think she had Gene's baby inside her and she could imagine a whole beautiful life together. She was going to wait two weeks then do a home pregnancy test, and when she told Gene he would be happy, too and everything would be settled. They would be settled. But she was only four days late, devastated when she felt the cramps and saw the blood. Those four days were full of dreams. She believes there was a baby inside her then, a baby she lost, and she believes it was a girl. This could be a second chance.

"If all we did was report it, nothing would happen, right? The people who left her there would get a slap on the wrist. A warning not to do it again. There would be no consequences and nothing to stop them from leaving her alone in the car the next time they feel like it. We definitely did the right thing, taking her instead of reporting it. You know that guy with the pony tail? He must have been the father, in there flirting with that girl, buying lottery tickets. Who knows what would happen the next time? She could die."

"Since when do we report people? Since when do we call the cops on people?" Gene is staring at her now, waiting for the right answer.

"We don't. I'm just saying, that's what people are expected to do if they see something like that, just call the cops and stand back and watch them do nothing, right?"

Gene nods once, focuses again on driving. They take a right at the gas station and now they are almost home. They pass the three duplexes all exactly alike on the outside then she can see their apartment building on the left, not where she wants to live forever, with other people's sounds and smells.

Jenny glances in the back. The girl looks like she is asleep again and Jenny tries to remember what they have to eat at home. "Let's get something to eat for when she wakes up." The store isn't far from

14

here. "I could run in and get a few things. Or you could, if you want me to stay with her."

"We're not stopping anywhere. We're going home and figuring out what we're gonna do with her."

He isn't angry, but close. He is definitely done talking now. He needs time to think.

Chapter 2

The car had been parked almost right in front of the package store. A dark blue Plymouth Fury, like they used to see at Salisbury Beach on Friday nights. Classic Car Night. The same guys or couples out showing off their shiny Mustangs and Thunderbirds and Vettes, cars they don't make anymore and will never make again. Someone obviously took care of the Plymouth, which was why she noticed it in the first place, how clean and shiny it was, even the hub caps polished. Then she noticed how open and vulnerable it looked with all the windows down, how everything was exposed and inviting to anyone walking by.

She and Gene had been up all night, which made her super perceptive and sensitive, so the smallest details became as clear as if they were under a magnifying glass. It was warm beginning-of-summer air, light and easy to walk through. Jenny looked up at the sky as a cloud passed in front of the sun, a small thin cloud she could see through. Her sunglasses tinted everything just right.

They had left the van down the street just past the diner, and started walking as if they knew where they were going or had somewhere to be. Jenny had one arm looped through Gene's and she swung the other one, feeling all pleased with life when a couple crossed the street and walked just ahead of them. They were both young and skinny and wore baggy jeans and tee-shirts with faded words and they didn't seem to notice Jenny and Gene behind them.

"Are you kidding me?" the girl yelled. Jenny got the feeling the girl didn't know where she was.

"What?" The boy was angry, too.

"That was our rent money, you idiot." She shook her head and kept walking, barely keeping up with him.

The boy shrugged and walked ahead of her easily, as if she didn't matter, as if she didn't exist.

"That was our rent money," she said again. Her voice wasn't as strong. "You knew that." She ran up to him and grabbed his arm and Jenny stared at them as the man shook the girl off and kept walking without another word, as if she was the one who spent the rent money.

Gene walked a little faster, veering around the girl who just stood there watching the guy walk away. Jenny kept up with Gene, turned to look at the woman, younger than she thought at first, then just tightened her grip on Gene's arm and wondered how people ever got to that point in a relationship and why anyone would stay.

They walked on, down the street and past the bank, not open yet. A kid who looked about fifteen was inside, punching numbers into the ATM. He didn't look up when they walked by. Gene didn't trust machines and Jenny didn't either. Still, she would like to know what it felt like to push in just the right numbers and have money slide out into her hand.

She supposed Gene had some money saved somewhere and was waiting for the right time to tell her, when they needed it, when they were ready to buy a house. Something saved from his pay when he was in the service. But she didn't know how to ask him; he would have to offer it. They had been living off her unemployment and his government check and they were doing okay. She signed her check over to him and he took care of the rent and the electric, booze and drugs, put gas in the van and gave her a twenty each week. They didn't spend much on food. It was too easy to get for free from the store or someone's car, plenty for the two of them, or they got burgers and fries at a drive-through, a large cheese pizza for eight bucks on Tuesdays.

Gene believed the government would take care of him after serving, but they didn't do much for a private with only one tour. He still put his life on the line and that should mean something. She knew he appreciated her helping out. It was the least she could do.

Gene was saying something about crashing soon, but Jenny wasn't ready yet so she gave him her sweetest smile and pretended she didn't hear him. He almost smiled back, put his arm over her shoulder. It weighed her down and made it harder to walk, but she automatically reached her arm around his waist and got in step with him. She still wanted a couple more hours. No crashing. Ease on down. A joint, a couple beers, a bowl of cereal, then bed.

He took his arm off her shoulder as they got to the store, a few yards past the Plymouth. It reminded Jenny of a police car. She bent down to look in the windows, noticed it was unlocked but no keys hanging in the ignition or lying on the seat. Not that she would steal the car, but she would have loved showing Gene a handful of keys right then. Whenever she saw keys in a car she grabbed them and threw them into some bushes down the street or into a trash can, sometimes down a sewer.

There were no keys or cash, but she grabbed the lighter on the dashboard, shoved it in the pocket of her jeans. Then she looked in the back for any shopping bags or boxes. A bag of food would be nice.

That's when she noticed the little girl. She turned to say something to Gene but he was at the door of the package store, reaching for the handle. She saw it all in slow motion.

"You coming?" Gene called.

Jenny straightened up, stepped back from the car and put her hands in her jeans pockets. "I'll wait out here."

"What do you want?"

"Anything. Everything." She smiled and watched him pull the door open and go inside.

That must have been the moment Jenny realized what she was about to do, what she needed to do, not just for herself, not just for the little girl, but for all of them, including the people who left her there. It wasn't an actual decision or something she thought out. Looking back, it doesn't seem like there was one specific moment, but a series of moments, everything running just below the surface, all her thoughts and reasoning and feelings, with some force guiding her, helping her do the right thing.

Jenny looked at the sleeping child, the little angel face turned towards her, so peaceful, even with her neck at such an uncomfortable angle. She turned and glanced at the window of the package store, with its signs advertising Seagram's and Corona and Budweiser. A cold beer would have been nice right then, something to take away the dry mouth and taste of coffee.

She could just make out a man inside talking to the woman behind the counter, pointing up to the rolls of lottery tickets hanging like colorful snakes. He was a short man, wearing a tee-shirt and cargo shorts, a skinny ponytail trailing halfway down his back. He must be the father, not even checking over his shoulder for a second to see if his little girl was okay. Across the street she saw two guys wearing white shirts and ties, one with a suit coat slung over his shoulder. They didn't pay any attention to her as they talked, didn't notice her at all. Everyone had their own life to live.

It only took a few seconds to open the car door. It was a heavy door but it didn't make a sound. The girl was buckled into a car seat and Jenny squeezed the plastic piece that held the straps in like she had done it a hundred times before. Then she pushed the button on the front, slid out the buckle. The straps over the little girl's shoulders were already loose and slipped off easily. Jenny picked her up and eased her out as carefully and gently as if she were her own sweet child. She weighed nothing at all and when the little girl rested her head on Jenny's shoulder and didn't wake up, maybe that was the moment.

She closed the door gently with her hip. It wasn't closed tight but it held, and Jenny walked down the street, away from the package store and Gene and the car and whoever left this little angel. She walked without looking back once, without letting herself think. Just feel. The rhythm of her steps, the slight weight of the child. Hold on. Not too fast, not too slow. If she can just get around the corner before anyone comes they will be safe.

The girl slept on. Kids can sleep through anything.

"Hey, wait up!" Gene was at her side with a freshly lit cigarette in one hand, a 24-pack in the other. "What the hell did you do? Who's that? Jesus, Jen." He was a little out of breath and she had all the energy in the world and wasn't about to slow down now.

"Shhh. Don't wake her up." Jenny walked a little faster, held the girl tight. "She was all alone in the car. Someone left her all alone in the back seat of that car. I think it was that guy in the store. Did you see that skinny guy with the ponytail? I think it was him."

"What guy? What car? What the hell. Jesus, Jen. I leave you alone for two minutes."

"Someone left her in that car. You know that nice blue one I was looking at? So I took her. She was all alone and I saved her." They turned the corner and she felt safer. She slowed down a little and tried to catch her breath.

"You just took her. Jesus. Whatever's not nailed down."

Jenny didn't understand why he was so angry, why he couldn't see what she was doing. "It wasn't like that. Well maybe it was in a way, but it was different, too. It wasn't like I thought about it or planned it. She was all alone. Remember how you told me once about having to react when you were in the war, how you had to make split-second decisions, life or death decisions, without thinking too much? That's what I did. I couldn't just leave her there."

She glanced at him and he still didn't look like he understood, not exactly, and she didn't really blame him, but the look in his eye said he was at least a little proud of her, almost the way he looked at her when she pocketed that bottle of gin. He had told her then she had skills.

Once they were across the street and around another corner Jenny knew the man wouldn't find them. He would have no idea, if he even bothered to look. "People think nothing of leaving their kids alone all the time," she said. "And as long as the kids aren't dead or they don't get caught they do it over and over again until something does happen. They go shopping for a couple hours or to a casino for the day then you're reading about some poor kid dying in a hot car."

She wasn't sure where all that was coming from, if it had been stored in her brain or her soul, but it was rising up from somewhere deep and pouring out of her. The more she talked the faster she walked, as if she knew exactly where they were headed, and Gene miraculously kept up with her and seemed like he was listening. It was amazing the little girl didn't wake up, but Jenny held her close, protecting her like she should be protected.

Gene took a final drag from his cigarette, threw the butt in the gutter and laid his hand on Jenny's shoulder, stopping her. She stepped back towards a brick apartment building and stared at him, her mouth so dry.

"You always get away with it, don't you?" His voice was low and calm, not angry or upset anymore, just stating a fact.

"Will you take us home?" She smiled. It seemed almost funny but she wasn't sure why. Usually when she took something it seemed funny like this at first because she got away with it, because it was so easy to fool people. Then she felt guilty afterward and wished she could go to confession so she could let it go and not think about it anymore, get forgiveness so it didn't weigh on her.

Of course Gene would laugh at her, say she didn't need to tell some priest what she had done. Mostly she told Jesus in her mind she was sorry and made herself believe it was enough. *What's done is done*, her grandmother used to say. And for the most part Jenny was able to make herself forget what she wanted to forget.

But this was different. It wasn't done; not even close.

Gene looked at her and the little girl in her arms like they were one person, someone he didn't know. "The van's back at the diner."

"We'll wait here." Jenny stroked the little girl's head, barely touching her hair, so soft and fine, the color of straw. She kept her voice a whisper and Gene did, too.

"Okay Jen. You got away with it. Now you can put her back. We're not bringing a kid home."

"We can't bring her back. How would we explain it?"

"Then just put her down here and someone will find her."

"We can't leave her here. That's worse than leaving her in that car. She was in trouble. In danger. She could have died. And now we can't just leave her here alone. We can't."

All of a sudden it felt like they were surrounded. People walking to work, kids walking to school, more traffic. Gene looked around and seemed to notice it at the same time. Everyone staring at them, walking towards them then past them, their eyes darting across her face like they were recording her image in their brains. But they didn't know. How could they?

Gene glared at her, trying to get into her head. Jenny was shaky and out of breath and the girl was thankfully, impossibly still asleep. For the first time in her life Jenny knew she was doing something important, something that mattered, something that would make her parents see beyond her mistakes and forgive her. She realized she couldn't let go of the little girl and that's when she started to cry. Not cry exactly, just tears spilling out of her eyes, out of nowhere. She hardly ever cried. It wasn't allowed when she was a kid.

"What?" Gene took a step back and looked around, then back to her. He didn't like crying either.

"Can you just get the van, please? And can you get a coke or something? She'll be thirsty when she wakes up. I'm thirsty, too." She was also getting scared but wouldn't tell him that.

"Stay right here. I mean it, Jen. Don't go anywhere. I'll be right back."

She watched him walk away, a man on a mission. The little girl was starting to get heavy and Jenny leaned against the side of the building and looked at her head, her little shoulders, and willed her to stay asleep just a little longer.

Jenny pictured the man coming out of the store with his beer and his lottery tickets, then his surprise and hopefully his guilt when he noticed the empty car seat. Did he know right away she was gone, or did he drive off before he even noticed? Maybe he was still in the store talking to that girl behind the counter. She imagined him calling the cops and saying what? *Well you see I left my little girl in the car for just a few seconds while I ran into the store for some milk. I was gone less than a minute and when I came out she was gone.* Liar.

Then Gene was back. And in the space of those few minutes Jenny knew she was doing the right thing. The only thing. A woman walking by with her own little girl smiled at her and Jenny looked her right in the eye and smiled back like it was a natural thing. Mother to mother. It was a day of connections. A life changing day.

Gene got out of the van and slid open the side door. It was almost like Jenny walked on air, smooth and slow and gentle. She laid her down and covered her with the flag and smoothed her hair back gently, the way a loving mother would, and it came to her then that her name would be Margaret, after her grandmother.

Chapter 3

Gene pulls the van around to the back of their apartment building, the red brick still in shadow. He parks in their usual spot to the left of the dumpster, close to the building and out of sight of the security camera. It was the first thing Gene checked out when he got back. He said Uncle Sam lost the privilege of watching him when they decided he wasn't good enough to serve his own country anymore. It's one of the ways he has changed, noticing security cameras and having all these negative opinions about the government.

Jenny doesn't talk about the government. It's one of the many things she doesn't understand or have control over and doesn't like to think about.

He turns off the ignition, but instead of opening his door and climbing out, walking inside with her where they can sit and have a cold beer or maybe just go to bed, slip under the cool sheets and lie down for a while, he turns towards her, rests his arm on the back of his seat and glances in the back, then stares at her.

"So." He pulls out the crumpled pack of cigarettes, takes the last one out. "You got a plan here?" He looks straight at her, no emotion or judgment, just ready to listen to what she has to say.

She doesn't have much. She really has nothing. She doesn't want to be in charge of this anymore. Gene is the one who makes the plans.

The little girl starts whimpering like a hurt puppy. If she would just shut up Jenny could think. She pulls out two beers and hands one to Gene. She opens hers and drinks almost half of it down. Not ice cold, but still good.

"Do you? What do you think we should do?"

"You're the one who took her." His tone, his expression, doesn't change. He isn't exactly accusing her of doing something wrong like some people would, like everyone always has. He just wants to help her figure things out by stating a fact and waiting for her to explain, but she isn't prepared. She used to be so good at explaining.

The last couple miles home had been silent as Jenny tried to picture the three of them in the apartment, tried to see ahead at least a few hours. She tries to hold onto a thought for more than a few seconds, but as soon as one picture starts to form it swims away just far enough so she can't grab hold of it. She has been running on pure feeling all day, maybe every day since Gene got home, maybe every day since she met him, and she isn't back to anything even close to real thinking yet. Thoughts come from nowhere and then are replaced by another and another, on and on, one thing turning into another. All she knows is their lives are all moving together now like some grand plan unfolding, but it's not her plan. It's not all up to her. Maybe none of it is.

What had she been thinking about right when she opened that car door, when she saw the little girl waiting for Jenny to come get her. What was she thinking when she had her in her arms? There was no thinking, just pure feeling. It felt good.

It's hard to remember now exactly how it all happened, like an accident right in front of you and even though you couldn't take your eyes off it you still can't be sure what happened. It was a huge rush; she remembers that. But now not so much.

She takes another swig of beer, getting warmer already. "I didn't have a plan. I wasn't thinking too far ahead. I wasn't really thinking at the time. Just doing. You know how I get sometimes. When I saw her I felt this emotion, like I had to save her, and then when I had her and was walking away with her, I knew I was supposed to."

"You were supposed to kidnap a kid?"

"Save a kid."

"From what?" He already knows the answer to everything and is just waiting for her to figure it out, say it out loud so it sticks.

"From everything bad that could have happened to her. From whoever left her in the car. From the people not taking good care of her. If people have kids they should take care of them, right? So maybe I thought just for a minute that we could save her together, that we could take care of her." He stares at her, really listening. "Maybe this is the only good thing I have ever done." Those words sound true.

"So you want to take care of someone else's kid. Some kid you pulled off the street, you want to keep her. You're out of your mind." He takes his eyes off her, looks around outside, his eyes everywhere but on her. He sighs, turns to look in the back again and the little girl stops crying.

"Just because we saved her doesn't mean we have to keep her. Unless you want to." Jenny looks down at her lap, scrapes at a spot of yellow on her jeans. Dried mustard. When did she have mustard?

Jenny smiles. "You know how I get when I see something just asking to be taken. I just needed to do it."

Gene sighs, combs his fingers through his hair, off his forehead, behind his ears. Jenny waits while he takes a pill from his pocket, washes it down with his beer. What about her?

She looks in the back at the little girl still in the corner, as far away from them as she can get. When she meets Jenny's eyes she says, "My go home?" She is still crying, but at least she's not screaming.

Jenny looks back at Gene. "You mad at me?"

He shakes his head slowly. He doesn't seem mad. "We'll make it work. You're something else. Can't help it, can you, Jenny girl?" He reaches out and touches her face, her hair, so gently it makes her want to cry. He loves her no matter what and that is exactly what she tried to explain to her parents, how Gene had so much more to offer than money and so-called security. She has all the security she needs just by him loving her so much.

She leans into him, whispers. "Let's go in and relax. She'll be better when we're inside." Jenny is ready to lay down now, take a little nap. Her eyes are burning and her body feels heavy. They could all take a nap together and figure things out when they wake up.

"Not yet. I need to think." Gene looks outside, scans the parking lot, deserted but for three cars, everyone else gone off to work. He reaches past Jenny into the glove compartment, gets a fresh pack of cigarettes, opens them and offers her one even though she hardly ever smokes. He lights them both and she takes a drag, feels the burn as the smoke fills her lungs. He always knows exactly what she needs.

He reaches for another beer and she gets one, too. The day isn't ruined, not by a long shot.

They both turn as the back door of the building squeals open and the maintenance guy walks out. He glances over at them then walks to the dumpster and hurls two huge black bags into it, walks back inside keeping his eyes down. "Put your window up in case she starts screaming again."

Jenny takes one more drag, throws the rest of her cigarette out the window then puts it up. "Do you think we should just give her back? We can call the cops, tell them we were just trying to help her. We can actually tell the truth, that she was alone in a hot car and we didn't want anything to happen to her. The guy who left her in the car will be the one who gets in trouble, not us. We'll be like heroes." Even as Jenny says this she knows she couldn't do it. The girl will go right back to the people who left her alone, not ever realizing how Jenny tried to save her and change her life forever. When she lifted her into her arms and carried her away from danger she felt as strong and right as she ever had in her life.

Taking the girl was something like grabbing people's keys or money. It makes people think twice and pay attention and not be so stupid next time. She changes people's lives forever. And now it feels like there was a purpose all along. She thought it was just the rush, the getting away with it, even though she knows she's not really getting away with anything and some day she will be punished because Jesus knows. He will forgive her, though, for everything, if she does the right thing for the girl. This could be her chance for redemption.

"So what do you think?"

Gene looks straight ahead and Jenny takes a swallow of beer and waits.

"You're seriously thinking about calling the cops," he says. His eyes are on her now. "You." His voice isn't soft or loving.

She should have just let him think. She should have kept her mouth shut. If she could call anyone it would be her grandmother, the only one who ever listened to Jenny, the only one who ever took her side with her parents. *Leave the girl alone.* She must have said that a thousand times. There isn't another person in the world who would understand why Jenny did what she did and take the time to help her figure out how all this should work.

She drinks down the rest of her beer. It doesn't taste as good as the first one. Now she wants something sweet and tries to remember if they have any cookies.

"You could call," she says softly. "You wouldn't have to say who you are. Just tell them where she is and hang up. They can't trace the call if it's only a few seconds. They would call you a good Samaritan. Wait, I know. Let's take her to the park and while she's playing we can leave and call the police from a phone booth. Or call a newspaper."

"That's a fucking great idea. Let's bring her out for people to see us. I'm sure she'll just start playing in the park like nothing happened. Then we can call the police on ourselves, or better yet, get it in the newspaper. Those are great fucking ideas."

Jenny hates it when he swears like that, swears at her. She is starting to feel the weight of what she's done, the guilt she always feels, but worse this time. Now Gene is mad at her and he thinks she is stupid and maybe he is realizing he doesn't love her after all. He used to think she was so smart.

Her voice is barely a whisper "I'm sorry." She puts her hand on his leg. "Don't be mad."

He reaches over and puts his hand on the back of her neck, squeezes just a little too hard. "Too late to be sorry, Jenny girl. We'll make it work. If we handle this right we could come out of this okay. They always have rewards for lost kids. We'll see what they're willing to pay to get her back."

Jenny pulls away. That isn't what she did it for. He makes it sound like kidnapping. "You want to give her back to the people who left her in the car? They'll just do it again and next time maybe she'll die and this will all be for nothing."

He stares into the back. "Not our problem. Never was."

Jenny isn't sure about that but she takes a deep breath and relaxes a little now that Gene has taken charge. It's funny how everything can shift like that. Still, she wants him to know this isn't some random thing. "But it felt like I was supposed to save her, like she was left there so I could find her. Did I tell you I saw the face of Jesus last night? I did, right? That was part of it, I think, like he was telling me I had something important to do, maybe the most important thing I ever did in my life."

Her words sound good and as close as she can come to being sure, but it has taken all her breath and now the van feels like a prison, full of the smell of cigarettes and beer and the little girl in the back who is sleeping again. How can she just go to sleep like that? "How about I carry her in and we can talk inside. She's sleeping. We can figure everything out after we just rest a little."

Jenny pulls the handle and just as the door opens, the woman who lives downstairs walks by the van towards the dumpster. She is carrying a white trash bag that looks only about half-full. She turns towards the van and waves and Jenny closes her door and waves back. When Jenny looks into the back of the van, the girl is still there, getting more real every minute.

"You stay here," Gene says. "I'll be right back." He doesn't sound mad anymore, or nervous. He must have a plan and Jenny is amazed at how he can do that so quickly and without talking it all out. Not a word. He was always the man with a plan. That's what his friends called him. The man with a plan.

Jenny wants to go inside, too, but she doesn't say anything, doesn't want to spoil it. All of a sudden he is outside the van without a sound and she is alone with this sleeping girl. She is responsible.

She locks the doors and sits back, takes a deep breath and closes her eyes for just a minute. She thanks God for Gene, for sending her someone who loves her so much and takes care of her. Her parents were so wrong about him.

Even though she tries not to think about her parents they intrude whenever they want, just like they always have. If only they had just tried to be a little more open to Gene, everything could be different.

He only came inside her house twice. The first time was when they met him and the second time was when they insulted him. After that he met her down the street and she had to sneak out, but that made it all the better, all the more meaningful. Her father called him a bum and her mother said he wasn't suitable. With all their talk about how much they loved her and didn't want her to throw her future away on someone like Gene, all they really wanted was to control her life. They didn't want her to be happy. They wanted her to be miserable like them, as if that was what it meant to be married.

Not that she and Gene had any plans to get married. They weren't the kind of people who needed a ring and a fancy wedding with people they didn't even know and a piece of paper signed by some stranger that said they were husband and wife. It was like they had a bond before they even met.

How different it would be if they had just given him a chance, if they had just taken the time to get to know him. They would have liked him. But all they saw was the way he dressed and his long hair and his motorcycle and that was it. They wanted her to marry some preppie kid who either had his face in a book or played golf and drank scotch, talked politics and knew what fork to use.

Her mother called Gene a thug one day. "Where did you ever meet such a thug?" Her mother hated anyone she thought would contaminate her neat little world. Once Jenny started laughing she couldn't stop and her mother just walked away. *A thug.* She couldn't wait to tell Gene.

Jenny remembers every detail about the day she met Gene, outside Vic's Variety with two candy bars in her pocket, one paid for and one not. He was at the curb, checking the front tire of his Harley and he turned around and stared at her when she walked out. He told her later the first thing he noticed about her was her hair, how shiny and soft it looked and how he wanted to pull his fingers through it, but she didn't believe him. As soon as she left school that day she had rolled up her skirt at the waist and unbuttoned the top buttons of her white blouse. Of course he noticed more than her hair.

She stood outside the store for a minute and stared back at him, then sat on the step that led to a door she had never seen anyone use and opened her candy bar and her heart.

Chapter 4

Gene slides open the side door of the van, startling Jenny awake. She turns to see him throw in a black trash bag and his duffle bag, which makes the little girl start crying again. He slams the door shut and slips behind the wheel without a word, hands her a plastic grocery bag before he turns the key in the ignition. He backs out and drives slowly to the parking lot exit and waits for a school bus to go by before he pulls out onto Lincoln Street.

She had been dreaming of another place, another time. "Where are we going?" she asks, pulling open the bag he handed her, hoping for something sweet.

"We can't stay here." He doesn't even look at her.

Jenny pulls out the milk, smells it, then gulps some down. It's cold and perfect. "Why not?"

When he stops at a red light he turns and gives her that look like she's supposed to know, like it should be obvious, but it's not. The same look her mother gave her when Jenny asked why not? Why was she not bailing her out of trouble just one more time? Why wasn't she helping her? Why wasn't she acting like a good mother?

"Why not?" Did she already ask this?

"You don't think the neighbors are ready to call the cops on us again? All they need is one more excuse, like a kid screaming. They know we don't have a kid."

Jenny glances in the back. The girl is just sitting there, staring at her and the milk. She looks so lost and sad. "She's not screaming." She puts the top back on the milk, checks out what else is in the bag – the rest of the cheese, two boxes of crackers, a bag of chips. Did they eat today? She remembers pie for breakfast, but was that today?

Gene checks the mirrors, the gauges, the mirrors, his eyes everywhere at once.

"Does this mean we're not giving her back?"

"Not yet we're not. We need to handle this right. We have a golden opportunity here."

Jenny stares at him, wants him to say more. A golden opportunity for what? To take care of the girl? To be a family? She wants him to say it but he focuses on driving and his own thoughts. "Wait. What do you mean 'yet'? We're keeping her? What are we doing?" She takes a handful of crackers, holds out the box to him, but he shakes his head so she sets it down. "Do you have another joint?"

He pulls one out of his pocket like magic and hands it to her. They smoke slowly, deliberately, and Jenny watches her town go by. She doesn't look in back again, doesn't want to see the sad, sad face of the girl again right now.

She studies the houses surrounded by chain-link fences that make her think of prisons. There are two men on a roof, their backs shiny and muscled as they hunch over their work, in a world of their own, oblivious to the danger. It probably never crosses their mind they could fall.

The only roof she has ever been on was the flat roof of the brick projects where Gene lived when they first hooked up, not so different from where they live now. They were the only ones up there and stayed away from the edge so no one would see them. It was their special place where at first they held hands and kissed and later Gene brought a blanket and laid her down and took off her clothes so gently, his eyes taking her in and appreciating her, loving her before they even made love then slipping inside her, still gentle and loving so she wasn't afraid.

The look on her mother's face when she got home that night said she knew everything Jenny had done. No words, no way, but somehow she knew. There must have been something in Jenny's eyes or the way she walked or looked that told her mother she wasn't a kid anymore. The next morning she asked Jenny if she was proud of herself and she called her a slut. That was another time her grandmother had said *Leave the girl alone*, though Jenny didn't feel like a girl anymore and she didn't feel like a slut either.

She turns to Gene, back to reality. "This has been a really long day. Don't you think this has been a long day?" Jenny rubs her face, pushes her hair back. Each time she blinks it feels like there is sand under her eyelids. "God. This morning feels like a hundred years ago."

Gene nods, reaches over and squeezes her hand. "Relax."

He takes Route 40 out of town, winding back roads with trees on both sides, a few houses, some close to the road but not so close to neighbors. It isn't long before Jenny feels like she is a million miles away from everything and they are safe.

She opens her window and takes a deep breath through her nose, the clean air with the smells of earth and trees and a coming rain. She glances in the side mirror and sees a black car coming up fast behind them. Chasing them? When she looks over at Gene his eyes are on the road but she feels him slow down a little and move to the right to let the car pass. Jenny sees a leg, a bare foot up on the dash. Kids.

Then the little girl appears between their seats, standing behind the console like she rose from the dead, dried tears and dirt and snot smeared on her face making her look like an orphan. She smells like pee. "My hungry."

Whoever she belongs to sure didn't teach her how to talk. Jenny opens the glove compartment and fishes around until she finds a wet-nap. Then she grabs the bag and climbs in back, hopes the girl doesn't start screaming again. How did her face get so dirty?

The girl is silent and still while Jenny cleans her face as gently as she can. Her skin is so white and tender. She and the little girl sit facing each other and Jenny unwraps a piece of cheese, holds it out to her like a peace offering. The girl looks like she is going to start crying again. Maybe she always looks like that.

"Here. It's for you. Cheese. Don't you like cheese?"

The girl takes it and the two of them eat and stare at each other. Jenny is going to have to take care of her now, feed her and get her some clothes and make sure she brushes her teeth and goes to bed early. She will teach her how to be a good girl.

All the implications and responsibilities make her tired and what she needs to do right now is lie down. She is drained and stoned and needs just a little rest. Just a little rest is all she wants and it isn't too much to ask after all she has done today. Naps with her grandmother were the best, the safest place in the world. Just for a little while she needs to close her eyes; then she can think.

The girl stares at her while she eats. She's a quiet eater, and neat for a little kid. Jenny lies down on her side, uses the blanket for a pillow and watches her eat. When she is finished Jenny opens her arms for her to join her just like her grandmother used to do and it makes her feel like her grandmother's spirit is right there with her, guiding her to the exact right thing to do, and like a small miracle the girl lies down next to her. Her face is inches from Jenny's, her pale skin, the delicate features, the sad, wet eyes that still look so scared.

"My go home?" That tiny voice.

"Don't worry about anything, sweetheart. We're going home." Jenny puts her arm around the little girl, closes her eyes and melts into the movement of the van. Her thoughts go from her grandmother to her mother then to her father. If only she could go back and do things different, be different, just be his little girl. She didn't mean to be bad. Or maybe she did. She was fourteen, old enough to know being with your own father was wrong. Part of her, most of her, just wanted to see what he would do.

It took her a long time to realize her mother saved her. If she hadn't walked in on them that day, Jenny and her father would have gone through with it. It makes her sick now to think of it. They had reached the point where turning back wasn't an option. What she can't understand, though, is how her mother forgave Jenny's father, but couldn't forgive Jenny.

When Jenny wakes up and looks around, the girl is sitting way back in the corner again with the flag over her. She is awake but not crying, her eyes wide and watchful. They are still driving, along a narrow country road now, trees and more trees, trees so close to the road that's all there is. The road is bumpy and curved and narrow and Jenny wishes she were the one driving.

When she climbs up front, into the passenger seat, Gene looks at her and smiles and she smiles back. "Where are we?"

"Almost there. Good snooze?"

She pulls the mirror down and checks out her face, her eyes, smooths her hair back. "How long was I asleep?"

"Almost an hour."

"I guess I needed it. Where are we? Looks like we're in the middle of nowhere." Jenny opens a beer and takes a sip. It's warm now, but good. She doesn't mind warm beer. She just wants to sip on it. "Do you have any more speed?"

He hands her the bag with only two left. The only time he gives her the whole bag is when it's almost gone. She washes them down with the beer. "So do you know where we are? Where we're going?"

"Heading north." His voice is a little hoarse and either he doesn't want to tell her where they are or he doesn't know. Maybe he doesn't want to say anything the girl can hear. He's always thinking.

"Want me to drive for a while so you can sleep?"

"I'm good."

Jenny doesn't really care where they are; she will just enjoy the ride. So many trees. There are probably animals in those trees watching them right now.

He slows down as they pass a brown house that almost blends into the trees behind it. There is a tall flag pole out front with two flags whipping in the wind. An American flag and a gray and black one with someone's profile. POW/MIA. Gene nods towards it. "That's it. Ray's place."

They pull onto the side of the road a little way beyond the house and Gene checks the mirrors even though the road is completely deserted. He always says you can never be too careful. He makes a u-turn back to the house with the flag, pulls into the gravel driveway that curves around to the side, trees blocking the van from the road. It looks like a nice enough house, though the POW flag makes Jenny uneasy.

Gene had told her about Ray, his buddy from the service, how he had a house up in the boonies in New Hampshire and how Ray was down in St. Pete for a while with his mother. He told Gene where the key was and asked him to keep an eye on the place if he ever came up this way, check on it from time to time if he could, or even stay there if he wanted. Guys trust each other so easily. He hadn't said much more about Ray, just that he was a good guy. All his buddies are good guys. Jenny is glad Ray isn't here, that they have the place to themselves.

It feels good to get out of the van, finally, stretch her legs. She breathes in the air, so different here, clean and sharp, pine trees and grass. Gene slides open the side door of the van and the little girl stands there, waiting and looking like she is about to cry again. Jenny has heard enough crying today to last her a lifetime.

While Jenny reaches in for the beer, Gene lifts the girl easily and carries her up the stone steps, sets her down and retrieves a key from under a rock by the door. Then they are inside, standing in a spotless kitchen with knotty pine cabinets and walls. It's so beautiful.

The little girl stands close to her, leans into her leg like she is afraid. She already understands that Jenny will protect her. That's something.

"My go potty."

Jenny smiles. "Me first." She walks down the hall, finds the bathroom. She forgot she had to go so bad. The little girl follows her and stands in the doorway, doing a little dance. How did she get so dirty again? She doesn't ask for help, so Jenny walks back to the kitchen where Gene is looking through the cabinets. "This is nice."

He looks past her. "Where is she?"

"In the bathroom. 'My go potty' she said. I wonder how old she is. We'll have to teach her to talk better."

"We won't have her that long."

"What do you mean? Why not?" Why would they bring her all the way up here if they weren't keeping her? Does she even want to keep her? They will have to talk about it, but it seems he has made up his mind.

"Someone will be looking for her and want her back. We'll hang low here until we hear something. There'll be something on the news and then we can figure out how we'll do this."

"Do what? You think someone will look for her up here?" Jenny looks around as if someone is going to appear. She pushes down the fear as she pictures the police at the door. There must have been a camera that saw her taking the little girl. Cameras are everywhere, someone always watching. "Do you think they'll find us? Do you think they have us on their camera and it will be on the news?"

They hear the toilet flush and tiny footsteps on the linoleum. Jenny whispers now. "If they see me taking her out of the car they'll think I was kidnapping her, won't they? They won't understand I was saving her."

How could she have thought they were safe? She starts shaking now as she tries to remember who was around. Those guys in the white shirts. That woman who smiled at her. Surely she would recognize her, standing there holding the girl and smiling like an idiot. How could she be so stupid?

Gene holds her tight, keeps his voice low and soothing. "The only camera was inside. If they have anything it will be the guy with the ponytail, the one you said was probably her father. They might have me in there buying beer, but I paid in cash and kept my head down. You probably had her by then anyway. Plus the van wasn't anywhere near there. We're all set. We'll make out on this." He touches her under the chin, lifts up her head so their eyes meet. "Hey. It's time we caught a break. Don't worry so much. Relax. We're fine. We need to stay cool." All the time he is talking he rubs her back and she tries not to be so afraid.

"I know it sounds crazy, but I didn't expect anyone to really look for her except her father. At least right away. And if he called the police I figured he would be the one who got in trouble for leaving her alone. But they might even call the FBI, right? If they think it's kidnapping?" God she hates that word.

"Right now they'll be checking the father's story. They'll definitely look at him first, then they'll question the rest of the family, the neighbors. They'll look for witnesses. And they won't find anything to connect us because there isn't anything. Nobody noticed us. Nobody pays attention. Nobody wants to get involved."

"I paid attention. I got involved." She wants him to love her for it.

"I know you did. And we couldn't have planned it better. It will probably be on the news tonight, tomorrow at the latest. Her face will be all over the place but not so much up here. People mind their own business up here."

"How do you know?"

"It's New Hampshire, Jen. Live free or die."

The little girl is standing in front of the kitchen sink looking up at them. She is so small and scared and out of place. Whatever is going to happen Jenny just wants it to be over. She wants to fast forward with her and Gene set up in their own place, a place like this, and the little girl back where she belongs or even in a better place, and they will start their own family. The girl's parents will appreciate her more after almost losing her and take better care of her. Sometimes it takes a scare like this to make you realize what you have and almost lost. Or maybe social services or whoever will take her away and give her to a better home. Mostly Jenny hopes it turns out for the best for this kid, that what she did isn't for nothing. It can't be. She thinks of Jesus' face and knows she did it for him. He loves little children best of all.

"Come here, honey." Jenny crouches down, keeps her voice calm and sweet. "You okay?"

"My go home?" Her eyes are full again, ready to spill over.

"Pretty soon, okay? We're going to take care of you for a while, okay? Are you hungry sweetheart?"

The little girl just stares at her. Jenny moves to pick her up and she backs away. "My go home." She's not asking now and Jenny sees she might be more stubborn than she thought.

"I'm not going to hurt you. I saved you. Jesus. You think I would hurt you now?"

"Jen." Gene touches her shoulder. "Leave her alone. She's still scared."

Since when is he such an expert on kids? Jenny turns and walks over to the refrigerator, a stainless-steel side-by-side like her parents had. She stares into it and blinks back the stupid tears. She won't let the kid bother her. Like Gene said, they won't have her for long. But why doesn't she like her?

This is probably the cleanest refrigerator Jenny has ever seen. It must be brand new to be this clean. There is beer. Their beer? A jar of hot cherry peppers, a brown jug of maple syrup and a jar of strawberry jam. She is starving. They should have stopped to get some food. A sub or pizza would be perfect right now.

In the cabinet over the counter she finds an unopened box of Ritz crackers and it is like finding gold. She takes it down, pulls out the strawberry jam and a paper plate, finds the silverware and starts spreading jam on the crackers, popping the first one in her mouth, enjoying it while she works. She turns to Gene, but he is not looking at her. Instead he picks up the little girl without saying a word. Jenny's father used to pick her up like that, carry her. It makes her want to cry. Does Gene love this little girl already? The way Gene holds her and how the girl has her arms around his neck. It must feel so good to both of them, but what about her? No one is holding her.

She follows them into the living room carrying the plate as if she is serving guests at a party. They are all quiet as they walk around the house, like a family looking to buy or rent it. Maybe this is just what Gene wants after all, and definitely what they all need. Jesus brought them all together to save each other.

There must be a hundred books in the living room. Shelves take up one whole wall like a library, a recliner sits in the corner with a floor lamp next to it and an old side table with dozens of rings on the surface. She easily pictures her father in his recliner, a glass of scotch on the table next to him, on a coaster of course, reading the newspaper with his glasses halfway down his nose, pretending he doesn't watch her walking in and out in her short shorts and low-cut tops or her tight little green dress.

Jenny runs her hand across the top of the soft beige couch in the middle of the room that feels like velvet and faces a big-screen television. It is like two separate rooms – the library and the den. Jenny sits in the padded rocking chair in front of the window, also facing the television, then gets up and pushes open the curtains to let in some light. The windows are dirty, the sky gray. No one will even know they are there.

Gene sets the girl down on the couch while he and Jenny check out the two bedrooms off each end of the living room, taking their time. No hurry. They are safe now. There is a double bed and a dresser in each room, a few things in one of the closets – three flannel shirts, a camouflage vest. Two pairs of well-worn boots are lined up on the closet floor. There is another small bathroom with a shower off the bedroom. Like the kitchen, everything is spotless. *Immaculate*, her grandmother liked to say. They stand next to the bed and Jenny pulls back the spread to see there are no sheets. She likes making beds.

"So he lives here alone?" Jenny walks to the dresser, opens the top drawer. A couple of folded black tee-shirts, a pair of boxers.

"Far as I know. Looks that way. What are you looking for?"

"Sheets." She closes one, opens another, jeans, sweats, socks. "Everything is so neat."

"Service will do that to you. Come over here."

She stands in front of him, between his legs and he wraps his arms around her. "We're lucky to have this place to lie low with her until we hear something. Something will be on the news and we'll figure it out from there. We'll see who she belongs to, what they're willing to pay to get her back." He is talking to himself as much as to her.

"We can't hold her for ransom," she says. That word sounds so dark and sinister.

"Not ransom. A reward. She's our ticket out, Jen. I'm figuring the reward will be ten, twenty grand at least, maybe more depending on their situation. We can use the money to get ourselves set up somewhere. I kind of like it up here. No one bothers you."

"You're not mad at me?"

He lets go of her and she steps back so she can see his face. He doesn't look upset at all, just tired and full of thoughts. "Jenny girl. No point in being mad. We'll make it work. We'll come out of this just fine."

She sits next to him on the bed, kisses him, lays back onto the pillow and opens her arms. This is all she ever wanted. Instead of lying on top of her Gene turns toward the door and the little girl is standing in the doorway. "My thirsty." Her voice is so tiny, so timid. What lousy timing.

Jenny rolls onto her side. "Come here, honey. Do you want to take a nap?"

"My thirsty."

Jenny stands and reaches for her, but the little girl backs away. So what? Jenny takes a deep breath and walks past her to the kitchen, opens cabinets until she finds a thick brown coffee mug. Better than a glass. She fills it from the tap and holds it out to the little girl. She gulps it down, then stares at Jenny.

"What's your name, honey?" Jenny crouches down but doesn't get in her face.

"My Addie."

"Addie? That's a funny name. How about Margaret? Do you like Margaret?"

"My Addie. My go home." Her eyes are dry and her voice is angry. What right does she have to be angry?

"Not right now, okay? We're going to take care of you for a while. Isn't it nice here?" She straightens up and looks around, touches the clean counter, wonders if there is something wrong with the girl. She can't talk right and maybe she doesn't even understand what Jenny is telling her. And of course she has no idea what happened except she was taken away from her life and here she is with two strange people. No wonder she's scared. She doesn't understand.

She could at least try to understand, though. Jenny has done nothing but take care of her, give her something to eat and drink. She even took a nap with her for Christ sake. What else does she want from her? She saved her life. "Be a good girl, okay?" She keeps her distance until the little girl's eyes start to fill up again and when Jenny steps towards her the girl throws the mug on the floor between them. When it shatters she starts crying, then Gene is there, scooping up the little girl who clings to him and cries.

"What are you doing?" He looks at Jenny as he rubs the little girl's back just like he rubbed Jenny's a few minutes ago. Then he looks down at the shattered cup, shakes his head. "Come on, Jen. Clean this up before she gets cut."

"I didn't do it. She did. She just threw it on the floor." Now Jenny is close to tears again. She always gets blamed for everything.

"She's just a little kid. What are you giving her a cup like that for? Isn't there a paper cup? A plastic cup? Jesus."

Jenny swallows. It's not right. It's not her fault. "It's all I could find. She threw it on purpose. She's the one who should clean it up." She doesn't like her voice, whining and complaining, and even though she has more to say she stops and stares at him and holds back the tears.

"Come on. She's only a kid. Just clean it up, okay? We need to make sure she isn't hurt, that she doesn't say we did anything to her."

Jenny turns away, stands at the counter with her back to him, spreads a thick layer of jam on a cracker and slides it into her mouth. It is starting to get dark outside but she can make out a little clearing with a picnic table sitting there, a fire pit, trees and darkness beyond that. It is a whole new world and she is not sure if she likes it or not.

She sighs and picks up the biggest pieces of the shattered mug, looks around for a broom. She opens a door that leads to a basement. The steps are steep and it's dark and there is no way she's going down there, then she sees a broom and dustpan hanging on the wall to her right. Jenny likes sweeping floors. There's something steady and comforting in it. Tonight they will get some sleep and tomorrow they will get groceries and whatever else they need. She will try to trust God and Gene that everything will happen just the way it's supposed to.

Gene walks in the kitchen without the girl just as Jenny empties the dustpan into the trash. She will sweep again to make sure she got it all. There are television sounds coming from the living room. A cartoon? "I'll get the stuff from the van." He walks past her to the door.

"Did you bring any of our dishes?" she asks, knowing he didn't. There was one bowl that was her grandmother's, something Jenny took to remember her by. It's the only thing she had saved from her other life and now it's gone, left behind like it didn't matter.

"I only brought what we need. Clothes and shoes and stuff from the bathroom."

Jenny nods, knowing there is nothing she can do about it. They can get all new stuff. They have one credit card not maxed out yet and an offer for a Visa she got in the mail is in her purse. It's so easy for people to get credit cards these days. Plastic. Just fill this out and sign here.

While Gene is outside Jenny stands in the doorway of the living room. The little girl is curled up on the couch with an afghan over her. Maybe Ray's mother made it for him, squares in shades of orange and gold and green. The girl is quiet, staring at the television screen. What kind of life did they take her from? It's so odd how she likes Gene and not her. Maybe it's a test. She will find a way to make the girl like her before she goes back. It is important that this girl likes her, trusts her and chooses her over Gene. That's the way it should be. She'll be the mother and mothers should come first.

50

She turns back to the kitchen and makes some more Ritz and jam, puts some on a paper plate and brings them into the living room along with a cold beer. There is a cartoon on the television, a little boy with dark hair asking them to repeat *vamanos* over and over while he swings through the trees. *Vamanos.* Then Gene is in the doorway.

"I'll be right back. You okay with her?"

She was just starting to relax. "Where are you going?"

"I won't be long." He steps over and sets another beer on the coffee table. "You'll be fine."

"You're leaving me here alone? Why can't we all go? Or you stay here and I'll go. She doesn't like me anyway. She likes you."

He steps to the back of the couch, massages her shoulders. "You'll be fine, Jenny girl. I won't be long."

She loves when he calls her *Jenny girl.* Those two words, the way they float out of his mouth, make her somebody.

"News will be coming on in a few minutes. See if there's anything yet. I'll bring you back something."

It takes her a few seconds to realize what he means by seeing if there is anything, why they are there in the first place hiding out. One minute ago it felt natural and normal to be there, but now she feels the fear. It will only be okay if they are all together. "I don't want you to leave. We need to stay together. Let's all just go."

"We're not taking her out. You know that. That's the stupidest thing we could do right now."

She takes a deep breath, a swallow of beer. "She needs some things. Pajamas, a toothbrush, some clothes. You said we need to show people we took care of her. And if we get caught we can just say we saw her wandering down the street by herself so we took her home and took care of her until we could find out where she belongs. Right?"

"Make a list. "I'll get what we need and pick up some food."

The label on the girl's shirt says 2T. Jenny isn't sure what the T stands for but she tells him to get size two clothes and pajamas. And underwear. In a few days she will be back where she belongs, wearing new clothes, and people will know they took good care of her. "Oh, and get some shampoo, too, and a toothbrush. And some milk. And cookies. And cereal. Do you want me to make a list? Bread. We need bread. And peanut butter, okay?"

Gene fishes a joint out of his shirt pocket. He lights it, takes one hit and hands it to her. "See if you can relax. I'll be right back."

In less than an hour Jenny is unpacking the food. She loves unpacking groceries when she's high. She smoked half the joint and had two beers and one hit of speed she found in her pocket and feels more like herself again.

It's like they are different people with this little girl, a family. They are responsible people living their life. Gene got all the right things – milk and orange juice, macaroni and cheese and hot dogs, Cheerios and bread, peanut butter, bananas, and those mini chocolate chip cookies Jenny loves.

"How was she? She say anything?"

"Not a word. I didn't try to talk to her again. I just left her alone. I found sheets and made both beds. Nothing on the news yet. After we eat I'll give her a bath."

They have cereal and bananas and toast for supper, a quiet supper, relaxing and perfect, then

Gene says, "I have a couple things to do. You put her to bed. I'll be home to watch the late news."

Jenny almost complains, but stops herself. She will show him she is fine. He always comes back and is always glad to see her. Jenny isn't sure she's entitled to more than that. Hopefully, one day he won't want to go anywhere without her.

In a minute he closes the door softly behind him and Jenny turns to look at this little girl who is becoming hers now, like a prize she won at a carnival. She pulls the tags off the pajamas Gene got for her, pink with little purple and white ponies.

While she gives her a bath and combs her hair she wants to ask the girl questions about where she is from, get some idea if her family has money, but is afraid the girl will get upset and start asking to go home again. She tells her how pretty she is, how nice her hair is, and what a good girl she is.

In a little while the two of them are on the couch watching another cartoon. The girl is content and clean and Jenny feels like she accomplished something that would have seemed impossible yesterday. Her parents should see how responsible she is.

She lights the other half of the joint, has one more beer, then she has her arm around the little girl and holds her close, the two of them in their own world, safe from anything that could possibly hurt them right now. The girl isn't afraid of her anymore and Jenny feels something complete in her, something she has never felt before. She puts her to bed at nine with a kiss on the forehead, tells her again what a good girl she is, how she will take extra-good care of her and not to worry about anything. She tells her a dozen times that she is safe. If she feels safe then everything else will follow.

Chapter 5

For more than a week there is nothing on the news, nothing in the newspapers, no one banging on the door. Each day that goes by Jenny knows she should be thankful they haven't been caught. She tries not to think about what people would say, what the police would do to her. Jenny can't believe how long they have kept her, how deep they are into this.

Her mother said she took things because she wanted attention, but that wasn't it. She got plenty of attention. Too much sometimes. It has always been about the rush of the moment, of being in control and not getting caught.

But this is different. The rush is long gone, faded into not even a memory now, and all that's left is a sense of being on the other side, as if something has been taken from her, but she can't quite figure out what it is. Maybe her freedom, or her belief that she was ever in control.

She is restless and sick of being trapped in someone else's house out in the middle of nowhere. Gene goes out every day, either to get something they need or just to get out for a while, while Jenny stays with the girl. It's starting to feel like she is being punished. And it's not over yet, not even close.

Then there are moments when Jenny feels such a connection to this little girl she finds herself praying, making deals with Jesus, promising to never ask for anything ever again and to never steal ever again if she can just get away with this one last thing. She tells Jesus she was only trying to help this little girl, to save her, and sometimes late at night when Gene is asleep next to her and the little girl is asleep in the other room, Jenny thinks that this little girl is a precious gift from Jesus.

The first two days, Gene stayed in front of the television smoking cigarettes and an occasional joint, drinking coffee and whiskey and beer, always pacing himself, switching between channels. Now it feels like they should be doing something, going somewhere, calling someone. Moving. Not just sitting around waiting for something to happen. It's not like Gene to just wait like this, but Jenny doesn't know what else they could be doing either.

Giving the girl back isn't an option anymore, if it ever was. Gene says the ball is in their court, as if they are playing a game and Gene is the one who started it. Every day they are sure it will be the top story. Breaking news. But there is no mention of a missing child, no tearful parents on the news begging for their little girl to be returned safely. No FBI manhunt. In a way Jenny is disappointed. It shouldn't go unnoticed or unreported. It shouldn't have been that easy.

"What do you think is going on?" Jenny asks. "Do you think no one wants her? That no one cares? Do you think that guy wanted to get rid of her? I mean she's a person. She must belong to someone. Someone should report her missing."

The girl has been sleeping for hours while Jenny and Gene are in their usual places on the couch, a pizza commercial on television. She loves this television. Their empties are on the table in front of them, wrappers from their subs. The eleven o'clock news is more than half over and still no story.

"They're probably just waiting to hear from whoever took her, waiting for a ransom call. It's a good sign, Jen. Whoever she belongs to is playing it smart, probably getting money together so they're in a position to get her back. I give them one more day before they go to the media and offer a reward." He drinks the last of his beer, stands and stretches.

Jenny stands, too, and looks up into his face. "But what if they don't?"

"They will. Let's go to bed."

"But what if they don't? Will we keep her?"

"They will. Don't worry." He clicks off the television, puts his arm around her and steers her towards the bedroom.

Jenny doesn't want to see the parents on television crying fake tears. And she sure doesn't want the little girl to see her own face on television and ask questions Jenny doesn't have the answers to, at least not yet. She mostly keeps her in the kitchen or in the bedroom.

Gene got her some coloring books and crayons and the girl seems content doing this for hours. Sometimes Jenny colors with her and it relaxes her. The girl takes a nap every afternoon after lunch and sleeps for an hour and a half. Jenny sits by the bed and watches her sleep or reads a magazine. She doesn't like being out of her sight. She's a good kid.

When she's awake she is a watchful kid, though, like she is waiting for something to happen any minute, waiting for Jenny to do something, as if taking care of her isn't enough. If only that look would go away, like she's going to bust out crying any minute. But she hasn't cried since that first day and she hasn't mentioned Tony again. Out of sight, out of mind. It is a little creepy sometimes how she stares at Jenny, like she knows every little thing Jenny has ever done and that her punishment is right around the corner.

Jenny wants to call her Margaret in the worst way, but it would probably make Gene mad. She needs to be patient, so she doesn't call her anything except honey and sweetheart and she. Except when the girl is sleeping and Gene isn't home she tries it out, whispers, *Don't worry, Margaret. Everything is going to be fine. Mama's here. Mama's here.* Jenny says it over and over and believes the girl takes it in on a deep level.

She doesn't ask her any questions about her name or her family or where she is from. She is young enough to lose all her memories; maybe she already has. None of it matters anyway.

It doesn't seem possible or anywhere near right that they will actually give up this little angel, swap her for money. Maybe the people she belongs to would learn a lesson, though, after almost losing her, and be better parents.

"I need to get out of here." Jenny stands in the doorway of the kitchen wearing her white capris and red tank top. While the girl sat in front of the television with her toast Jenny put makeup on and has her hair down the way Gene likes it. It is another beautiful day, warm and breezy, a day they should be outside.

Gene looks up from the newspaper for just a second, but doesn't say anything. She crosses her arms. Can't he see how desperate she is, how good she looks? "I'm going stir crazy. You get to go out every day. How about we go for a ride, the three of us? We can stop at a park or something, get some exercise. I really need to get out of here." She tries hard to keep her voice strong, not whiny. "Maybe we could go somewhere for lunch. There must be a place we can get a couple beers, a burger. That's all I want. Okay?"

The more she talks the tighter the spring inside feels. When she got up that morning she felt hopeful; now she feels angry and desperate and why can't he see that?

Gene keeps his eyes on the newspaper. "You looking to get caught? We're here to lay low, not to go out drinking or playing in a park." He looks up at her now, notices how nice she looks and his voice changes a little. "You don't think people will notice us with a kid? It's only been nine days." He walks over to her, puts his hands on her arms and looks into her face. "We have beer, and if you want a burger, I'll get you a burger. There's a grill around back. We can have a cookout and run around the back yard, okay?" He puts his hands in her hair like she knew he would and kisses her.

This is one of those times she wishes they were alone, but right on cue the girl walks towards them, then past them, climbs up on a kitchen chair and opens her coloring book and crayons. Then Gene sits across from her and gets back to his newspaper though they both know there is nothing there. He has even been reading all the want ads. *Just in case.* Just in case what?

"So that's it?" Her voice is angry now and she doesn't care. "You're telling me to go run around the back yard? Really?"

Gene sighs, looks at the girl then up at Jenny. He doesn't care how good she looks. "Go out back for a while, sit at the picnic table and read one of your magazines. Just relax."

So that's it. She's dismissed. She glares at Gene and then at the little girl, just coloring away without a care in the world, no idea how Jenny saved her. And for what? No one ever appreciates what she does.

She snatches the green crayon out of the girl's hand and throws it on the floor, pushes the coloring book and the open box of crayons and a spoon onto the floor, too, then walks out. Before the kitchen door slams behind her, she hears the girl's surprised voice. "My color book." Too bad.

Jenny stands in the back yard facing the trees, her arms crossed over her chest. Her ragged breath seems loud, all she can hear besides the birds. There must be a million birds in those trees and who knows what else could walk out any minute. She is being punished for all her sins. She will never leave this place, never have a normal life with Gene.

She listens for the door to open, for Gene's footsteps behind her. She wants to feel his arms around her, wants him to care, ask if she is okay, apologize for not understanding. Then she will tell him a cookout would be perfect. But he is not coming out to see if she is okay. He is making sure the girl is okay. It's all about the girl now.

It's cooler than she thought, the sun mostly blocked by the trees, but Jenny walks quickly down the driveway, past the van and out to the street. Too bad she didn't think of grabbing the keys, then she would be off and he would be the one waiting at home for her.

As she walks she feels the isolation of the area. No cars, just her footsteps on the sand and twigs and pebbles on the side of the road. No sidewalks. Not even another house yet. Of course not. Who is stupid enough to live around here? She keeps walking as fast as she can, her arms still crossed over her chest and hopes it won't take Gene too long to realize she is gone and come after her. She pictures him and the girl pulling up in the van, relieved to see her, saying they were worried. That's what it takes sometimes to make people realize how much they care.

A chipmunk startles her when it scurries out of the trees and across the road not far from her and the leaves are loud as the wind picks up. She hasn't gone too far but is out of sight of the house when she hears a car coming up behind her. She doesn't turn around. All she feels is relief that he would come so quickly, that he must have changed his mind and they can go out after all, the three of them like a family. That's what this is all about.

A black pickup rattles past her and around the bend and then Jenny is totally alone again. After a minute she slows down then stops to catch her breath, looks up at the white sky beyond the treetops. A bird soars high above her. It could be an eagle or a hawk. She doesn't know much about birds but right now she wouldn't mind being one.

When her breathing has slowed down she turns and walks back to the house, taking her time, pushing the hurt down. It doesn't matter. He is doing the right thing staying with the girl. He knows Jenny can take care of herself.

When she walks into the kitchen Gene is still sitting at the kitchen table doing the crossword now and the little girl is coloring again, everything picked up off the floor like it never happened.

"Feel better?"

She does. Getting out helped, and walking into the kitchen at that moment with Gene and the girl waiting for her feels as close to coming home as anything ever has. "Yes." She goes to the girl who looks up at her with those scared eyes, smooths back her hair. So soft. "I'm sorry, honey. You okay?"

"My okay," she says, the sweetest words Jenny has ever heard. She is the first thing Jenny has ever taken that matters, the only thing she has ever wanted to keep. Here they are, overnight parents. It gets more real every day. A gift from God. All she needs to do is show she is worthy of it, that she deserves it. All the petty things she has stolen ever since she can remember must have been leading up to this.

She picks up Gene's coffee and takes a sip, the whiskey warming her. "I'll have one of those."

By the end of the second week they are into their routine. Gene goes out each morning and buys the Concord Monitor and the Boston Globe, milk and cereal and juice if they need it. He is so good at making sure they have everything they need. When he comes back from the store he lays the papers on the kitchen counter for Jenny to take the first look, then he and the girl have cereal or waffles.

"Look and see if we're wanted yet," is what he says each morning. Jenny listens for signs of blame in his voice but there are none. He almost seems content, as if this is what he had in mind all along. On their second day he had brought out the clock radio from the bedroom and set it on the kitchen table where it stays tuned to a news and talk station.

They are a quiet family and sometimes Jenny goes for a whole day without a thought to where the girl came from. It matters less each day. She is theirs. No one else wants her.

Jenny finds a cookbook in one of the cabinets and tries cooking. She bakes a chicken one night, with baked potatoes, and it makes her feel close to her grandmother and to God.

By the fourth week. Gene starts going out in the afternoon and after he is gone a couple of hours Jenny waits at the window, wondering what she would do if he never came back, if he decided to just keep on driving, head up to Canada or out to California without her. She doesn't believe he would do this, but there are a lot of things she didn't think could happen, like being here in the middle of nowhere in someone else's house with someone else's child. She wouldn't blame him if he left. This was never part of the deal.

The girl is asleep on the couch, the flag covering her like a blanket. Funny how she latched onto that flag and funny how Gene let her have it. Jenny wants more than anything to be with Gene right now, riding along the deserted roads with the windows down, sharing a joint, listening to country. She wants that freedom again and for a minute she hopes someone comes forward soon, someone she wouldn't mind giving the girl back to who will pay them well for taking care of her all this time. Then they can put all this behind them and be better for it, stronger. But most of the time when Jenny looks at the girl, this innocent little angel, she can't imagine giving her to anyone.

Jenny walks around, examines the titles of the books as if she is shopping in a book store or visiting the library. Lots of history books. World War I, World War II, Korea, even the Civil War. None of them appeal to her. The fiction might be okay if she could focus long enough to get into the story. There are even some authors she has heard of like Mickey Spillane and Hemingway. She pulls down *A Farewell to Arms*, reads the first page, closes it and puts it back. She has never been a big reader, another disappointment to her parents and teachers. She takes down random books and flips through them. Sometimes people hide things in books – money or letters or important papers – but she hasn't found anything yet but a yellow hand-written receipt from a place called *Books by the Lake.*

She opens drawers looking for small things Ray won't miss, things he threw in and forgot about. Matches from places in Florida she will probably never see. Del Ray Beach. Miami. She would like to see Miami. A pen from a Holiday Inn. A magnet in the shape of New Hampshire.

Jenny looks for a sign every day and then she sees the card in the drawer of the night stand. It's a picture of Jesus, looking so sad, his heart exposed and bleeding. *Sacred Heart of Jesus Pray for Me.* She holds it close to her face, looks right into the eyes of Jesus staring back at her, giving her that look like she should know exactly why she is there and what she should do. She presses the card to her heart and closes her eyes, asks Jesus to please help her do the right thing.

She walks back out to the living room and sits at the end of the couch, puts her hand gently on the girl's little leg, leans back and closes her eyes. She can easily imagine it is just the two of them alone together in the world.

Then she hears the van crunching the stones in the driveway, the door slamming, Gene's footsteps. She could never live without him.

"Anything on the news?" he calls.

Jenny tip-toes out to the kitchen. "She's sleeping," she whispers. "You know it's her nap time. Where did you go?"

Gene smiles and checks her out like they are meeting for the first time, leans down and kisses her and she tastes the whiskey on his tongue. It isn't fair he can go anywhere he wants, sit down at a bar, order a beer and a shot and have a random conversation like he doesn't have a care in the world, while she is waiting here for him, taking care of this little stranger who isn't a stranger anymore.

She likes the way he is looking at her, though, his wanting-her look. She keeps her face tilted up for another kiss and then her shirt is open and her bra is unhooked and he is at her jeans now and she is against the counter unbuckling his belt.

"She's right in there," she whispers, her eyes wide as if she couldn't possibly do anything with a kid sleeping just a few yards away.

"You said she's sleeping." Then her jeans are down to her ankles and she pulls one foot free and his hand is between her legs and Jenny doesn't care if the Queen of England is in the next room. All she knows and wants is right here right now and then her legs are wrapped around him and he is inside. It is quick and good and when the little girl walks into the kitchen a half hour later dragging the flag with her, Jenny and Gene are sitting at the kitchen table with their third cold beer and a bag of salt and vinegar chips, Garth Brooks singing to his sweetheart on the radio. Everything is as right as it possibly could be.

Gene smiles at the girl and his eyes light up, his voice tender and sweet. "Hey there sleepyhead. How ya doing? Have a good sleep?" It is the voice he sometimes uses late at night when he and Jenny are lying in bed and he is in the mood to share his dreams for their future, about buying a piece of land in Wyoming or Colorado, having a little farm, maybe a couple horses. He picks up the little girl and sets her on his lap, reaches over to the counter and picks up a plastic bag Jenny hadn't noticed. The girl finds a book inside with a princess on the cover and a little doll with eyes that close when she lies down. Jenny used to have a doll like that.

"My have it?" she asks.

"All yours."

The girl puts her arms around Gene's neck, hugs him like she has known him all her life, then sits in her own chair with the doll and book and the three of them are a family. A good family.

"Let's call her Margaret," Jenny says. There won't be a better time than this.

Gene lights a cigarette. "Margaret? That's an old lady's name."

"It was my grandmother's name."

He blows smoke up towards the ceiling and smiles. "Your grandmother was cool."

"So it's okay? We need to call her something, right?"

Gene shrugs, turns to the girl. "That okay with you?"

The girl looks at him, not sure what they are talking about. She lays her doll on the table and the eyes close. "Baby sleeping."

"That's a nice baby, Margaret," Jenny says, trying out her name. It suits her, even though she is just a little girl. Her grandmother was a little girl once, too.

"My not Margaret. My Addie."

"You're Margaret. That's your new name. It was my grandmother's name, and now I'm giving it to you."

The girl stares at her, picks up her doll and hugs it.

"Margaret is a nice name. And we could give you a nickname if you want. How about Meg? Or Maggie? That's kind of close to Addie." She turns to Gene. "Right? What do you think?" He is focused on the newspaper now, reading through the obituaries. Just in case.

"Well that's it. Okay? You're Maggie. We're going to call you Margaret or Maggie, okay? That's your new name."

"Meggie?" the girl says. It sounds right.

"Okay, sure. I like that. Meggie." Jenny picks up her beer, holds it up in a toast. "To Meggie."

Chapter 6

It has been raining for three days straight, a steady rain that feels like punishment or torture. Margaret doesn't seem to mind being cooped up, coloring or making little puzzles or playing with her stupid little doll. Gene doesn't seem to mind either, but he comes and goes as he pleases, so why should he? Jenny is the one who is like a prisoner here.

Gene walks in with the newspapers like he does every morning, and a little white bag he hands to Margaret. She pulls out a jelly donut and smiles at him before she takes a bite.

"Where's mine?" Jenny asks. "You only got one?" How could he be so uncaring, so oblivious?

He pours himself a cup of coffee from the pot that Jenny made, and sits down. "I thought you were watching your weight." End of discussion. He opens the paper and scans the front page, as if today there will be something.

Jenny stands with her back to the counter staring at the back of his head. "I love jelly donuts. You know how much I love jelly donuts." She feels herself pouting, close to tears, but doesn't care. It would have been such a nice surprise. "I haven't had a jelly donut in a really long time." It is like she doesn't exist anymore.

Gene looks up from the paper. "Jesus. You want me to go get you a jelly donut?"

Jenny turns and walks down the hall into the bathroom without a word. She doesn't want him to think she is crying over a stupid jelly donut. All she wants is for him to think about her, give one thought to her once in a while. She washes her face and brushes her hair, puts on just a little mascara before she goes back out, hoping he has snuck out to get her a jelly donut. But he is still sitting there, the paper open now. Nothing on the front page.

He looks up and stares at her for a few seconds. Finally. "You okay?"

"No. I'm not okay. I'm going stir crazy. I have to get out of here. And don't tell me to go out back. Can we just take a ride, please? Just go out to lunch? No one is looking for her and even if someone saw us you said people up here mind their own business. She's good. She won't be any trouble. You know she won't. I need to get out of here or I'm going to lose it."

Gene gets up, puts his arms around her and uses his caring voice. "One more day. If we don't hear anything by tomorrow we'll figure something else out. It's been over a month now. I don't get it. The news should be all over this." He smooths her hair, whispers. "You think you can be patient just one more day?"

She sighs, pulls him closer. "You promise? Tomorrow we go somewhere, do something, no matter what?"

He kisses her. "Promise." He looks into her eyes to see if she is okay, see if she is going to lose it, so she gives him a smile before she walks into the living room and turns on the television. One more day. She can do one more day. Their life has been on hold too long.

When Margaret joins her on the couch she sits close and Jenny puts her arm around her and changes the channel to cartoons. She doesn't mind cartoons. She studies that little face and wonders why no one wants her, how her parents or whoever had her let her go just like that; it's not like she's any trouble. When Gene said they would figure something out he probably meant dropping her off somewhere, getting rid of her if they aren't going to get a reward. Poor little thing.

The next morning there is finally a story on the news, as if they heard their ultimatum. Jenny and Margaret are sitting at the kitchen table matching cards from a deck she found in a kitchen drawer. There was nothing in the morning paper, and now Gene is watching the news at noon.

"Jen!" he calls, and she knows.

"Stay here, honey." Jenny's heart is pounding as she joins him in front of the television where a woman is saying something about a missing girl. Two-and-a-half-year-old Adeline Jenkins, who has resided in a foster home for the past six months. The woman is from the Massachusetts Department of Children and Families. She doesn't look much older than Jenny, but she is dressed in a dark blue suit with a white shirt underneath, open at the collar. Well aren't you the professional. What have you been doing all this time?

The woman says the details about exactly when the little girl went missing and the circumstances involving her disappearance are still unclear at this time, but her office is doing everything they can to find her. Her office? The woman asks anyone who has any information to call the number at the bottom of the screen. A policeman steps up to the microphone, a big man taking questions as if he knows anything. Then Margaret's face fills the screen only they're saying her name is Adeline and she doesn't look quite like that anymore. Her hair is a little longer now and her face is a little fuller and she doesn't have that haunted look in her eyes all the time. Anyone can see they have been taking better care of her than her parents. Foster parents.

The policeman is saying they are pursuing a number of leads and that the foster parents, as well as the DCF employee assigned to the case, are under investigation. Then the regular news-woman is back, the face Jenny knows so well. She wears a pretty blue dress with silver jewelry and she turns to the man next to her and tries to look genuinely concerned. "I hope this story has a happy ending, Jack."

"My hungry." Margaret is standing in the doorway and Jenny rushes to her, picks her up and carries her back into the kitchen as the newswoman reminds anyone with any information to call the number on the bottom of the screen. Jenny holds Margaret tight, sits at the kitchen table and just holds her. Margaret puts her arms around Jenny's neck, rests her head on her shoulder.

Finally. This is the closest Jenny has ever come to feeling like a real person with a true purpose in life. People become mothers in all sorts of ways and Jenny feels a divine spirit at work, Jesus or her grandmother or some invisible force in the universe that is making all this unfold just as it is supposed to. This could be her only chance to be a mother, her chance to redeem herself for everything bad she has ever done, all the mistakes she made.

This little girl, her Meggie now, really did need to be saved and Jesus chose Jenny to be her savior. She breathes in the baby shampoo smell of Margaret's hair, touches the soft skin of her arms and knows like she has never known anything before that this child needs her and only her.

While she fixes Margaret a peanut butter and jelly sandwich she wonders what Gene is thinking, what he will want to do now that they know she doesn't have a family to go back to, no reward. *Please Jesus don't let him want to desert her, send her back into the system.* Commercial sounds float in, a man screaming about some cleaner, and now that they know people are actually looking for her she expects Gene to shut off the television, come out and tell her what they will do now, where they will go. He has had enough time to think about it and probably not only has a plan, but one or two backup plans. No reward. She is secretly glad.

They don't talk about it until Margaret is taking her nap, and Jenny is the one to bring it up. "Doesn't look like she has anything to go back to." She keeps her voice calm and rational, afraid to show how excited she is, how validated. Or is it vindicated? She will be good and patient and not complain again about being here.

They sit at the kitchen table, the television silent for now, the rain pelting the windows and trees. It's a comforting sound, protecting them from the world. "Doesn't look like there will be any reward, right? They just let her slip through the cracks. It looks like we're all she has, the only people in the world who care about her."

Gene sighs, plants his hands on the table and looks at them as if they have some answers. "She's not our kid. Not our responsibility."

"I know, but in a way she is. We've been taking care of her. It's probably the first time she ever felt safe and loved. I know you like her. And she likes you. A lot. More than she likes me. And she hasn't been any trouble."

He looks up at her and frowns "She's not our kid," he says again. "Not our responsibility."

Jenny feels his mood darkening and knows she should just shut up and let him think but she wants to have some say in this. "But I think when I took her I kind of made her our responsibility, didn't I? I didn't mean to at the time, but that's what I did." While she waits for her words to sink in and hopefully make a difference, she opens the freezer and takes out the vodka, pours two shots and sets them on the table.

"Maybe we'll have our own kids someday, when we're settled somewhere and have jobs. We're nowhere near ready for a family right now. You know that." He throws back his shot and holds out the empty glass for a refill.

Jenny wonders if he means her, if he means she is the one who is nowhere near ready, if he means she isn't capable of taking care of a child, this child or any child. Doesn't he see how natural it is for her? He should have seen Margaret with her arms around her just a little while ago and how tightly she held onto Jenny.

"But you like her. You've been buying her things and I can tell she really, really likes you, maybe even a little more than she likes me. Maybe little girls are like that. They always love their daddy." Why didn't her own parents understand that?

"I'm not her daddy." He says this not with anger, but like she said something crazy.

"I bet you're the closest thing to a daddy she ever had." Jenny doesn't know how she knows this, but it is something she is sure about. She wants him to tell her what a good mother she has been, but all he does is throw back his shot while hers is still untouched.

He pushes his chair back and stands. Their talk is over He is going out to wherever he goes and for the first time in a long time Jenny has an awful feeling he is seeing someone else. Someone he likes to talk to. Someone he likes to be with. Someone normal who doesn't cause him trouble. It scares her.

He sets his glass in the sink. "I need to think, make a plan."

Jenny stands and grabs his arm, holds onto it. "Let's make a plan together." She drinks her shot, feels the burn spread from her throat down to her chest. "You're not going out now, are you? We have a lot to talk about."

Gene glances out the window, then down at her. "I won't be long."

"Actually," she says, "let's not even talk." She pulls off her tee shirt and drops it onto the floor, puts her arms around his neck and kisses him. When she goes for his belt he pulls away.

"Hold that thought. I won't be long."

"No." Her anger spreads through her whole body and her voice is louder than it needs to be. "You can't just keep going out like this, leaving me alone. That's not what couples do." He needs to stay. She needs him to want to stay. She stands in front of him, looks into his eyes and isn't sure what she sees. It doesn't look like love; it looks more like pity.

"You're going to wake her up." His voice is flat.

"You're mad at me now? It was fine as long as you thought there was something in it for you, but now that there isn't it's all my fault? Everything is always my fault. I won't say I'm sorry. I saved that little girl. *We* saved her. She's ours now."

He picks up her tee-shirt from the floor and his eyes soften a little. "Jen, she's not ours and you know it. You grabbed her off the street. I know you probably didn't mean to, just like you don't mean to do a lot of things, but that's the truth and now I have to clean up your mess." He leans in to kiss her but she turns away.

He shakes his head, sets her shirt on the table. "I won't be long."

All she can do is stand there and watch him leave. She wants to shout after him to not bother coming back, when all she wants is for him to turn around and come back to her.

The story is on the news only one more day before it's replaced by breaking news about Michael Jackson, who has been accused of molesting a little boy. He denies it, of course. He loves children. He has children staying with him all the time, children sleeping in his bed with him. Jesus. It never stops.

The Globe continues to carry Margaret's story and picture, expanding it, covering it from every angle, from investigating procedures at the Department of Children and Families to child predators, to children who run away from foster homes. She is not even three. The people who had her, who were supposed to be taking care of her, never reported her missing so they could keep getting payments. And now the police and the public are starting to believe they did something to her. They have removed the four other foster children from the home and two things are becoming clear, at least to the media: DCF did not do their job, did not check on these people until it was too late, and the foster parents had something to do with the girl's disappearance.

It never crosses anyone's mind that maybe, just maybe, someone took her because they wanted to save her from the life she had, that someone would actually want her and take care of her. Of course no one even thinks of this angle to the story; they only want to write about the worst it could be. She tells this to Gene and he laughs.

Margaret is sleeping on the couch and Jenny and Gene are sitting out back at the picnic table, drinking vodka and lemonade from blue plastic cups that match the sky.

"Yeah, that's why you took her. You're a real Mother Theresa. My little klepto." He touches the tip of his cup to hers and takes a swallow.

"Don't call me that. This is different. There's a reason."

"Same reason as always, right Jenny girl? You can't help it." He smiles his beautiful smile and Jenny is so glad he isn't mad at her anymore that after a moment she smiles, too.

Two days later there is another story in the Globe. The foster parents and the circumstances surrounding the girl's disappearance are still being investigated. The focus is not only on the foster parents; the social worker assigned to their case was fired and the procedures and staffing at the DCF are under attack. There are articles about them being severely understaffed, about inadequate follow-up. Caseloads are so heavy they can't possibly investigate every claim or properly check on families with foster children. Even the director might lose her job or resign.

Jenny can't believe she put all this in motion, but is glad, even proud of herself for helping to make such a change, not only for Margaret, but for all the other little foster kids who aren't being taken care of. They will continue to search for Margaret, but now it seems they believe the foster parents did something horrible to her.

Jenny pictures Margaret's little face on a milk carton and on fliers stuck in envelopes along with coupons or stapled to telephone poles. *Have you seen me?* Her face and statistics will be plastered on the walls of police stations, given out to people, photocopied over and over again until it doesn't even look like her anymore. It's a big story now and she and Gene need to be really careful.

Gene talks to his buddy Ray the next day. They have never used the phone on the kitchen wall; Gene said there couldn't be any calls out. It all leaves a trail. When it rings Jenny knows it must be the police or the FBI or someone from DCF looking for Margaret. Gene's face is serious while he says everything is fine and how much he appreciates it and when Jenny realizes who he is talking to she relaxes and goes back to cutting Margaret's waffle.

Gene says, "Okay. I'll see you soon," and Jenny knows Ray is coming back from Florida. She had been secretly hoping he wouldn't come back at all, that he would stay down there at least for the winter and the house would be theirs and they would become a real family. There wouldn't be any rush to make a decision right away and the longer they had Margaret the more attached Gene would get. And she would grow and change enough so people wouldn't recognize her. Now Ray is coming back.

"How long til he gets here?" she asks.

"He's stopping in Atlanta to see his sister. Probably be here in maybe a week. He said we can stay on as long as we want, but I wouldn't put him in the middle of this."

"Middle of what?"

He frowns and takes her hand, walks her into the bedroom where they sit on the edge of the unmade bed. "You know we have to do something with her before he comes back. Ray's not big on kids, especially kidnapped ones."

"Don't say that word. You know that's not what happened. At least call her Margaret. Or Meggie. I don't see why we have to do something right now. I mean I think it's too dangerous right now while the story is still so big in the news."

"Kidnapping is a federal offense and I don't plan to spend the next thirty or forty years in jail."

"We can figure it out. We can make it work." She turns to him, puts her arm around his neck and presses into him. "Let's make a plan. Let's go somewhere, the three of us."

He takes her arm off him, pulls back to study her face. "We are going somewhere. The two of us."

Everyone wants to tell her what to do, everyone wants to be in control of her life like she isn't smart enough to make decisions. "We didn't talk about it yet, not really. It isn't just up to you. We've been good, the three of us. There has to be a reason we have her."

"You know we can't keep her. And you know why we have her. You never think you're gonna get caught, do you?"

Jenny shakes her head and looks towards the doorway, expecting Margaret to be standing there, wishing she would be, but the doorway is empty. She feels herself getting angry but keeps her voice low. "If we give her back you know they'll just put her in another foster home. They don't care. She's not even three yet and who knows how many foster homes she's had. You don't think I can do it, do you? Be a good mother?"

"You're not her mother."

There is so much Jenny wants to say but it won't do any good. He's not listening, not hearing her and not caring what she has to say or how she feels. She needs to get out of there. She stands and faces him. "I need to go to the store."

"What do you need? I'll get it."

"Female things. I need Tampax and pads and I want to ask the Pharmacist what's good for cramps. Do you want me to make you a list?"

His mouth tightens and his eyes look like they don't believe her. He hesitates a few more seconds. "There's a store about fifteen minutes down the road. It sells just about everything. Go left out the driveway and stay on this road til you come to an intersection. It's no more than a mile. Take a right and you'll see it on your right. You need to be careful, Jen. I mean it." He fishes the credit card out of his pocket and hands it to her. "Get beer, too, and a bottle for Ray. And come right back."

"I won't be long." She likes throwing his words back at him. She walks out before he changes his mind, into the kitchen where she kisses Margaret on top of her head and tells her she is going to the store like any normal mother, grabs the keys and is out the door.

As soon as she turns out of the driveway and is out of sight of the house Jenny feels like a new person, a powerful person, a person in control. She drives a little fast with the windows down, the radio on country. The road dips and curves like whoever put it in was pretty wasted.

There is half a joint in the ashtray and no other cars on the road. She lights it and takes a deep hit, thinks about what she will get at the store as she drives past a house with a low stone wall in front, a trailer for sale in the driveway, then further down a white house she would like to have, with a front porch with two rocking chairs and plants. A peaceful place. No chain-link fences, plastic furniture or ugly office buildings. Just her and nature. Maybe she is meant to live in the country. As long as there are a few places to go, a couple of stores and bars, she will be all set.

She thinks about Gene and Margaret back at the house, which right now seems like it is a million miles away. And she thinks about her conversation with Gene and wonders why she is fighting so hard to keep Margaret, whether she really wants her or whether she just wants to win for once.

Gene was right about the store having a little bit of everything. She pulls out a shopping cart and takes her time going up and down the aisles, stops and looks at the shampoo and conditioner. She studies the hair dye, finds one that is supposed to be mild. Organic. Everything is organic these days. She chooses a soft dark brown. Chestnut, it's called, the same color as hers. Gene will be so impressed she thought of this.

As she goes through the rest of the store a few people nod or smile or say hello. So friendly here. She pockets a box of toothpicks, puts a new lipstick in the cart, tampons and hand lotion and a little stuffed dog for Margaret, white with black spots. Then she gets maple cookies, a case of beer, a bottle of orange vodka she will put in the freezer and a bottle of Wild Turkey for Ray.

She waits at the register behind a man buying a newspaper and a can of chewing tobacco, notices the jar on the counter, just sitting there holding change and folded bills. She never has any cash. There is no one behind her and she puts her purse up on the counter, studies the rack that holds lollipops and chooses a bright pink one. Bubblegum. Margaret can have it while Jenny does her hair.

As the man in front of her puts the tobacco in his pocket and takes the newspaper, the young man behind the counter tells him to have a nice day. He actually sounds like he means it. She loves how friendly people are up here.

Jenny watches the young man scan each of her items and when he tells her the total she pulls her credit card out of her wallet and hands it to him. Once everything is bagged and in her cart, he hands her the receipt and tells her to have a nice day. "You too," she says with a smile.

Instead of going right back to Ray's, Jenny goes the opposite way, just to see what's down the road. She is free now and not in a hurry to get back. She passes a store with tractors and lawn mowers and grills out front, then a little way further a pizza place where she stops and gets two large Italian subs and a small cheese pizza. She will be the one to make everyone happy today. On the way back to Ray's she sips on a beer and finishes the joint and feels happier than she has in a long time.

As soon as she pulls into the driveway Gene is outside and doesn't look happy. "You get lost?"

She steps out of the van, gives him a quick kiss and a smile, and together they carry everything inside. It feels good to be the one missed.

Margaret loves her puppy, and as soon as they are sitting at the kitchen table eating the incredible lunch Jenny brought, it starts to rain and it seems perfectly planned. The windows are open to the sound of the raindrops hitting the trees, the leaves and branches. That's all. Even the birds are quiet. They are going to be all right. They are a family.

They enjoy their subs and beer and Margaret eats two slices of pizza, crust and all. She is such a good girl. She and Gene share a joint after they eat, then Margaret is ready for her nap. Maybe she and Gene can lie down, too, and the day will be perfect. People always say how hard it is having kids, all the time it takes and how much work it is, but it is all so easy. When Gene is in the bathroom Jenny pours two shots of vodka and opens two more beers, undoes another button on her shirt.

Gene walks back into the kitchen, glances at the table and smiles, sits back down and throws back his shot. "When Ray gets here we'll stay maybe one more night then take off. We still have a little time to figure out where we'll head. Probably a good idea to get to another state. We can tell Ray she's your niece."

He seems as content as she is now and Jenny is proud of herself for making that happen, for making him see they are a family. She nods as if it is exactly what she had been thinking. He must have decided this while she was gone, while he was alone with Margaret. She drinks her shot, cold and hot at the same time.

"Do we have enough money to do that?" she asks. They will plan this together. "I like it around here, don't you? Everyone seems so nice."

He takes a swig of beer, looks around the kitchen. "There's not much to do, probably not much for work. I thought we would move on to a city, maybe something in upper New York." He smiles at her, finally. "I thought you were going crazy here."

"I told you I just needed to get out for a while. I think I could get used to it. We could probably get lost up here."

He smiles a lazy, drunk smile. "We have to do something with her before we go anywhere. I'm thinking we can bring her to a church or a library or something. Probably not a library. A church. Has to be a church around here."

Jenny stares at him. He can't possibly mean it; he couldn't just leave her somewhere. Not their Margaret. She takes a swallow of beer and wants to say the right thing, but doesn't trust her voice right now.

"She's a good kid," he says, as if she doesn't know. "Someone will find a home for her. Someone up here will probably just take her in, like we did. No paperwork or foster home. Now that it's been on the news there's probably a lot of people feeling sorry for her, lots of people wanting to take her in." He lights a cigarette and Jenny tries to find the right words.

"I thought you liked her, though. I thought maybe you were coming around to keeping her. She's crazy about you."

"Liking her and keeping her are two different things, Jenny girl. I like a lot of people. Doesn't mean I want to live with them. Come over here."

Jenny sits on his lap, puts her arms around his neck and he rubs her back with one hand, slips the other hand up her shirt.

"You didn't think we were keeping her, did you? We talked about this. Time to cut our losses. We're not gonna raise someone else's kid just because they don't want her. She's not our problem."

He kisses her, unhooks her bra, and as much as she wants him she's not finished talking about Margaret.

She slides off his lap, retrieves the bottle from the freezer and pours two more shots. She drinks hers down, walks to the doorway and stares at the little shape curled up on the couch under the flag, asleep and innocent and trusting them to do right by her. She loves that flag and Jenny loves that little girl.

She turns back to him but doesn't sit down. "You could actually do that? Just drop her off and leave her somewhere? Does that mean you could do that to me, too?"

Gene steps over and puts his arms around her. "You know better than that. You're my girl. She isn't ours. We took care of her for a while, got her out of a bad situation, and now it's time for someone else to step up. Time for us to get back on the road."

Chapter 7

When Margaret wakes up from her nap, Jenny has everything ready. "I have a surprise for you."

She has Margaret sit on a chair with her back to the kitchen sink, four books under her to make her the right height. "Just like at the salon."

She follows the directions on the box, except for the part about not using it on children under five. After she rinses it out, she says, "You are going to look so beautiful." Jenny carefully combs Margaret's hair, parting it in the middle while Margaret sits very still, as if she is used to getting her hair cut.

Jenny has never cut anyone's hair but her own, but she knows she can do a good job. She tells Margaret to close her eyes and combs some of her hair down in front of her face, cuts bangs, then cuts about five inches all around so Margaret's hair barely reaches her shoulders. When she carries her into the bedroom and stands in front of the mirror, Margaret touches her hair and looks at Jenny in the mirror and smiles. It is one of her few smiles, a gift for Jenny.

"See? You have the same hair as me now." They could easily pass for mother and daughter. "Let's go show Gene."

"Hey. Look at you," is all he says. He smiles at Jenny and she can tell he is proud of her for thinking of changing her looks like this.

With the weeks that have passed and her new haircut, Margaret looks way different than she did the day they got her. Her face has filled out and she has grown taller. And now her hair. Even her own mother probably wouldn't recognize her.

It's the first time Jenny has thought about the mother. She thought about the guy in the store and she thought about the foster parents and the social worker, but she has never really thought of Margaret's birth mother. She must have been a really bad mother to have such a good kid taken away from her.

They all sit on the couch together and watch old episodes of Seinfeld, eat Ritz crackers and strawberry jam like they did on their first day as a family.

Jenny thinks of their life before, how free they were, and sometimes she wants that back but mostly she doesn't. Now that she knows what it is like to be a mother, how easy it is and how full her life is now she wants less and less to go back to their old life. The three of them feel just right and Jenny wonders if Gene will ever want to settle down. This might be her only chance. If they keep Margaret they won't have a choice; they will have to settle down somewhere and have a life together, be a family. She is already a great mother.

Later that night, after a supper of waffles and sausage, Margaret is sound asleep in bed and Jenny and Gene watch the news. Gene doesn't mention it anymore, but he probably still has some hope someone will come up with a reward for Margaret. Something. You never know who might step up.

Then there is breaking news. Everything is breaking news. Jenny thinks it will be something about Margaret, and in a way it is. A 9-month-old boy was found dead in a car outside an apartment building. The father discovered his son in the car and called 911, but the infant was pronounced dead at the scene.

Jenny covers her mouth with her hands. "Oh my God! Oh my God. See? Oh my god. I knew it. I told you. Do you see now?"

"What?" Gene asks. "What are you talking about?"

"If we weren't there she would have died. Shhh. Listen.

There are no more details at this time. We will keep you up to date as more information becomes available. Turning to local news, a heartbreaking story about a bold theft that leaves a family devastated.

Jenny is still standing in front of the television when she sees her own face on the screen. There she is earlier today in the store, smiling at the guy behind the counter, pulling the jar close, hiding it behind her purse and slipping it into the side pocket. They play it over and over, telling the world it was a collection jar for a local girl with leukemia, and then there is the girl's mother saying how awful it is and asking what kind of a person would do such a thing.

Jenny feels something in her stomach rising up to her throat, something like guilt, but also anger for all the judgement coming at her.

Gene stands up and turns to her, grabs her arm. "Are you kidding me? Jesus, Jenny. Jesus."

"What? I didn't know there was a camera."

"You didn't know there was a camera? Are you kidding me? There's cameras everywhere. I told you that a thousand times. I can't believe this."

He's standing now as the newsman asks people with any information to contact the police. "I let you go out one time and this is what you do?"

"You *let* me go out? What am I, in jail?" She starts pacing. She had forgotten all about that stupid jar. Just a minute ago they saw how a little boy died in a car and she knew it was a clear sign she did the right thing and she wanted Gene to see it, too, and then he would know they were meant to save her, but now he's mad at her about a stupid jar and there is nothing she can do or say to make it better.

"You're something else, you know that? Can't let you out of my sight for a minute. You trying to get us caught?" He faces her now. "Where is it?"

Her purse is hanging on the bedroom doorknob, where she always keeps it. It's a nice big one, brown and soft like real leather. She walks over to it and pulls out the jar, notices for the first time the picture of the girl. A smiling little blonde girl who doesn't look like she is sick at all. It's probably a scam.

"It was just sitting there. Then it was in my purse and I was walking out." It's not like it should come as a shock to him.

Gene pours out the jar onto the kitchen table, a nickel rolling onto the floor. While she sits there like a guilty kid, her arms crossed in front of her chest, he counts and folds the bills, stuffs them in his pocket and leaves the change scattered on the table. Why should he get to keep it? She doesn't say anything.

"We need to get on the road first thing in the morning now. We need to bring her somewhere and then we'll head north. If someone saw the van, noticed the Mass plates and even part of the numbers, we're screwed."

"No one saw anything. Remember how you said everyone minds their own business?" She wants to argue about bringing Margaret somewhere, wants to tell him she can't just leave her now, but he is too angry.

Her grandmother would be so upset to see this. Homeless and in trouble, on the run for being so stupid. With a little girl who isn't really theirs, even though Jenny tries to believe she is, that somehow they were meant to have her, be a family. She needs to make him see this. "Where will we go?"

Gene shakes his head. "Away from here. And you need to stay out of sight. No more stores for you until we get at least a few towns away."

"Don't be mad at me. We got some cash, right?" She wants to ask Gene how much money was in the jar, wants to ask him if he has any money saved from being in the service, but she feels like she has no right. And it would diminish her, diminish the trust they have in each other. She scoops up the change, mostly quarters at least, and spills it into the bottom of her purse. Splitting the money with him like this makes it seem again like they are in this together. She watches Gene as he peels the girl's face off the jar, crushes it into a ball and shoves it into the trash along with the jar.

In the morning Gene isn't next to her when she wakes up. Jenny starts to sit up, then lies back down. Her head is aching and her mouth is so dry. She shouldn't have had that shot right before she went to bed, but she needed to calm herself and calm Gene and it seemed to work. He didn't say anything else about the jar and to Jenny that is forgiveness.

When she opens her eyes again Gene is standing in the doorway all shaved and showered and dressed. He never has a hangover. "Hey sunshine. I'm going to the store. Try to be ready when I get back."

He turns and is gone before Jenny can ask what she needs to be ready for. She tells herself the same thing she tells herself every day when she wakes up with such a godawful hangover, that she will cut down on the booze and stick to pot and whatever else Gene can get. It's the booze that kills her.

She uses the bathroom, then walks out to the empty kitchen and pours herself a cup of coffee, stands in the doorway and sips it while she watches Margaret. She is sitting on the couch with the doll in her lap, talking more than she ever has. "My love you. My your mama. Mama love you." Such a sweet kid, so used to her new life. Not just used to it, but happy, happier and more content than she ever was in that foster home. Jenny walks over to her, kisses the top of her head. "Hi sweetie."

Margaret looks at Jenny, picks up her doll and hugs it. Jenny can't imagine not having her in her life, not seeing her in the morning or putting her to bed at night. "You love your baby, don't you?"

Margaret nods, looks at her doll. "My her mama."

"I'm your mama. Did you know that? Can you call me mama?"

Margaret stares at her with those scared eyes. "Mama?"

Jenny feels her eyes filling. She puts her arms around Margaret, pulls her onto her lap. If Gene sees them like this, if he hears Margaret call her mama he couldn't possibly take her away, leave her

89

somewhere. He has to change his mind. "Yes. I'm your mama."

She remembers all the times she sat by Margaret's bed when she was sleeping, whispering her name, saying her mama was here and not to worry. She doesn't deserve it. Or maybe she does. Maybe she deserves it more than anyone else.

She kisses the top of her head and slips her off her lap. In the kitchen she pours herself another cup of coffee and carries it into the bathroom to have after her shower. *Mama.* Will it be enough to make Gene change his mind?

Gene is back in about an hour with two iced coffees, a newspaper, a black suitcase, a little pink backpack for Margaret and a pint of coffee brandy. Jenny is out of the shower, where she has gone over and over in her mind what she could say to Gene, how she could make him see they can't just leave Margaret somewhere after saving her. It wouldn't make any sense. If he loves her enough he will see how much Margaret means to her. He has been saying Margaret is not theirs, but she is. He will say they don't want the responsibility right now, that they have no jobs, no place to live and what kind of life is that for a kid? Jenny doesn't have the answers, just a need to show she can be a good mother, a need to prove she is a good person. Divine intervention is what she really needs.

"Thought we'd pack right this time." Gene sets the suitcase and backpack on the bed, pulls Jenny in for a hug and kisses her. "You good?"

"She called me mama."

He looks at her and smiles, opens her shirt and kisses the tops of her breasts.

"She did. She called me mama." Jenny pushes away from him a little but he pulls her back and laughs.

"You're my mama." He kisses her on the forehead and steps away, opens the suitcase. "We need to get a move on."

Jenny follows him out to the kitchen where he sets the coffees on the counter and opens the newspaper. There is Jenny on the bottom of the front page. It's blurry, but they both know it is her, slipping the jar into her purse. *Stealing Hope* is the headline. Talk about drama.

She takes a sip of her iced coffee then takes the cover off and pours in some brandy and takes it into the bedroom. She puts her things into one side of the suitcase, leaves it open and takes the backpack to Margaret's room to pack her things, still not believing they are not taking Margaret with them.

She is leaving with a lot more than she came with, and whoever finds her will know they took good care of her.

Now Jenny is crying and can't believe she feels so awful about this, so sad. Two months ago she didn't even know Margaret existed, now it feels like she is losing her own child. All she ever really wanted was to have a life with Gene and now that doesn't seem like enough. But there is nothing she can do.

She picks up the flag and folds it carefully, puts it on top of Margaret's clothes, the pony pajamas, the book. She stands there a minute and wipes her cheeks before she zips up the backpack and carries it out to the kitchen where Margaret sits.

She's not coloring or playing with her doll, but just sitting there waiting, as if she knows what's going to happen and accepts it. They both have to accept it.

Jenny sits across from her for a few seconds and Margaret just looks at her with those sad eyes but doesn't say anything, doesn't ask what is going on, doesn't call her mama again. Jenny doesn't know what to say either, so she gets up and wipes the clean counter, gets the broom and sweeps the floor.

In a minute Gene is standing there with the suitcase in one hand, Margaret's backpack in the other. He sets them down in the doorway, pours a little more brandy into each of their coffee cups. A final, wordless toast, then he picks up the suitcase and backpack. "All set?"

Jenny takes a deep breath. "Come on, honey." She holds out her hand and Margaret climbs down from the chair and takes it. Jenny feels like she is going to lose it, but she can't. She will be strong. Gene is right; they have done enough. Even though Margaret doesn't belong to them, Jenny can't help but feel she might be sending her to her death. The little boy in that car didn't have a chance and now Margaret won't either. Once they are miles away from here she will be fine. They will be fine and Margaret will be fine and they will all get over it.

"Where we going?" Margaret asks. She hasn't been out of the house since they got there, except for the back yard, and she has no idea where she is. Now they are going to bring her somewhere and just leave her. They are no better than the people who left her in the car. Maybe worse because they know exactly what can happen.

"Church," Gene answers. "We're going to church."

"Church?" Her little eyes are so innocent, so trusting.

"It's where Jesus lives," Jenny tells her. Poor kid doesn't even know what church is. This is one more way Jenny knows she was meant to be part of Margaret's life, introducing her to Jesus. It makes Jenny think about seeing the face of Jesus the night before they found Margaret and it helps her to trust and hope it is all right and good, like they have come full circle in just a few weeks. She slipped that holy card in the back pocket of her jeans that morning. *Sacred Heart of Jesus, pray for me.*

"Jesus is God," she tells Margaret. "Well, actually he's the son of God, but he is the one who answers all your prayers. And sometimes his mother, Mary." Margaret stares at her and Jenny realizes she probably doesn't even know what prayers are. "If you want something, you just ask Jesus. He lives up in heaven, and if you ask him for something you have to really, really want it with all your heart, and it has to be a good thing, not something selfish. And you have to be a really, really good girl all the time. Understand?"

"My a good girl." Margaret is staring at Jenny with such sadness and hope, looking like she is going to cry. "Mama? My stay with you?"

"See? Did you hear that? Did you hear her call me mama?"

"I'll put the stuff in the van. Make sure we have everything, okay? We won't be back in this neck of the woods for a while."

Jenny lifts her up, notices how much heavier she is than that first day and wonders how she knows they are going to leave her. "You are with me, sweetheart. I'm right here. And you are such a good girl. You're a very good girl." She kisses her cheek and follows Gene out the door.

The church is called St. Augustine's. Gene saw it on one of his afternoons out and as far as he's concerned one church is as good as another. It is the first time Margaret has been in the van since that first day and she holds tight onto Jenny when they slide open the door to the back, so Jenny lets her sit on her lap up front. They drive in silence for the ten minutes it takes to get there.

It's a simple church, bright white with a steeple like you see in postcards of New England. Jenny looks up to see if there is a bell, but it just comes to a point with a cross on top nearly blending in with the pale blue sky.

Gene parks around the back of the church and there is only one other car, a faded green Volvo. Only now does Jenny begin to panic, only now does it seem like they are really doing this. She doesn't want to get out of the van. She wants Gene to smile at her and keep driving, but he turns off the ignition, takes a deep breath as he looks at Jenny and Margaret. "Let's do this."

Can't he see this isn't right, that this isn't what's supposed to happen? Margaret holds tight to Jenny's hand as they walk towards a wooden door, and Jenny tries to feel strong, in control, like a mother should feel. Maybe the door will be locked. That would be a sign. But it opens easily and they walk in like a family. She will kneel and pray and ask for God's forgiveness, though Jenny is sure God knows she didn't mean any harm to Margaret. God knows she never meant any harm to anyone in her life.

Jenny's heart is pounding as they walk to a pew in the back, trying to act like it is something they do every day, or at least every Sunday. It smells like incense and furniture polish.

There is no one there to see them, but Jenny knows they are being watched so she smiles and genuflects as she faces the altar like she did as a little girl. As she starts to step in, Gene puts his hand on her arm to stop her so Margaret can go in first.

It is good to be there; it is just where they are supposed to be and Jenny feels holy, bringing Margaret to Jesus. Jenny kneels and closes her eyes and says a Hail Mary, then an Our Father. She asks Jesus to send her a sign so she will know what to do.

When she looks over at Margaret she is sitting still, looking up at Jesus nailed to the cross, a few drops of blood on his face from his crown of thorns. The top of her head just reaches the back of the pew and her little legs stick out straight.

The windows are plain, no stained glass, no images of the saints. They must save that for the big churches, the expensive churches. There's a table, an altar with a white cloth over it, a simple white tablecloth. Come to the table of Jesus.

Jenny doesn't know how they can just leave her there and she doesn't know how they can take her with them to start their life together, always afraid someone will find them, afraid of every knock on the door. So she just closes her eyes again and says a prayer, not to Jesus or Mary, but to her grandmother in heaven. She prays they are doing the right thing, the only thing, leaving it all up to the powers that be.

Gene puts his hand on her shoulder and whispers in her ear. "Let's go. Tell her to stay here. Tell her we'll be right back."

Jenny touches the top of Margaret's head gently, the soft hair the same color as her own, looks into her sweet, trusting face. Margaret looks scared, like she knows what is going to happen, and Jenny uses her calmest voice. "Stay here, honey, okay? We'll be right back."

Margaret puts her little arms around Jenny's neck and hugs her tight. "My go too?"

"We'll be right back. I promise. You stay here and say a prayer, okay? Talk to Jesus in your head. We'll be right back." She gently pulls Margaret's hands away.

Telling lies in church. It doesn't get much worse than that. Jesus will never forgive her. Does he understand she has no choice? Does she have a choice? She's not sure of anything now but the feel of Gene's hand on the small of her back, gently leading her away. It's all she can do to keep from crying. She'll cry later, when she's alone.

Margaret stays still, her eyes on Jenny, and Jenny takes one last look at the altar, at Jesus on the cross, then follows Gene out of the church. She tries to make herself feel nothing, but the tears are there, for herself and for Margaret, but maybe mostly for herself. Margaret will be okay. They will all be okay.

They walk quickly to the van and Gene climbs in, slams his door and starts it up, breaking the silence of the deserted parking lot. Jenny looks up at the sky, looking for something – a sign? But there will probably be no more signs for her after this. There is still no one around. Hopefully the Volvo belongs to a priest who will find a good and loving home for Margaret.

As Jenny puts her hand on the door handle, about to get in the van and drive away with Gene to start their new life, she turns for one last look at the church and there is Margaret standing in the doorway, looking tiny and lost and alone. Jenny glances over at Gene through the window and it is almost like the day they found Margaret, as if time has slowed down so she can see it all clearly and know what is happening and they are back in the movie again.

Jenny hasn't gotten into the van yet. She can't seem to move as her eyes fix on Margaret, waiting. And Gene is waiting. Everyone is waiting. Jenny takes a step away from the van and opens her arms, watches Margaret run towards her, running for her life.

Chapter 8

Margaret knows she has to be a good girl all the time, even when she is alone, especially when she is alone, even walking home from school or waiting for her mother and Gene to come home. Jesus is always with her, watching her.

Sometimes it is a good feeling, like Jesus is keeping her safe, but sometimes it scares her to be watched all the time. Mama told her that Jesus sees everything and knows everything even what she is thinking, so she has to have pure thoughts. Margaret isn't sure what pure thoughts are, so she tries not to think too much about anything because God punishes bad girls. If she starts thinking about school and the mean girls, she pushes it all out and says the Our Father or Hail Mary over and over in her head. If she is good enough Jesus will answer her prayers and make everything all right, make mama and Gene stop fighting and love each other. She likes when they tell her what a good girl she is and what a big girl she is, but it still isn't enough.

Mama is upset or sad most of the time. She says she hates her life and can't believe they ended up in a trailer with no money. She walks around and cries and smokes and drinks and talks out loud, but not to Margaret. *How the hell did I end up here? I should be living in a decent place by now and I'm living in a goddamn trailer. Jesus Christ.* Margaret is so afraid for her mother's soul. She is the one who told her how important it is to be good, to love Jesus. She taught Margaret the Ten Commandments and what they mean, but she forgets sometimes. Sometimes Margaret doesn't know if she should stay out of her mother's sight or if her mother needs to hold her and cry, so mostly Margaret just watches and stays quiet.

That's something else mama and Gene like her to be, quiet.

She prays for her mother, even though she isn't sure Jesus will forgive her mother if she doesn't tell him herself that she is sorry for her sins. It doesn't seem like her mother means to sin, though, and Margaret makes herself believe Jesus will forgive her and not send her to hell.

When her mother is really angry it is at Gene because he should be doing something to make things better. She says they will never get out of the damn hole and Margaret pictures a hole big enough to swallow the trailer, a hole they sink into deeper and deeper until they are all buried too deep to ever climb out. Her mother tells him he needs to be a man, that it is about time he grew up and started taking care of his family.

"You're the one wanted a family so bad you couldn't wait til we were both ready to have our own, and you're the one can't keep a job more than a week." Gene says this a lot and it gives Margaret a funny feeling in her stomach and chest, like there is something heavy and dark there and she hopes it's not sin. It might be all her fault. Her mother told her so many times how much she wanted her, and even though she doesn't say Gene didn't want her, Margaret is pretty sure it's true, and that's why they fight about money.

When mama gets fired from jobs, she says the other women were jealous and didn't like her or, *You know I have to be here to take care of Margaret.* Margaret doesn't want to be any trouble, doesn't want to be the reason they fight, so when she isn't helping her mother with the cooking or cleaning she just tries to be invisible and have pure thoughts.

The fights end when one of them walks out. Her mother walks out when he talks about her sticky fingers as the reason she can't keep a job, but she doesn't go far or for very long like he does. She usually walks over to Darlene's to tell her about her problems and drink gin and tonics.

Darlene is the biggest person Margaret has ever seen and it scares her a little to be near her, as if Darlene might smother her if she gets too close. Darlene is her mother's only friend, and just like the girls in school, they don't want Margaret around when they are together, as if Margaret would ruin everything. Once when Margaret followed her mother just to see if she was okay, her mother told her to go home and leave her alone.

Whenever Gene leaves, her mother cries, but when her mother leaves, Gene winks at Margaret and says, *finally, some peace.*

It seems like everyone in the world is complaining, that no one is ever happy about anything. The people who call in to talk on the radio complain about gas prices or taxes or illegal immigrants; her mother complains about her life and Gene complains about mama.

They have some good days, too, when the three of them sit at the table and Gene and mama talk and drink and sing country songs playing on the radio, then after a while Gene takes mama's hand and they go in their room and close the door. This is when Margaret feels so lucky, like Jesus is listening to her prayers.

Then something happens and everything changes, as if a button has been pushed in her mother and she is a different person. When this happens, nothing can make her happy. After a while, with mama slamming doors and swearing, starting in on Gene about getting off his ass and finding a job, he turns off the radio and looks up at mama and says, *Enough, okay? Give it a rest. Jesus.* This makes mama either madder or sad. She either calls him names or starts crying and Margaret knows it is time for him to leave again. Her mother must know this, too, and Margaret wonders why she is like this, why she makes him leave. Then Margaret tells herself her mother can't help it and she says another prayer.

When the door closes behind Gene, everything feels different. Sometimes Margaret wonders what he would do if she went after him and asked him to stay, but she isn't brave enough to do it yet. She and mama end up alone again and Margaret waits to see whether her mother is mad at her, too. Sometimes she is and sometimes she isn't and Margaret waits to see which way it goes. She is almost eight now and is tall and very smart for her age. Some day she will know exactly what to do to make everyone happy.

After Gene leaves it never takes long for her mother to stop crying and talking to herself and change the radio from talking back to country music. She turns it up loud and knows all the words to all the songs. Most of the songs are sad, about people being lonely, about tears and heartache, cheating boyfriends and trucks and people left behind. Maybe it makes her mother feel better to know other people have troubles and are sad and left alone, too, except her mother isn't really alone.

Once Margaret reminded her, "I'm here, mama. I'll never leave you." She tried to hug her, but her mother pulled away.

"You don't know what you're talking about," she said. "Everyone leaves me."

"I won't. I promise."

"Right." You say that now, but when you get older you'll leave first chance you get."

If her mother isn't angry they sit at the kitchen table and Margaret puts together a puzzle or colors in a coloring book or practices her cursive. She likes to draw, and once she made a special picture of the trailer and the trees around it. She put in sunflowers and a rainbow in the background and the sun shining in the corner. Next to the trailer she drew the three of them holding hands, and at the bottom she wrote *My Family*. It made her mother cry and Margaret asked, "Do you like it?"

Her mother just went into the bathroom and ran the water like she always does when she wants to be alone. Gene laughed at first, then said it was a great picture and he put it up on the refrigerator with a magnet from George's pizza. The next day, the picture and the magnet were in the trash, so now Margaret colors in coloring books or just makes designs that don't mean anything.

When her mother is in a good mood, she tells her stories about when she was young. Margaret has heard them lots of times, but some of the details change enough so they are new stories every time. When her mother tells her stories Margaret feels special, like she is getting a present no one else is getting and that no one can ever take away.

She tells Margaret about being in junior high school and then high school, which both seem like magical places to Margaret. Her mother tells her how all the boys used to stare at her when she walked down the halls. Her face gets soft and happy and Margaret tries to picture her young. She tells Margaret how she used to sneak out of the house at night when her parents were sleeping, about meeting Gene and walking around, going up on the roof of his apartment building and lying on a blanket, looking up at the stars. She even tells Margaret about her first kiss when she was only twelve, and Margaret hopes she will have her first kiss when she is twelve, too. She says when she and Gene first met it was like magic. "I never wanted anyone else," she says. "From the minute I saw him I knew. And it was the same for him."

Mostly she likes to tell Margaret how pretty she was, how the other girls were jealous because all the boys wanted to be with her. "My own mother was jealous, for Christ sake." She blows smoke towards the open window, then smiles at Margaret. "Another story for another time." I was too pretty; that was my problem.

She tells Margaret about the mean girls, always trying to make her look bad and calling her the worst names and spreading rumors. She pulls her fingers through her hair as she talks and her eyes get watery. Margaret doesn't know what to say to make her mother happy again. Only Gene can do that. She tries sometimes, though.

"You're still pretty, mama. You're beautiful."

It makes her smile, but it is a sad smile. "Lotta good it does me, huh?"

Margaret wishes Gene would walk in right then, wishes as hard as she can that this one time he would only be gone only a little while and come back. Then he and mama could talk and be happy and she would feel safe again.

"You better smarten up when you start meeting boys," her mother says. Her voice sounds a little mad now and Margaret stops making her puzzle and looks at her mother so she can see she is listening, that she is a good girl. "You go for someone who's nice to you, someone who treats you like you are the most important thing in the world. And pick someone who's smart and has a plan for the future, a career ahead of him. Never mind what he looks like. You see how I ended up. Did I go for the nice ones, the ones who would have treated me like a queen? Course not."

Her mother looks away, takes a sip of her coffee and whiskey, then a drag of her cigarette, but Margaret knows she's not done. When her eyes are on her again they are her angry eyes as if Margaret just said something she wasn't supposed to, cigarette smoke filling the space between them. "I was just a kid. What did I know? I wanted the bad boy. Jesus, was I in love with him the first time I saw him. All the girls wanted to be with him but he wouldn't give them the time of day. I saw the way they stared at us when we were together, all jealous because he chose me. Lucky me."

After her mother is quiet for a few minutes. Margaret says, "Do you want me to make you a sandwich, mama?"

"I don't want a goddamn sandwich. I want a goddamn life. That's what I want. Can you give me that?"

There is nothing Margaret can say. When she thinks it's okay, when her mother seems to be lost in her thoughts or opens a magazine and has forgotten all about her, Margaret goes in her room, picks up her doll and lies down facing the wall. She stares at the yellow spot in the paneling until she is invisible. In a little while her mother might come in and lie down with her and she and Margaret fall asleep. Before she drifts off into sleep, mama always says, "My Meggie," and holds her close and everything feels almost right again.

After Gene is gone two or three days, Margaret watches her mother brush her hair and put on mascara and red lipstick. At first Margaret thinks Gene must be coming home today, then her mother just says, "I'll be back. You be a good girl. Stay in and watch t.v." It almost seems like she is talking to herself.

"Where are you going?" she asks.

"For a walk."

"Can I come?"

"Not today. Just be a good girl. He's out having a good time for himself. Why shouldn't I?"

"But I'll be good, mama."

Her mother laughs. "I know you will, but you can't come. I'm going to see the doctor." Then she leaves and Margaret watches t.v. and waits like a big girl. Her mother is only gone a couple of hours, and when she comes back her eyes are shiny and she is happy, so Margaret is, too.

And even though it feels like all they do is wait for him, Margaret and her mother are always surprised when the door squeaks open and Gene walks in like he has only been gone for a few minutes, like he had just gone to the store for cigarettes and a newspaper. It's always in the late afternoon, just when Margaret has given up hope for another day, just as she is thinking about what they might have for supper. A bowl of cereal or toast with peanut butter, but then there he is, standing in the doorway holding a pizza box in one hand and a suitcase of beer in the other. Every time Gene comes home it is the happiest moment of Margaret's life.

"Where's my girls?" he shouts, looking over Margaret's head as if she isn't right in front of him. Mama walks out of the bedroom or bathroom and Margaret knows she is happy to see him, too; she can tell by the way her eyes get bright again, like the girl she used to be in her stories.

But her mother holds onto her anger as if they had their fight just a few minutes ago or as if she doesn't love him. He usually wears a new jacket or shirt or boots, and he always has a new haircut. Margaret wonders if this is what mama means by him having a good time for himself. At first mama ignores him, but it doesn't take long for her to talk. She has been silent for days and is full of things to say by the time he comes home.

"You glad to see me?" he asks.

"Must be nice," mama says.

"Don't be like that."

"Do you ever think I might need something, too? Do you ever think I might like to go out and have half a life?"

He doesn't say anything for a minute or two while she walks off some of her anger, pacing and talking to him and to herself about not having a life and how this isn't what she signed up for, then he tries again and puts on his best smile. "Come on, Jenny girl. Better get a slice before Margaret and I eat it all."

Margaret watches the spray when he opens two cans of beer and hopes he will give her some. Everyone seems to be moving all at once as Margaret clears her coloring book and crayons from the table, puts away the rest of the beer and takes three paper plates out of the cabinet. Gene pulls off two slices, one for himself and one for Margaret, then turns on the radio. At first he hums, then one of their favorite songs comes on, like the radio knew exactly when he would come home. He sings along and Margaret can breathe again. Everything is perfect now, or will be as soon as her mother comes around. It is something her mother needs to do, though, acting for a little while like she is still mad, acting like she doesn't like him. Margaret is glad for this, though. She likes being the one who welcomes him home.

Gene fills the trailer with talk of where he has been and what he has seen, details and hints of his life for the past two or three weeks he has been gone. Mostly he tells about looking for a decent job, buddies with leads and how he landed a gig with some construction guys and worked in Vermont and even New York, doing grunt work until they didn't need him anymore. In the winter he says he worked in kitchens or did odd jobs at resorts, painting or carpentry or plumbing. Gene can do anything. She wants to be like that when she grows up, able to go anywhere she wants and to work at all kinds of interesting jobs.

Her mother picks up her beer and drinks it down, crosses her arms and pretends not to be interested, finishes her beer and gets another one without a word or sound except the door slamming behind her when she walks outside. Her mother wanting to be alone one more minute doesn't make sense to Margaret, but it makes a difference when she is out of the kitchen, out of the trailer. She takes all the bad feelings with her and Margaret has a few precious minutes alone with Gene.

Even though Margaret tries not to expect anything so she won't be greedy, Gene always brings presents for her, something he pulls out of his pocket when mama isn't there to see. He leans in close and says, "Gotcha a little something. For taking care of her for me." He winks and tilts his head towards the door and his voice makes her feel grown up and responsible.

It is always a surprise and Margaret loves whatever he brings her. When he holds it out she puts her hand under his and he opens his fingers slowly, like it's magic. It doesn't matter what he brings – sugar cubes wrapped in white paper or a little box of three or four crayons and a menu from a restaurant with puzzles on the back, sometimes a little bar of soap wrapped in paper. It doesn't matter. She loves everything Gene gives her and she loves the smell of him when she hugs him, cigarettes and beer, whiskey and coffee and aftershave, all mixed together. She loves the way his arm feels when she touches it, the dark hair and the muscles.

Nothing bad will ever happen as long as Gene is here. Sometimes he says he doesn't know what he would do without her and sometimes her mother tells her that, too. Both of them say the same words to her, but Gene is the one she believes the most.

Margaret likes to study Gene and he doesn't seem to mind, doesn't ask what she's looking at like her mother does. She notices how he takes big bites of pizza and talks before he swallows all his food. She stares at him as he tilts his head back to drink from his can of beer, watches his expression as he lights a cigarette, the way he sucks it in and holds it for a few seconds before he blows a stream of smoke towards the ceiling. Margaret tells him how she learned in school that smoking is bad for you, that it causes cancer. She can say things like that to him, things she would never say to her mother.

"It's a bad habit," he says. "Don't ever start. Once you start it's too late to stop. They put chemicals in it to make it impossible to stop."

"But you could try," she says. "You and mama could try together. She smokes a lot, too." A girl in school said her grandfather smoked a lot and died from lung cancer and now Margaret worries that mama and Gene might die from it, too.

"How was she?" His voice is lower now, in case mama walks in. She doesn't like when people talk about her.

Margaret shrugs. "She was sad. And mad. And she didn't eat much." Margaret leaves out the part when her mother goes out to see her doctor and have a good time for herself. If he knows she is sad and upset maybe he'll stop leaving them.

He reaches over and touches the back of her head, smooths her hair and looks at her. He is the only person in the world who seems to really look at her. "I know it's not easy on you. But I'm back now and things will be okay." He kisses her forehead and pours her some beer in a juice glass, and when mama walks back in he winks at Margaret like they are special friends with a secret.

Her mother still acts angry and won't look at either of them, so for a little while his stories are just for Margaret. He talks about drywall and forms and scaffolding and he sounds like the smartest man in the world. And Margaret loves the moment when he takes a roll of money out of his shirt pocket and sets it in the middle of the kitchen table. Her mother snatches it up and shoves it into the back pocket of her jeans without looking at it or counting it, as if someone else was going to get it. She takes a big sip of beer but still doesn't sit down. She turns on the faucet over the kitchen sink and wets the sponge, wipes the counter around the sink even though Margaret already cleaned it. Margaret wonders what she is thinking.

Her mother goes into the bathroom and in a few minutes she is back out with her hair brushed and pink lipstick on, still pretending to be mad until he pulls her onto his lap and feeds her a bite of pizza, slips his hand under her shirt and kisses her neck. He whispers how much he missed her and Margaret knows it's their time now.

When her mother laughs and calls him a son of a bitch, the ache that had settled in Margaret's chest since Gene left begins to soften and gives her room to breathe again.

They used to tell her to go outside and play, but now she leaves before they even ask. Sometimes she takes a paper cup with beer in it. As long as they are together again and she isn't in charge of her mother anymore, Margaret feels warm inside and as safe as she can be. She walks around outside but doesn't go far, then she sits on the rock and digs in the dirt with a stick until one of them, usually her mother, calls her in to help clean up and get ready for bed.

Chapter 9

Early Saturday morning, as soon as Margaret gets up and heads to the bathroom, she turns to see Gene pick up one of her sneakers and hold it out for her mother to see. It is filthy and there is a hole where her big toe began pushing through a couple of weeks ago. He holds it out with the very tips of his finger and thumb as if it is poison. "You see what she's wearing on her feet?"

Margaret remembers when the sneakers were new, the long walk to Valu-Mart last October. The leaves were all orange and red and yellow, but it was a hot day like summer instead of fall. Gene told her it was Indian summer and to enjoy it while it lasted.

How beautiful her mother looked in her yellow sundress and her shiny hoop earrings. She had lots of earrings, but those were Margaret's favorite. She had made Margaret wash her feet and change into clean clothes, but didn't tell her why. That was the day her mother told her the big secret, that she was going to have a baby.

"Don't say anything to anyone," her mother said. "We're not telling anyone yet."

Margaret didn't know who she would tell except maybe Amy, her friend at school, but they didn't really tell each other secrets. The only other person would be Gene, but he must already know. "How come?"

"Just for now. Until it's safe. So no one gets any ideas about doing anything about it."

Margaret tried to figure out what she meant, what ideas someone would get. The only things people did about babies was feed them, give them a soft place to sleep and hold them when they cry and change their diapers. The words made her feel a little afraid, but mostly she was happy because her mother was happy.

Kids in school talk about new baby brothers or sisters who took their place, who got all the attention, and Margaret could tell they were jealous and it's a sin to feel that way. She would never feel that way about her little brother or sister. She knew right away she would love the baby and help take care of it and be the best big sister in the world. When she took her mother's hand they smiled at each other and Margaret hoped the baby would make mama this happy all the time and that she would never be angry or sad again. And Gene wouldn't go away anymore. Margaret was so happy that day.

Now Gene tells her to stand up and she does as she is told and looks at the floor, her hair hiding her face while Gene talks about her skinny body and her ruined sneakers, how soon she will be walking around in her bare feet.

"You think I don't know?" her mother says.

"So that's what you want?"

Margaret stares at the gray swirls in the linoleum, wishes she had kept her sneakers cleaner, wishes her feet would stop growing. This fight is different from the others. Usually it is her mother who's upset about not having enough money to buy what they need, but now Gene is blaming mama for not having enough money. Margaret uses all her energy trying not to be afraid something awful is going to happen, that maybe Gene is going to leave again and this time he will never come back. She can't figure out whose fault it is; sometimes, like now, it feels like it is hers, that everything would be okay if she wasn't there. When she gets bigger she will get a job and bring home enough money so they can all be happy. Gene says they need to do the right thing. He is always so sure about everything.

Mama's hands rush to her belly, big now from the baby growing inside, and her voice is shaky. "I can't believe you. How can you even ask me to do this?"

"All I'm asking is for you to think about it. If you think about it you'll see it's the right thing."

"I won't. Don't even ask me to. I won't." She puts her hands over her ears and turns in a circle, something Margaret has seen her do before when she is upset. Then she stops and crosses her arms over her chest, turns her back on both of them, goes to the sink and turns on the water.

Margaret knows she is crying and Gene is going to leave, but he doesn't have that look in his eyes like he is already someplace else. Instead of walking out the door, he steps over to mama and puts his hand on the back of her head, smooths her hair, then rubs her back.

"We're talking about twenty grand here, Jenny girl. Starting over and having a better life. Isn't that what you want?" He makes his voice so nice.

Margaret turns and walks down the short hallway to the bathroom, closes the door softly. Whatever they are talking about scares her. It has something to do with her and she remembers things she has heard, mama talking about giving her back and Gene saying she was the one who made the choice. Her mother always says she had no choice. It's too hard to imagine who they would give her back to. Everyone knows babies come from God and you can't just give them back. Even so, Margaret knows sometimes her mother would do it if she could. It's her own fault for being so skinny and not taking better care of her sneakers.

She stands on her toes to look at herself in the mirror, her pale eyes and hair, her long face. Kids in school are mean to her sometimes. They call her ugly or ask what she is looking at if they catch her staring at them. All she is doing is trying to figure out how to be, how to act. They have something inside that she doesn't have, something that makes them belong. If she could figure out how to talk to people and how to act right and say the right thing, maybe she could have a friend, not like Amy who is only her friend sometimes.

She hopes she will be pretty like her mother when she grows up so all the boys will stare at her and want to go out with her, but she will choose the smart one, the nice one who will love her more than anything and take care of her. And even though her mother said not to go for the good-looking ones, she wants someone who is handsome like Gene. Sometimes she loves Gene more than she loves her mother, which doesn't seem right since she is pretty sure he isn't even her real father.

They only talked about it once but the words stay in her head. Gene had been home for a while and when he was in the bathroom, Margaret asked the question she had wanted to ask for a long time. *How come I call him Gene?*

That's his name.

I know but how come I don't call him daddy?
Because you call him Gene.
But isn't he my daddy?

Right at that moment Gene appeared and he smiled and touched the top of her head. *I'm as close to a daddy as you're ever going to get.*

She wonders if he will say this to the new baby someday. She picks up her mother's comb, pulls it through her hair but stops when she comes to a tangle and sets the comb back down on the edge of the sink.

When Margaret walks back out to the kitchen, mama and Gene are sitting at the table. It is getting dark outside now and rain taps on the roof and the windows. The only light on is the one over the stove, so it feels cozy in a way, but still something isn't right. The radio is off and the sound of the rain and the darkness outside closes in, so it feels like they are separate from the rest of the world. Margaret doesn't know whether to sit at the table with them or not, so she goes to her room and lies down on her bed with her doll and listens.

"Do you have any idea what you're saying? Do you even realize we're talking about a person here? This is our baby." Her mother's voice is a loud, angry whisper.

"We're talking about a hell of a lot of money here. We're talking about doing what we need to do. It's an opportunity and we have to take it. You tell me *I'm* selfish. Who's selfish now?"

"All we need is for you to get a job and start taking care of us. You said you would always take care of me. You promised." Mama sounds so sad.

"Don't put it all on me. You're the one got us into this in the first place. You had to have a kid right away, you had to keep her even though we weren't

115

ready. Well you kept her and now we're stuck here. And here you are wanting another one." Gene's voice is angry, too, then it gets softer so Margaret can barely make out the words. "This is our chance, Jen. We can get out of here, find a decent place to live and really start over. That's what you keep saying you want."

It is silent then and Margaret can't focus on the yellow spot enough to disappear. She wants to get up and go to her mother but is afraid to move. She wants to sit on her mother's lap even though she is getting too big for that now. They say she is a big girl but sometimes she doesn't feel like it; sometimes she is scared like a baby. She waits for more, wonders if they are all done talking, listens for the sound of the door.

Her father's voice is calm now. "I have to let Sam know by Saturday. One way or the other. Otherwise, they'll just find someone else. There's plenty of people in our situation, plenty of girls willing to give their baby a good home. That's what you should be thinking about. I know it's hard, but it's the only way."

"You don't know anything. It's not the only way. We can make it work. You know we can."

"Jen. We can't take care of one kid, never mind two."

"You are one son of a bitch. It doesn't matter to you one bit that this is our baby. Just hand it over to some strangers for a few bucks so you won't have the responsibility. You said we would have kids of our own someday. You promised. Well this is some day. This is our baby."

"It's twenty grand, Jen. That's a hell of a lot more than a few bucks. It means a whole new start for us. I promise. All you ever talk about is getting out of here, having a decent life. We won't ever get another chance like this."

It's silent for a few seconds, then her mother says, "What about Margaret?"

Margaret takes a deep breath and holds it.

"What about her?"

"She's a good girl. She's quiet and does what she's told. Anyone would love to have her."

Gene laughs for about a second, not even really a laugh. "Come on. They want a baby. And what makes you think you could give her up now if you couldn't do it five years ago?"

Margaret wants so much to understand what they are talking about, what they mean, but knows she could never ask. They would tell her she shouldn't have been listening, that it is none of her business.

Part of her doesn't want to know. Does her mother really want to give her away? She pictures her mother's face when she is upset, how her forehead scrunches up, how she presses her lips together tight to hold everything in and it looks like she hurts all over. Gene is the strong one and he will win. He always does whatever he wants, always gets his way.

Margaret lies very still, almost not breathing. Mama says she is a good girl, a quiet girl. Why would she want to give her away? It seems like they can only keep one, either her or the baby, so they have to give one of them away. Even though she doesn't eat much, she eats more than a baby. But she doesn't need diapers and diapers probably cost a lot of money. She is a big girl now and she can take care of herself and help take care of the baby, too. And she takes care of her mother when Gene is gone. That's probably why Gene wants to keep her and not keep the baby. She wonders what twenty grand is.

"Sam says they're good people," Gene's voice is all soft again. "He checked them out completely. The guy is some kind of college professor and they're really well off. Big house, big yard. They can't have a kid of their own and want one really bad. They'll give it a real good home, something we can't do right now. Once we're all set we'll have one of our own. I promise."

"You can't promise anything."

It gets quiet again and Margaret tries not to be so afraid. There is nothing to be afraid of, nothing to cry about. That's what Gene always tells her. She waits again for the sound of the door closing behind him, her mother crying. As soon as Gene is gone she will get up and go to her mother, tell her how good she will be. She will tell her not to be sad, that she will help take care of the baby and everything will be all right. But there is no sound of the door, no crying either. Just her father's voice again.

"We will. Soon as we're on our feet, when we have a decent house to bring it into. We'll have as many as you want, I promise. But we just can't have another kid right now. I gave in with her, didn't I? I knew how much you wanted her and you see where it got us. If we don't do this, we're screwed. We're way behind on the rent, they're gonna shut off the electric any day now, and forget about propane this winter. We're out of choices here. You think about it, okay? I'll be back in a little while."

"Where are you going? I'm coming with you."

"I won't be long. You need to stay with her."

'She's sleeping. She won't even know we're gone."

In a few seconds Margaret feels her mother in the doorway of her room watching her. She keeps her eyes closed, her breathing soft and even and then she hears the door squeak open, then closed, their footsteps on the gravel.

She is all alone, but not really. Somehow her little baby brother or sister is with her. Brother. She would really like to have a brother, telling her not to be afraid. Somehow she knows it is a boy and Margaret makes a picture of him in her imagination, like little baby Jesus. It isn't the first time she has been alone, and it is one more way she can prove she is no trouble. She tells herself they will be home when she wakes up and makes herself go to sleep, but first Margaret asks Jesus and Mary to please not let her parents give her or her baby brother away to strangers for a few bucks.

Chapter 10

It is hot and sticky again today. Between the heavy air and her belly Jenny can't seem to take in a good breath. She sips her coffee and glances at Margaret sitting across from her. They had the last of the bread and the last scrapings of the peanut butter for breakfast. Gene is doing this on purpose, making everything as bad as it can be so she will give in. She isn't stupid. Or maybe she is. She must be; why else would she be here?

They look up at Gene when he walks out of the bathroom smelling of soap and after shave, his hair combed straight back. He has a clean white tee-shirt on and jeans and looks like he just stepped out of a magazine. The heat doesn't bother him, doesn't even make him sweat.

He spreads his hand on top of Margaret's head. "Go play outside like a good kid so we can talk."

Jenny doesn't want to talk, doesn't want another word about the baby or Sam or the right thing. As if he knows or cares about the right thing. She is so sick and tired of being told what's best. What's best for them. What's best for the baby. No one knows or cares what's best for her. Do this. Don't do that. There is never a choice. Why doesn't she ever have a choice? All she wants is to have this baby, her and Gene's baby, and have a semi-normal life. She has even been praying, actually praying to God that something will happen, that Gene will step up, come through and realize he can't sell his own child. Jesus God almighty, please.

It's her punishment. For the way she treated her parents. For abandoning her grandmother. For almost having sex with her father. For every bad thing she has ever done in her life. She hardly ever thought about punishment because she hardly ever got caught, and when it did cross her mind, she figured her punishment would come after she died, and that was so far off she had time to change some day, make up for everything and get forgiveness right at the end. That was her plan.

But she should know better. God is up there just waiting to pounce. He let her create this baby, to have Gene's baby inside her, and now he will make her give it up. It doesn't matter how much she prays now.

She watches Gene pour himself a cup of coffee, stir in sugar and the last of the milk, acting as if he doesn't have a plan, isn't getting his words just right. Everything out of his mouth lately sounds rehearsed and fake.

She looks around the trailer and asks herself for the millionth time how the hell she let herself end up here. The cheap paneling and little windows she can't quite get clean. Tiny rooms with hardly any privacy. Just sit around, eat, sleep, fuck. Not that she thought they would end up in a mansion, but something better than this, just a little apartment of their own. They could be happy. She thought they would be. Just temporary, he said. At the time she was more than okay with it. They were together, had their own place where no one knew them and no one suspected anything. Jenny felt safe. Now all she feels is trapped.

"We have to let Sam know today." Gene's voice is strong and sure. He is always so goddamn sure of himself. He sets his mug on the table and sits across from her, leaning in and looking her in the eye, acting so sincere. "I need to let him know one way or the other. Whatever you want to do, Jen. It's up to you now, but we have to decide today. We can keep living like this, or we can make a new start." He takes a sip of coffee. "Your call."

It takes Jenny a minute to find her voice. She has hardly spoken for days, and when she does she sounds sad and weak, as if she has gotten smaller, so insignificant she is beginning to disappear. "You never wanted a family, did you?"

He sighs. "Our luck is finally turning around. We just need to do the right thing."

"Why do you think you always know the right thing? Why is what I want never important? Why is what I want never the right thing?"

Gene frowns, then looks at her like he is confused. His mind is completely made up, probably has been from the time he knew she was pregnant. "You really want to keep this baby? Fine. You take care of it when it's hungry and screaming and cold this winter. You figure out how to get diapers and clothes and whatever else it needs." He stares at her then looks away as if this is all her fault.

There is nothing she can say and she doesn't want to talk anyway. She doesn't even want to look at him, so she lifts herself out of the kitchen chair, her eyes on the door, and walks outside, letting the door slam behind her. At least he doesn't try to stop her and he can't see her crying.

Margaret looks up from where she sits on the ground, first at Jenny's face, then at her belly. "Hi mama."

Jenny eases down into the folding chair next to the steps, wipes her wet cheeks with her hands and pushes a couple of stray hairs off her face before she pulls a cigarette out of her shirt pocket, puts it in her mouth and lights it. Her one of the day. She squints as the smoke reaches her eyes and after a couple of drags she throws it down, crushes it under her flip-flop. She hears the refrigerator door open then close, the tab being pulled off a can of beer, then the radio. Talk. Blah blah blah. She watches Margaret drawing with a stick in the dirt.

"What are you doing?"

"Making a house. See? It's a big house like the one we will live in some day." She moves her stick over the middle of the drawing. "This is the kitchen, and these are rooms for all of us around it. Which one do you want?"

Jenny leans down as much as she can, points to the biggest square, on a corner. "I'll take that one." If only it were that easy.

"Okay. I'll make it pretty for you." Margaret digs deeper into the dirt, then outlines the house with pebbles and bits of gravel. It reminds Jenny of that house in the middle of nowhere. His buddy Ray's house, the POW flag out front. She liked that house. That house was perfect. Why couldn't they have a house like that? Everything was so good then. They had their whole future open in front of them and everything was possible. Their life had meaning then. Now she is stuck. Just so goddamn stuck.

"We used to have a house like that. You probably don't remember."

123

Margaret stops and looks up at her, her face blank. "Where is it?"

Good question. "It was a long time ago. You were really little. You didn't like me very much then. Do you remember that?" She thinks of Margaret throwing that cup on the floor and Gene getting mad at her as if it was her fault. Everything is her fault.

"I always liked you, mama."

"Well you didn't then. I guess I can't really blame you."

Jenny wonders about the people in Margaret's life before. Do they still think about her, wonder where she is? If she didn't die that day, Margaret would be living in some filthy place sharing beds and blankets and who knows what else with a dozen other foster kids. At least she has her own bed, her own room. At least she has a pretty normal life and is going to school. Plenty of kids have it a lot worse than this. She would probably be dead by now if Jenny hadn't saved her.

Margaret takes the top off a dandelion and places it carefully in the house, in Jenny's room. "How do you like it?" Always so eager to please.

"Come here, Meggie." When Margaret stands in front of her Jenny studies her face, the pale blue eyes that have always looked a little haunted, a little scared. She licks her thumb and runs it across Margaret's chin where there is a smudge of dirt. She is a good mother. She puts her hands on Margaret's arms, so skinny. "Look at me. Are you hungry?" What a stupid question.

Margaret shrugs and looks down.

Jenny lets go of her, pushes her hair off her face again and lets the tears spill down her cheeks. "Shit." Margaret looks like she wants to cry, too. "Help me up."

Margaret reaches her hands out and Jenny grabs them, lifts herself up and stands there for a minute, not looking at Margaret, but at her belly, picturing the baby inside. She takes Margaret's hand, puts it on her belly and holds it there. "Feel that?" Just a little shift in position. He doesn't have much room to move around anymore.

"Does it hurt?"

Jenny shakes her head, can't even look at Margaret. She walks back up the three steps into the kitchen where Gene sits with the newspaper and a sweaty can of beer. She stands there with her hands on the bottom of her belly and wishes she could keep him. "You win. Call him."

She walks past him before he has a chance to say anything or even look at her, slams the bathroom door and turns on the shower, swears to herself this is the last time he will ever get his way.

Sam comes late that afternoon. He brings hamburgers and French fries and beer, Popsicles and a telephone. It has been more than three years since Jenny has seen Sam, since he brought Margaret's birth certificates, showing her and Gene as her birth parents. One from Lawrence General Hospital signed by a Dr. Sherma with the date and time of Margaret's birth as if he had delivered her, and a certified one from city hall in Lawrence. It had made Jenny so happy to see them, amazed at how real they looked. Sam said, *Of course they're real.*

He never asked any questions and Jenny never asked how he did it. All Gene said was he went to school with him and has known him forever. Jenny has trouble believing he is a real lawyer. And here he is again, fixing things.

Sam tries to make it seem like a celebration as he opens the bags, filling the trailer with his deep voice, asking how everyone has been, if it's hot enough for them. "And look at you, little lady, getting so big." He rubs the top of Margaret's head. "So who's hungry?" he asks, as if he doesn't know.

From the time Sam gets there, Gene doesn't stop talking. He unwraps a hamburger right away like he hasn't eaten for days, takes a big bite, then opens a packet of ketchup and squirts it all over the fries. All of a sudden he is so happy, so relieved, back to the old Gene. He goes on and on about the Red Sox, how they are only two games out of first and how they will all go into Boston to see a game before the end of the season. "We'll take the train to North Station, have dinner at a nice Italian place in the North End, then head over to Fenway."

He makes it sound as if he has been there a hundred times, as if he is some big shot. He puts his hand on Jenny's leg and squeezes it gently. "How does that sound?"

Jenny stares at him. "We're doing this so we can go to a goddamn baseball game? Pour me a beer." If she gives up this baby it has to mean something.

"I don't think that's good for the baby," Sam says, his voice low and concerned. He looks at Gene when he says this, not Jenny.

"One beer isn't going to do anything," Jenny says. "German women have a beer every day when they're pregnant. You think I would hurt my own baby?"

"I promised them a healthy baby is all."

"Healthy?" She laughs. It's a real laugh and it feels good. "You came to the wrong place for healthy."

Sam stares at her, not sure whether this is a joke or a way out. Jenny smiles as she remembers back when she used to have such mood swings and temper tantrums, how upset her mother was when Jenny acted out, how badly she wanted a diagnosis so she could pin Jenny's bad behavior on it, how she saw doctor after doctor until she heard something she could live with, something that would tell the world it wasn't her fault. All the meds in the world didn't change a damn thing.

Gene takes a glass from the cabinet, drops in a few ice cubes and sets it in front of her. Her throat is so dry. He pours the rest of his beer over the ice and pushes it a little closer to her. The fizzing and cracking are loud, and they all stare at the glass as if they had never seen beer on ice before. Jenny takes a swallow, then another.

"Come on, Jen. Relax. We're almost there." Gene puts his arm around her shoulder.

"*You're* almost there. I'm not." Jenny rubs her swollen belly, wishes she could just walk out of there, wishes she had options. She looks at the phone Sam brought, lying on the counter. There isn't a person in the world she could call.

Sam stands, wipes his mouth with a napkin and clears his throat. "So, what do you say we get this show on the road?" He looks at his shiny gold watch as if there is somewhere important he needs to be.

Gene stands, too, picks up the wrappers and napkins and empty ketchup packets, shoves them into the trash by the door, throws the empty cans into the box next to it. Sam takes the Popsicles out of the freezer, rips open the box and pulls one out for Margaret, holds it out to her. "Here you go, sweetheart. Why don't you take that outside while the grownups talk for a few minutes?" All of a sudden he's in charge. Party's over.

Margaret touches Jenny's arm. "Do you want anything, mama?" It is the first thing she has said since Sam got there.

"No. Go ahead outside."

Margaret stands there and stares into her face, keeps her hand on Jenny's arm as if she wants to protect her somehow from these two men who want to take her baby away.

Sam sets his briefcase on the table, snaps it open and pulls out some papers while Margaret walks slowly to her room and gets her doll before she steps outside, turning to look at Jenny once more before the door closes behind her.

Jenny signs the papers quickly without reading them. She doesn't want to know what they say because she will never be able to forgive herself for agreeing to something so unthinkable. Gene doesn't read them either, anxious to get this done before she changes her mind, anxious for the money. It doesn't seem possible they could sign their baby away like this.

Jenny finishes the watery beer and opens another one without looking at Gene or Sam, takes it into the bedroom and leaves the door open. She sits on the edge of the bed and takes a long swallow.

In a few minutes she hears Sam's voice. *Tell Jenny she's doing the right thing. Plenty of time to have kids when you're on your feet.* She listens to their footsteps, then Gene's voice to Margaret. *Take care of her, okay? I'll be back.* She listens to Sam's car doors opening and slamming shut, the wheels crunching the stones in the driveway, then silence. She thinks of the house Margaret scratched out in the dirt and lets the tears come and spill down her cheeks as she finishes her beer. She sets the can on the floor by the bed and lies down on her side, facing the wall.

"Mama? Are you okay?" Meggie's voice is soft and afraid and Jenny wonders how much she understands about what's going on. She's not a kid who asks questions, not a kid who makes waves or ever complains, and Jenny is grateful for that. She feels her little hand on her shoulder.

"Lay down with me, Meggie." Jenny shifts a little closer to the wall to make room but doesn't turn around and then Margaret is lying up against her, her little arm around her waist, her little hand on her belly. The little brother or sister she will never know.

"Are you okay, mama?" she asks again.

Jenny can't find her voice for a few seconds. "Tired," she whispers as she realizes just how tired she is, not just physically, but so tired of her life, so tired of feeling helpless and trapped. Here she is, lying in bed with a little girl she pretends is hers, carrying a baby she has just signed away to strangers and she has no idea where Gene is. He got what he wanted and took off.

Mostly she is tired of pretending. Her life has become such a joke.

It's dark when Jenny wakes up alone, and it only takes a few seconds for what she did that afternoon to rush back and make her feel like someone beat her up. She is hot and sweaty, her tee-shirt stuck to her like skin. In the bathroom she splashes cold water on her face, pats it dry and looks at herself in the mirror. Her sadness shows in her eyes, her mouth.

She wonders what Gene would do if she said she changed her mind, what Sam would or even could do about it. She could say they forced her to sign the papers, that she did it against her will and has no intention of giving her baby away. Gene can deal with whatever happens with Sam and she could find a safe place, people who would help her, a church or convent where they would take her in. Do they still have those homes for unwed mothers? And what about Margaret?

There is a tiny knock on the door. "Mama? Gene's home. He got food."

Gene got food. Now that he has what he wants they can have food. What a fucking great guy. She shakes her head, opens the door to see Margaret looking up at her. She looks sad and lost, too. Jenny brushes her hair back before she walks to the kitchen where there are four plastic grocery bags on the table, a case of beer on the counter. Gene is outside, pulling out more bags from the back of a cab. A cab. She hears him tell the driver to keep the change, then walks back in with two more grocery bags. He's a goddamn big shot now.

After he sets the bags down he steps over to her and leans in for a kiss but she turns her head away. He smells like garlic and beer. "How ya doin? I got us some stuff. We're gonna be okay now."

"Okay? We'll never be okay. Not if we do this. How can you think we will ever be okay?"

"Come on, Jenny girl. It's a done deal." He doesn't look at her when he says this.

He pulls out a beer and opens it, sits at the table and turns on the radio. The voice tells them the Red Sox are losing to the Jays three to nothing. "Have a seat. You look hot. How about a nice cold beer over ice? Here, have a seat."

She doesn't sit. She is so done with him telling her what to do. "How did you get all this? You were actually holding out all this time just to force me into signing?"

"Sam gave us an advance. We'll be all set now." He takes a swig of beer and smiles at her like they have just won the lottery. It is hard to believe it doesn't bother him at all, hard to see how happy he is.

"How much?" Her voice is stronger now than it has been in a while.

"Enough."

Jenny watches the lump in his neck as he tilts his head back and drinks. She is so thirsty, but she doesn't move, doesn't sit. She watches as Margaret starts putting the groceries away without a word. "How much? she asks again.

"Don't worry about it. We're all set, okay? Relax." He changes the radio station and Kenny Chesney sings about cruising down the interstate and how forever feels. Jenny stares at Gene, a stranger to her now, then watches as Margaret unpacks the potato chips, cans of spaghetti and meatballs, peanut butter and strawberry jam and bread, eggs and bacon and milk.

Margaret looks over at her. "Do you want me to make you something to eat?" She's such a good girl.

"I'm not hungry." Jenny walks to the sink and lets the water run until it is cold, fills a glass and drinks it down while Gene tells them how good it felt to walk into the grocery store and get any damn thing he wanted, how for once he didn't have to count the change in his pocket to make sure he had enough.

"You shoulda seen the look on the girl's face when I handed her a hundred, like she didn't believe it was real. Same one that made me feel like shit when I was a buck short last time. I just looked at her and said I'd take my change in twenties."

"So where's the rest? Where's the twenties?" Jenny asks. If she just had some money she would be able to leave.

"Don't worry about it. I'll take care of everything now. You just relax and have that baby."

That baby. Like it's nothing. How could she have been so stupid not to put anything away? If she had just put away a little money each time he brought home something she would have enough to leave, get on a bus and just leave. But there were so many desperate times they needed every nickel.

The way Margaret looks at Gene makes Jenny sick. Her hero.

The next few days are quiet. Jenny either lies in bed or sits at the kitchen table staring out the window. There is nothing much to see but a few bushes and trees, sometimes a bluebird or a cardinal. Two squirrels chase each other across the yard and up the side of a tree. It has been cloudy and hot, a quick shower each afternoon not lasting long enough to cool things off, just making the air even more close and humid.

Margaret keeps Jenny's glass full of either iced beer or ice water, makes her peanut butter and strawberry jam sandwiches she hardly touches. She rubs Jenny's back and combs her hair and sometimes Jenny tells her to leave her alone and sometimes she doesn't have the heart or strength to. When Gene turns the radio on Jenny shuts it off. When he tries to touch her she pulls away, and when he tries to talk to her she ignores him, so they all live in a silent sadness. No one mentions the baby.

Chapter 11

When Gene comes into Margaret's room his voice is soft, but rough, too. He is telling her to get up. Get dressed. Margaret was having a nice dream, sitting with her mother on a flat roof. It was nighttime and there were a million stars out. They were eating slices of yellow cake with chocolate frosting and her mother was telling her how pretty she was.

It is so dark Gene is a big shadow leaning over her bed and Margaret is afraid until she hears his voice. "Wake up. We need to go."

"Where are we going?" She rubs her eyes and blinks and is all the way awake now.

"Hurry up and get dressed. We need to go."

"Where are we going? Where's mama?"

"Come on, let's go. She's gonna have the baby. Get dressed." This is the first time Gene has ever sounded scared or nervous.

Margaret sits up, pulls on the shorts she wore yesterday, takes a tee-shirt from the top of the laundry basket next to her bed and slips it over her head. The baby is coming.

"Come on, we need to get you to Darlene's." He moves towards the door now and Margaret freezes.

"But I want to stay with you." They have never left her with Darlene. She has only been in Darlene's trailer once with her mother and couldn't wait to get out of there. She would rather be all alone than with Darlene. "Can't I go with you? I'll be good."

"You just be good for Darlene."

Then her mother is in the doorway carrying a plastic bag in one hand, her other hand on her belly. She doesn't look at Margaret or say anything. She doesn't seem to be looking at anything.

Margaret stands, the three of them crowded into her room now. "Are you okay, mama?" She touches her arm and her mother flinches as if she hurt her. "Mama?" Margaret stands close but doesn't touch her again. "Are you gonna have the baby now? I can stay with you. Don't make me go to Darlene's." If she has the baby right now, right here, they can all stay together.

Her mother sits on the edge of Margaret's bed, holds her belly and leans over a little, squeezes her eyes shut. Her face is pale and a few pieces of hair stick to one side of her face. "Jesus." Mama's voice is barely a whisper.

"Come on." Gene grabs her hand, holds it too tight, then they are out the door just as the headlights from Sam's car light up the road, the trees and bushes and steps. Gene raises his hand in a wave towards the car but doesn't stop.

They walk quickly, then her father is knocking on Darlene's door and Margaret's heart is beating so hard. She has been waiting for the day the baby would come and now it is here and this isn't how she thought it would be. She thought they would all stay together. She had it all planned in her head, how she would hold her mother's hand, put cool cloths on her forehead until it was time, then she would be with Gene, waiting for the doctor to say it's a boy and they could see them now. Margaret would tell them how she knew it would be a boy. When they walk into mama's room she would be holding a tiny baby wrapped in a blue blanket and she would be smiling. Margaret would hold him and be so careful. And he would look right up at her with his beautiful little eyes and know she is his big sister.

Margaret feels tears coming and blinks to keep them in, doesn't make a sound. All she can think about now is that they are leaving her. In a minute they will be gone. Gene is taking mama away to have the baby and they are leaving her there with Darlene. She knew something bad was going to happen, but she tried not to believe they would leave her. She has been so good, but it wasn't enough. She wasn't good enough.

How many times did she hear her father say they couldn't afford two kids? Margaret thought if she was just good enough and didn't eat much they would keep them both, and if they really, truly couldn't keep them both they would choose her. She grabs hold of Gene with both arms, presses the side of her face into his side and tries not to cry, but then she is.

The light over the door comes on and there is Darlene, huge Darlene filling the doorway. She wears a black tee-shirt that comes to her knees with big red lips on it.

"I guess it's time, huh? Well come on in here, pumpkin. You and me are gonna have a lotta fun." She reaches towards Margaret and Margaret backs away, tries to press herself further into Gene as he pulls her arms off easily and gives her a little push towards Darlene. *Please. Baby Jesus, please help me.*

Gene steps back now, leans down and kisses the top of Margaret's head. "Be good. We'll be back as soon as we can."

Margaret looks up at him and opens her mouth, but nothing comes out, then he turns and walks away while Darlene puts a hand on her shoulder and there is nothing she can do but watch Gene disappear into the trees towards their place and Sam's big white car. She hears the car doors slamming, the tires crunching on the gravel, then they are driving away and she is frozen on that spot in front of Darlene's door. She can't believe they just left her like that and it happened so fast she didn't even say goodbye to her mother.

"Come on, pumpkin." Darlene holds the door open and Margaret looks up at her again, her frizzy blonde hair and her fat arms that jiggle even when she isn't moving. Her stomach feels sick and her throat hurts. The smell of hot dogs comes out of the trailer and Margaret looks down at the ground, notices how Darlene's feet spill over the tops of her dirty pink slippers.

"Come on," she says again. "Come in and shut the door before the bugs fly in. And lock it. Just turn that little button. You can't be too careful around here." Darlene keeps talking as she shuffles away. "I'm going back to bed. You make yourself at home and I'll be up in a couple hours. If you want to watch t.v., just keep the sound off."

There is nothing Margaret can do but step inside and shut the door. She locks the door and stands there for what feels like a long time after Darlene has gone into her room and closed the door. She thinks about waiting a few minutes more until Darlene is asleep, then just opening the door and going back home, to her own room, getting back into her own bed and waiting there for Gene and mama. She tries to imagine what might happen if she did, if they would be mad because she didn't do what she was told. That's not what good girls do.

She walks over to the couch and sits down. Darlene's trailer is a little bigger than theirs, which doesn't seem fair since they have more people. She remembers Gene making a joke about a double wide and how it described both Darlene and her trailer. Margaret isn't sure if her mother actually likes Darlene or not; she heard her tell Gene how nice it was to have someone to talk to, someone who actually listens. She would never leave Margaret there to live with Darlene forever. They have to come back.

It's still not light out yet. The clock on the stove says 4:18. Margaret pushes off her sneakers and lies down on her side, closes her eyes and wishes for Gene and mama to come back. The couch is scratchy and Margaret wishes she had her pillow, realizes then she forgot her doll. If she had her doll she might not feel so sad. Then she thinks about fat Darlene sitting right where her face is and sits back up.

Darlene said she could watch television but she is nervous to turn it on in case she can't turn the sound off and wakes Darlene up. There probably isn't anything good on this early anyway. Their television broke a while ago, when it was still winter. Her mother said it was shot and Gene said they could probably get something for it, but it is still sitting out back of their trailer with weeds growing around it.

She will just wait. Her eyes are used to the dark now, and the light over the stove and the nightlight in the hall make it not so scary. There is a stack of newspapers and magazines on the stool next to the kitchen table and the table is clean and shiny.

She sits at the table and takes a Cosmopolitan off the top. It has a pretty blonde woman on the cover holding her shirt closed like she didn't have time to button it before someone took her picture. *Sexy Sundresses; 15 Ways to Surprise Your Man in Bed.* She flips through the pages quickly, barely glancing at all the beautiful women smiling at the camera. They have shiny hair and lots of makeup and their mouths are open a little like they are about to say something. Mama could be in a magazine like this. She puts it back on top of the pile and hopes again mama and Gene come back soon. She isn't sure how long it takes to have a baby, but it doesn't seem like it should take that long for him to come out.

After a few minutes she lies back down on the couch, her head on a pillow from the chair, and closes her eyes. It's okay to cry a little as long as no one is there to see her and ask what she's crying about.

"Why didn't you turn on the t.v.?" Darlene shuffles out, her slippers scraping the floor.

Margaret looks at the television, its blank screen, and feels ashamed. She had just sat up a minute before Darlene came out and was wondering if she could use the bathroom or if it would wake up Darlene. "I don't know."

"You're a funny kid. Your mum said you were a funny kid. You hungry? Why don't you get us something to eat. Right in that cabinet. Pick out whatever you want." She points to a white metal cabinet next to the refrigerator. "I hope you're not a picky eater. I don't make nothing fancy."

Darlene rests her cane against the counter, turns on the water and holds the tea kettle under it. She reaches up and pulls out the coffee and sugar from the cabinet. "I hope your mum's doing okay.

She's a good person. She hasn't had it easy, that's for sure. I hope you're good to her."

When Margaret opens the cabinet it looks like a grocery store, everything stacked in neat rows, the shelves full. No wonder Darlene is so fat. There are packages of donuts, some with white powdered sugar and some with chocolate frosting, bags of cheese curls, pretzels and popcorn and chips, chocolate cupcakes filled with whipped cream like some of the kids at school have in their lunches. There is peanut butter and jelly and boxes of macaroni and cheese, cans of spaghetti and meatballs and ravioli. It doesn't seem right that one person has all this food.

Margaret is starving. She wants some of those cupcakes, but reaches for a package of donuts so Darlene won't think she doesn't know what you're supposed to have for breakfast.

"I'll have a package of cupcakes," Darlene says. "I like a little chocolate in the morning with my coffee. Don't be shy, pumpkin. Take what you want. It sure is nice to have company, even if you don't say much. You always this quiet?"

It makes Margaret embarrassed and ashamed when people say how quiet she is, when they notice there is something wrong with her. "I like chocolate," she says, and hopes it is enough. She puts back the donuts and takes out two packages of cupcakes. She wants Darlene to tell mama and Gene she was a good girl.

They sit in the living room, Margaret back on the couch and Darlene in her recliner, eating chocolate cupcakes at eight in the morning, the time she would be sitting outside the trailer or at their own kitchen table maybe having a piece of toast. She has never had chocolate cupcakes and cold milk in the morning, just sitting and watching television like it is a normal thing.

It's cooler in Darlene's trailer and Margaret notices two little fans that fit right in the windows. Maybe that's what Gene calls a.c. When she looks over at Darlene she isn't that scary anymore. Fat people have always looked scary to Margaret.

Darlene pops the last of her cupcake into her mouth, takes a swallow of coffee, then looks at Margaret. "You want something else, pumpkin?"

Margaret stares at Darlene's pudgy face, her pale blue eyes. She smells funny, like food and sweat and flowers all mixed together. Maybe she can't fit into her shower. "No thank you."

"Nice and polite. I like that. You don't be shy, okay? You wanna get me a refill?" She holds out her coffee cup and Margaret is glad to be doing something, to be helping.

They watch the morning news and weather, some game shows and the news again at noon. The big story is about a little girl who went missing in Colorado. Her parents say she just disappeared in the night, and Margaret can't understand how someone could just disappear. When they show the little girl's face she looks so beautiful, not like any little girl Margaret has ever seen, but like a princess with her makeup and a fancy dress with sparkles and pretty blonde curls. She never knew little girls could wear makeup like that.

After the news and weather they move to the kitchen table and she and Darlene make macaroni and cheese from a box. Darlene teaches her how to play Scat, and while they play they watch *All My Children*, then *One Life to Live*, then *General Hospital*. Darlene tells the people on the shows what they should and shouldn't do, warns them that people are

140

lying or cheating on them, as if they are her friends. There are some people she likes and some people she calls sneaky little liars.

"They all have their secrets," Darlene explains. "Things they can't tell anyone, or think they can't, but it always comes out in the end. See this one?" There is a woman with long dark hair and a low-cut red sweater walking into a room where a man and women sit on the couch. They are surprised to see her. She is pretty, but she looks kind of mean. "She's the worst. Always gets her way, always gets the guy. She takes them away from the nice girls, then she dumps them or cheats on them."

"How come she always gets her way?" Margaret asks. "How come the guys don't want the nice girls?"

"Because guys are generally stupid. The sneaky little liars find a way to make the good girls look bad and the guys always believe them."

Margaret knows it's just a show, but it doesn't make sense that they would make the bad people win and the good people lose and the guys be stupid.

When the shows are over they watch Oprah, then more news. The same news over and over, and mostly about the disappearing girl in Colorado.

They have hot dogs wrapped in soft white bread for supper, with potato chips and pickles, then go back to the television for her police shows. Darlene shows her how to make a gin and tonic and sips on it while Margaret has another glass of milk. This must be what it's like to be rich. Margaret wonders how Darlene can be rich when she doesn't have a job, why she isn't in the hole like they were.

At ten Darlene shuts off the television and brings a pillow out from her room, sets it on the end of the couch. "You lay down now pumpkin and get some sleep. I see your daddy didn't think to bring you anything to sleep in. Well that's all right. I spent many a night in my clothes." She laughs. "I'll see you in the a.m. We had a good day, didn't we? It sure is nice to have company." She turns and starts shuffling away. "Nighty night."

Margaret lies down but there is no way she can go to sleep without her doll. She looks up at Darlene walking away, her cane tapping the floor and her huge bum swaying side to side.

"I need my doll." Her voice is so soft, so babyish, Margaret doesn't even know if Darlene heard her, but then she stops and sighs.

"You just go to sleep now. I'm sure your mum and dad will be back tomorrow and you'll have your doll." She turns again and walks away and Margaret pictures her doll, on her bed or on the floor, all alone in the dark, empty trailer. She should have asked earlier, when it was still light out. She isn't sure if she really wants to go outside by herself in the dark and she isn't even sure if the trailer is unlocked so she can get in, but if Darlene let her go she would. Darlene must have a flashlight and Margaret can run really fast.

"Can't I just go get her? Please? It will only take a minute."

"Not now, pumpkin. You can't go out there this time of night all by yourself. You don't know what's out there. You go to sleep now. You're a big girl. We had a good day, now don't go and spoil it, okay?"

Darlene closes the bathroom door behind her, making it even darker. Margaret listens to her pee and flush the toilet. She feels sick to her stomach and afraid of whatever she can't see in the dark. Sometimes they get mice in their trailer and she pictures a mouse now, climbing up on the couch. She pulls the afghan down from the back of the couch and covers herself even though she's not cold, closes her eyes and buries her face in the pillow. She has never slept away from home before. Kids at school talk about sleepovers, but she has never been invited and is glad.

She wonders what mama and Gene are doing, if they are holding the baby and have forgotten all about her and started their new life. Darlene is the only one who ever called Gene her daddy. Margaret wishes sometimes she could call him daddy, but she can only call him Gene. *As close to a daddy as you're ever going to get.* Even mama calls him Gene to her. When she isn't talking to him she will say *Tell Gene* this or that. She asks Jesus to please make them come back.

When Margaret wakes to the sound of the television, a man talking about wildfires in California, she doesn't know where she is at first, then she rubs her eyes open and sees the back of the scratchy green couch. She smells coffee and starts to remember.

"Hey there, sleepyhead." Darlene is standing by the couch, leaning on her cane. She smells like last night's hot dogs. "How about some breakfast?"

The next day passes almost exactly like the first one except Margaret is used to it now. They talk a little during commercials, and Darlene doesn't say much about her being quiet, doesn't make her feel bad about it.

After lunch Margaret thinks about asking if she can go get her doll again, since it is still early. Plus she could change her clothes and brush her teeth, but she is afraid to ask. She doesn't want Darlene to say she was any trouble. It would feel so good to just walk into her own room and lay on her bed and disappear until mama and the baby and

Gene come back. And if Darlene would give her some food she could make supper and have it ready when they come home. But she is afraid Darlene would get upset and say Margaret spoiled everything, tell Gene and mama she wasn't a good girl. If she just waits and is patient and does everything she is told, they will come back. It feels like they have been gone such a long time. Margaret promises Jesus she will never ask for anything ever again if they just come back. She won't even ask for her doll. She will just be good.

They have grilled cheese sandwiches and slices of bread-and-butter pickles for lunch, scrambled eggs and toast for supper. Darlene tells Margaret the secret to good cooking is butter. Real butter. She has a big block of it in her refrigerator.

"You be sure to tell your mum and dad how good I fed you," Darlene says.

"I will." Margaret hopes she hasn't eaten too much, but all this food tastes better than anything she has ever had in her whole life. Plus, Darlene keeps telling her to eat, to have whatever she wants. Put some meat on those bones.

Margaret decides she likes when Darlene calls Gene her dad. He seems like he is her dad, and calling him Gene makes it seem like he really isn't, but she tells herself it doesn't matter. She loves Gene so much most of her doesn't even want to know.

When Gene comes to get her it is after nine. She and Darlene are watching *America's Most Wanted* and eating cheese curls. They stare at the screen, listen to the man talk about a sex offender and a murderer, someone who preys on lonely women. They show a picture of a skinny man with a beard and small, mean eyes. Margaret doesn't like this show and she doesn't believe the man prays on women.

There is a flash of light outside for just a few seconds, coming from the other side of the trees. "There they are," Darlene says, as if she knew they were coming at that exact time.

Margaret is afraid to move until she hears the knock on the door, then she is up and Gene is standing in the doorway just like he never left, except he looks like he just got out of bed and came right there. Tears fills her eyes and then her arms are around Gene's neck and she is crying like a baby. She will never let go.

Darlene asks how everything went, if Jenny and the baby are okay. "So, boy or girl?" she asks. But Gene is looking at Margaret.

Everything's fine," he says. "How was this troublemaker?"

"No trouble at all. Ate like a horse, I'll tell you that. Didn't you pumpkin?"

Margaret can't find her voice; she just nods and holds onto Gene, watches as he hands Darlene some folded money and thanks her.

"So how's Jenny doing? I hope she didn't have too hard a time of it." Darlene leans on her cane and at that moment Margaret feels sorry for her. "And how's that baby? You didn't say if it's a boy or a girl."

Gene isn't even listening to Darlene, and the way he looks at Margaret she can tell he missed her, too. Then he looks at Darlene for just a second. "Everything's fine. Thanks again."

Darlene turns towards the television, ready to get back to her show, and Gene takes Margaret's hand. "You ready? You got all your stuff?"

Margaret wipes her eyes and nods, relieved to be finally going home.

"I'm sure gonna miss the company," Darlene says. "You come back and visit, okay? She was as good as gold."

Gene takes her hand and they turn to leave. "Thank you," Margaret says, her voice so small, then she and Gene are walking home. The crickets are loud in the darkness, the only sound besides their footsteps crunching in the dry grass.

"You give Jenny my best. Tell her I'll be by soon to see that baby!" Darlene calls after them.

Margaret and Gene walk away while Darlene is still talking and Margaret loves Gene more than anything in the whole world for coming to get her, and she loves Jesus and Mary for answering her prayers, just like her mother said they would. She takes a deep breath of the warm night air. It feels like she hasn't been outside in a really long time. "How's mama? How's the baby? Is it a boy?" She pictures her mother sitting up in bed holding the baby, feeding him and smiling, waiting for her.

"She's resting. You need to take good care of her now."

"I will." It feels so good to be walking with Gene, almost home. Now that she has a little baby brother she feels grown up. She will be such a good big sister. "And I'll help mama take care of the baby, too."

Gene stops, but doesn't let go of her hand. "You need to forget about the baby, okay? There is no baby."

Margaret stares at him. "What do you mean? Where is he?" They couldn't have given the baby away. They wouldn't. Mama wouldn't.

Gene crouches down and looks into Margaret's eyes. "He's in a better place. That's all you need to remember, okay?"

It takes Margaret a few seconds to understand what he means. The baby can't be dead. She felt him kicking inside her mother just a couple of days ago and Gene just told Darlene that everything was fine. Tears come again and she can't stop them. She can hardly talk. "He's in heaven?"

Gene doesn't like her to cry. He told her once he gets enough of that from Jenny, so Margaret never cries in front of him. Margaret is afraid he will be upset with her now, but when he looks at her he smiles as if she said something funny, then he wipes her cheeks and she smells cigarettes on his fingers.

"Come on. There's nothing to cry about. We're all better off, especially the baby. No more crying now. And don't say anything about the baby when we get home. The sooner she forgets about it the better. Try and get her mind off it."

He holds her hand tight again as they walk the rest of the way to the trailer. Sam's car is still there, the lights off now but the engine still running. She can see the outline of Sam in the driver's seat, but can't tell if he is watching them. When her father opens the door he lets her go in first and the familiar smells of cigarette smoke and beer welcome her home. It feels as if she has been really far away.

"Hey Jen, look who I found." Gene is trying to sound happy, but how could he be? Her mother is sitting in the dark on Margaret's bed, her legs folded under her and her back against the wall. Margaret stops in the doorway, not sure what to do or say.

Her mother takes a drag of her cigarette, the end glowing bright. Margaret can barely make out her mother's face, but she can see she's not smiling and her hair is messy. Gene turns on the light and right away her mother tells him to shut it off, then it is almost dark again. She is wearing her gray sweatpants and a gray tee-shirt and even though her belly isn't as big as it was before, it looks like there could still be a baby in there. Gene puts the light on over the stove and it is enough.

"Hi mama." Margaret wants to climb up onto the bed and hug her, but she waits when her mother doesn't say anything back. She is afraid again but isn't sure why. When she turns and looks at Gene he smiles, kisses the top of her head and turns towards the door.

"I'm going to get a few things. You take care of her."

Her mother doesn't say anything and Margaret is even more afraid than when they left her at Darlene's. But as soon as the door closes behind him her mother puts her cigarette in the beer can next to the bed and opens her arms. Margaret climbs up onto the bed and her mother is holding her and Margaret is holding back her crying, holds everything in her stomach and chest and throat as her mother hugs her, rocks her a little and starts telling her about the baby.

"He was so beautiful. My perfect little baby boy." Margaret knew it was a boy. Her mother takes a deep breath and when she lets it out it smells bad, like when the milk goes sour. She lets go of Margaret, lights another cigarette and hugs herself like she is cold. Her voice is sad as she tells Margaret about his perfect features and tiny fingers, how he only weighed five pounds, three ounces, but had good, healthy lungs. Later Margaret will ask her about when she was a baby, how much she weighed and if she was perfect, too. Her mother says she got to hold him for a few minutes before they took him away and she smiles when she says this, nods as if she is agreeing with someone. Tears are washing down her face as she talks.

"They didn't want me to. They said it would just make it harder, but I needed to hold him and tell him why I was giving him up, and he deserved to be held by his own mother, even for just a few minutes. He at least deserved that." She stops to blow her nose and Margaret waits and wonders if it is okay if she cries, too. "And who knows? Maybe when he gets older he will want to find his real mother, and when he finds me we will have that bond. He will feel it and I will know him no matter how old he is when I see him again. He might not remember me, but he will feel something, right?"

"Who took him away, mama?"

"People with money. People who can take care of him." She looks around. "He didn't deserve to be brought into this shithole. What kind of life is this?"

"It's a good life, mama." There is nowhere else Margaret would rather be.

"You don't know any different." Mama's voice is softer now, calmer. "He will, though. He will. He'll have a good life with lots of opportunities we couldn't give him. Options. He'll have a full life. He won't have to struggle. We sure as hell couldn't give him that."

Margaret can hardly believe she has a baby brother and that they gave him away. How could they just give a person away? She is glad he isn't dead and in heaven, but it's almost the same because he is gone. Their life isn't so bad. They could have taken care of him and Gene could have gotten a job so they could have food. She leans into her mother and lets a tear slip out.

"They'll take good care of him. They better." She reaches over and pushes Margaret's hair back from her face. "I did the right thing, Meggie. The only thing I could do. I have to believe that."

"We could take good care of him, mama. I would help." She is crying now, knowing she will never see her baby brother, never hold him or teach him things.

"I know you would." Her mother looks at her, smiles and smooths her hair back again. "We won't be so poor now. The people who took him gave us money so we can pay our bills and move away from here to someplace nice. I can't stand you being hungry al the time. You're all I have, you know that? Do you understand that? I want you to have shoes and clothes and nice things. If you look nice, you can make some friends in a new school. Looking good is important."

Margaret would rather have her brother than look good. She would give anything to have him here right now. Even though she has never seen him, she can picture him looking up at her. She really wanted to be a big sister.

"Didn't you want the baby, mama? Didn't you want to keep him?"

Her mother takes a deep breath and moves away from her. "We don't always get what we want. You should know that by now." She gets down from the bed, her hand holding her belly just like when the baby was in there, then she is gone, just her footsteps in the hall.

Margaret picks up her doll from the floor, its eyes closing as Margaret holds her like she would have held her baby brother. She sits there in the darkness, rocking a little and waiting for her mother to come back.

Chapter 12

They said ice would help when her milk came in, but they never said it would hurt this much. It feels like she is carrying around two gallon-jugs of milk instead of breasts, about to burst any second. As if she needs a reminder of not having her baby. As if she isn't in enough pain from giving her baby boy to strangers. *Here you go. Take my baby. Please take care of my baby.*

In her heart Jenny doesn't believe they had no choice. They both had a choice. There is always a choice. But she did it anyway. He got what he wanted – no baby to take care of and plenty of money in his pocket. Blood money is what keeps filling her head. Blood money. All he wanted was the money. And he conned her into thinking she was doing the right thing. Conned her into believing it was the only way. Not that she totally believed it, but she went along with the whole thing anyway. He wore her down. She is just so fucking stupid. And weak. And needy. So fucking needy. But no more.

Margaret's words keep playing over and over in her head. *Didn't you want the baby, mama?* A good question, an innocent question from the only innocent thing in her life and she doesn't have a good answer. She wanted the baby more than anything she has ever wanted in her life, but she sold him anyway. Nothing makes sense. She has a kid she just took off the street and kept, and she sold the one she carried for nine months and gave birth to. Her own flesh and blood. Nothing makes sense. If her mother were around she would tell her she got exactly what she deserved. Some twisted justice from a god she isn't even sure she believes in anymore.

Since she got home Jenny has only gotten out of bed to use the bathroom. Maybe she will just stay in bed forever, stay in the dark room and hide. She isn't sure what day it is or what time it is, and she doesn't really care. All she has been able to do is sleep and cry, take a few bites of whatever Margaret brings in for her. There is always a glass of ice water next to the bed. No sign of Gene. He is the one who should be right here at her side, bringing her flowers and making sure she is okay, but not Gene. He got what he wanted and now has no use for her.

Jenny finally makes herself get up and walk out to the kitchen. She must look like hell, but she doesn't care about that, either. There is Margaret, her little nurse, coloring at the table. And fucking Gene nowhere in sight, off somewhere spending the money. How could she be so stupid to think it meant a new start for all of them?

Margaret's face lights up when she sees her. "Are you feeling better, mama? Do you want something to eat?"

Jenny wants to scream. She wants to shake this kid, shake some sense into her, tell her to start thinking about herself and to stop trying to please everyone else all the time. It gets you nothing but a lousy life for yourself. Before she can say anything, though, she sees Darlene through the window, making her way over with a dish in her hand. That's all she needs right now. "Shit. Meggie, be a good girl and tell Darlene I'm sleeping." She walks into the bathroom and closes the door almost all the way, listens to the knock on the screen door. She doesn't feel like explaining anything to anyone right now. Why can't people just leave her alone?

"Hey there, pumpkin. How's everything? I made a nice mac and cheese, help your mum get her strength back. It's still warm. Is your daddy here? Where's your mum? I sure would like to see that baby. Must be a good little sleeper; I haven't heard a peep. Mind if I come in? I won't stay but a minute, just want to see the little one and see how your mum's doing."

"She's sleeping," Margaret says. "The baby's sleeping, too. I'll tell her you came."

"Here, can you take this?"

Jenny hears the screen door open and hopes Margaret doesn't let her in. *Just leave the goddamn food and go away.*

"I can wait a bit until they wake up. You and me can have a little visit. I brought the cards. What do you say to a game of Scat?"

"I have to do my homework."

"In the summer? You're too smart for summer school."

"We have to read and we have to write book reports," she says. "Everyone has to. And we have math, too." Jenny is amazed Margaret doesn't sound nervous, that she is able to lie so well.

"Well you be sure to tell your mum I came by, okay? And make sure she eats. I hope you're helping out around here. You tell her I'll be by again. Hey, is it a boy or girl?"

"A boy."

"I had a feeling it would be a boy. Your dad must be thrilled. What's his name?"

"We didn't name him yet."

Darlene laughs. "You didn't name him yet? Why not? Hey, what about Joseph? Joseph is a good boy's name. That was my brother's name, God rest his soul."

When it's quiet again Jenny runs the shower and lets the crying come. *It's a boy. We haven't named him yet.* They never will. She had thought about names. She would have named him Michael. She always loved the name Michael. It seems impossible she will ever be happy again.

She hates Gene and at the same time all she wants is for him to come home and hold her, tell her everything will be all right, that they will be all right. Make her believe it was worth it.

In the small bathroom Jenny realizes how bad she smells, how terrible she looks. Her hair is greasy and flat and dull, her eyes puffy and bloodshot from crying. What did she expect? She used to be so pretty. She is only 25 and she looks about 40. As she strips off her clothes and steps into the shower, Jenny looks down at her body, disgusted at the huge breasts hanging heavy, the fat belly and hips. Jesus. She used to have such a nice body. She knows she has to be strong now, has to get her act together. No more booze. No more drugs. And as soon as she can figure a way, no more Gene. She deserves better.

She stays in the shower until the water turns cold, scrubbing every inch of herself over and over, trying to wash off the guilt and the sadness and regret. If only she could do the same inside, especially her head, just clean herself out and start over. But she is already so empty. They scraped out her insides after her baby was born so there would be no trace of him ever being there. She can't let herself think about it anymore. If she doesn't let herself think too much maybe she will be okay.

"Are you feeling better, mama?" Margaret asks, hopeful and innocent as always. She hugs her around the waist like Jenny is the best person in the world instead of the horrible person she is, a person who just sold her baby, a person who lets this eight-year-old fend for herself while Jenny lays in bed feeling sorry for herself.

"A little." Jenny is amazed at this kid sometimes, how she does so much and asks for nothing. She glances at the clock, sees it is almost one. The sunshine is trying to come through the dirty windows, the day is half over, and Jenny feels like she has crawled out of some dark place. "Did you have breakfast?"

"I ate some cereal. Darlene brought us some mac and cheese. Do you want some?"

Jenny opens the refrigerator, sees four cans of beer, milk, the casserole dish from Darlene and a package of hot dogs. When was the last time she ate? "Sure. Let's have hot dogs, too." This kid has been taking care of her for so long. "You are such a good girl." She takes out the food and sets it on the counter, feeling a little bit like a normal mother, a good mother. When she opens the refrigerator again, she takes out the milk and a beer. She opens the beer and takes a swallow and finds herself appreciating Gene for leaving these for her. After all he has done, and who knows where the hell he is, she is thankful he left her four lousy beers. How pathetic is that?

She sits at the table with her beer, tired again when all she has done is sleep, and watches Margaret as she takes out the saucepan and puts two hotdogs in it, holds it under the faucet to cover them with water, sets it on the stove. She takes out plates and forks and mustard, sets the mac and cheese in the middle of the table.

It's hard to remember her life before. Before she had Margaret, when it was just her and Gene. It's hard to imagine not having Margaret, but if they didn't have Margaret, she would have been able to keep their baby. Their baby. Gone now. As gone as if she had miscarried.

If she could go back in time she would make better decisions and wouldn't have made such a mess of her life. She wouldn't have been so horrible to her mother, wouldn't have done what she did with her father. Talk about burning bridges. *Some things just can't be forgiven*, her mother said.

She finishes her beer while Margaret tells her about her conversation with Darlene and how she didn't mean to lie but didn't know what else to say.

"You did the right thing. Sometimes you have to lie. I don't want any company right now and I don't want anyone asking me about the baby. It's nobody's business."

While they eat, Margaret talks about staying at Darlene's, tells Jenny about all the food Darlene has and the television shows they watched and how she helped Darlene cook.

"Do we have real butter?" she asks.

"Sometimes. It's expensive."

"We had cupcakes for breakfast, mama, and grilled cheese and chips for lunch and she taught me how to play Scat. She has a real lot of food. How do you think she gets so much food just for herself?"

"The government," Jenny says. "She had some government job and is on disability now. She probably gets food stamps, too. She's someone who knows how to work the system. That's what we're gonna do. You and me."

She studies this honest sweet girl that she raised and right then she promises herself she is going to leave Gene. She has known it for a while, in the back of her mind. She isn't sure when, but she knows it is what she has to do.

While Margaret cleans up, Jenny takes a fresh beer into the bedroom and searches through all of Gene's things – his drawers and the back of the tiny closet, the pockets of his jeans and shirts. She even looks under the mattress. Though she doesn't really expect to find anything, she keeps looking, hoping to find even a little cash, a bank book or a key. It's time she stopped being so stupid, so trusting. When she finds nothing Jenny knows he must have put the money in an account and has the bank book with him. He probably has one of those cards, too, to get money out of one of those machines whenever he wants it. He isn't stupid. She is.

She sits on the side of the bed and drinks down her beer, feeling a buzz already. He will come home before he spends all the money; he won't leave her stranded. She will ask for half as soon as he comes home. No. Why should she ask? She will tell him she wants half of the money. She deserves a lot more, but will take half. And if something good comes out of all this, if she begins to have a say over her own life, she may feel a little better about the whole damn thing.

"Are you going back to bed, mama?" Margaret stares at her from the doorway.

"No." Jenny takes a deep breath, thinks about taking a walk down to see if Rick is around, if he has anything to take the edge off. Her doctor. But when she goes into the bathroom she gets a look at herself in the mirror. How awful she looks. And the only thing that fits her are her sweats, cut off to shorts, and one of Gene's tee-shirts. Even Rick wouldn't be desperate enough to want her. She hears a car outside and walks back out to the kitchen and stands at the door.

She watches Gene step out of the back of a yellow cab like some big shot. He looks good. The driver gets out, opens the trunk and pulls out some plastic grocery bags, two cases of beer, and sets them on the ground before he turns to Gene. She hopes it's cold. Gene doesn't notice her yet standing in the door as he hands the driver some cash and tells him to keep the change. Jenny turns around and walks back into the bathroom. He doesn't need to think she has been waiting for him or missing him. She splashes cold water on her face, runs a comb through her hair, almost dry now.

The screen door slams and Gene shouts, "Where's my girls?"

God help her, she is so glad he is home. After a few seconds Jenny walks back to the kitchen and watches as Margaret wraps her arms around Gene, presses her face into him like he is there to save them. He rubs the top of Margaret's head, then looks up into Jenny's face with an expression she can't quite read, a mix of love and concern and even a little uncertainty. Her eyes fill and she turns around, walks into the bedroom and sits on the side of the bed, tears spilling out, then Gene is there trying to put his arms around her as she pushes him away.

"Hey, you okay? How you doing? Feeling better?" He sounds so hopeful, so anxious to forget all about the baby, forget everything she went through. Forget they even have a son and put it all behind them. All she wants is for him to hold her, but she pushes him away.

"How do you think I'm doing?" Her voice is angrier than she feels but she doesn't care how she sounds right now or how she looks. Let him see what he did, what he made her do and what it has done to her. "I can't believe you just left me like that. Did you even think for one minute that I might need you here after what I went through? No. You don't give a shit about me." As she talks her words soften. She is still so tired.

Gene's eyes are glassy and he actually looks sorry. "You know I do. The doctor said you needed rest. I figured you would be sleeping the whole time I was gone. I wasn't gone that long. And Margaret was here. You feeling better? I got us some things." He reaches for her again and this time she lets him hold her.

Surprisingly, Jenny's tears are all gone now. She must have used them all up. She knows she should be really angry and unforgiving, but when she breathes in the smell of Gene's after shave, his new clothes, the whiskey on his tongue when he kisses her, all she can think about is right here, right now. She will try to put it all behind her, and maybe it will be easier than she thought.

She pushes her damp hair back and pulls back to look at him. New shirt, new jeans, new boots. "How much of it did you spend?"

"Don't worry." There's plenty. I got something for you." He smiles and pulls a baggie from his shirt pocket with a few small white pills. She doesn't ask, doesn't want to know what it is. He knows what she needs. "And I have a line on a car. As soon as it comes through we'll get outta here. How does that sound? Come on. Come on and have a beer with me. I missed you." He is a little drunk and she is on her way and everything will be okay.

She wants to cry again but takes a deep, ragged breath and lets him take her hand as they step out to the kitchen where Margaret is putting the food away. There is so much food and beer, and for a few seconds Jenny forgets about the baby, forgets how sad she is and how lousy she feels and sits at the table.

Gene sets a beer in front of her and turns on the radio and it could be now or a hundred other times. A commercial for auto parts. She pulls open the baggie and puts two pills on her tongue, washes them down with a swallow of beer.

"Pass me those chips." The salt and the crunch and the cold beer take the edge off and make her feel almost human again.

"You look good," Gene says. He smiles.

She loves his smile, even when he doesn't mean it. "I look like hell." Jenny pushes her hair behind her ears, wishing she had put on a little makeup, not for him but to make herself feel better. She is climbing out of a dark hole.

Gene reaches into a shopping bag, pulls out a green paper bag and a shoe box, hands them to Margaret. "Here, try these on."

He takes a swig of beer as Margaret takes her things into the bathroom, then he looks over at her, expecting what?

"Where's the money? I want half." When the words come out they sound desperate and crude and make it sound like selling her baby was exactly what she wanted.

"Don't worry." He takes another swallow of beer, his eyes half closed. "I told you I would take care of everything. We're gonna move out of here

160

soon as I find us a place. That's what you want, right?" His words slur into each other and she isn't sure if it's him or the pills she took, but she feels okay. Better at least. She can push the money situation tomorrow.

He pulls out a baggie, sets it on the table between them. "Scored us some weed, too."

Jenny takes a deep breath and watches him roll a joint, light it and take a deep hit before he hands it to her. She takes a hit and holds onto it while he leans back and then they both turn as Margaret walks out of the bathroom wearing a sleeveless yellow dress and blue and white sneakers.

She looks so damn happy, so excited to have new things and to have Gene home. It's always such a goddamn big deal when he comes home, while Jenny is the one to stay home and take care of everything.

Gene whistles and Margaret smiles as her face gets red. Jenny can't remember the last time she saw her smile like that. "Turn around," she says, and Margaret turns around like she thinks she's a model.

"Do you like it, mama?" She looks at Jenny with those needy eyes, asking so much more than Jenny has to give.

"Come over here." Jenny unties the bow in the back, ties it again so it is even, then puts her hands on Margaret's shoulders and turns her around to face her. "There. Don't get it dirty." She takes another hit off the joint and hands it back to Gene without looking at him, takes a sip of her beer. "What did you get me?"

He reaches into the shopping bag again and pulls out another green bag, but no shoe box. She needs some new sandals. "Here you go," he says. "I hope I got the right size." He looks at her with something like need, too. Everyone wants something from her and she has nothing left right now.

She takes the bag into the bathroom without a word. He is probably expecting her to be all thankful and loving because he bought her something with the money. It's her money, too. It is a bright blue dress, sleeveless and low cut. It's clingy material and is as much for him as it is for her. It's a little tight, but she keeps it on, likes the way her breasts look spilling out of it. Give him a thrill. It's all he is going to get from her until he gives her half the money.

She puts on bright pink lipstick, brushes her hair and walks out to the kitchen where Gene and Margaret are eating fried chicken, listening to the Red Sox game.

Gene whistles and Margaret tells Jenny how beautiful she looks, but Jenny says nothing, doesn't even smile.

Margaret has a shot glass in front of her, the film of beer coating the inside. "You shouldn't give her that." She takes the glass away and right away feels bad about it. The kid deserves something. "Ah what the hell. It won't hurt you." She refills the shot glass and puts it in front of Margaret, sits down.

"Have some chicken." Gene grabs two more beers from the fridge, sits back in his chair and stares at her. "Looking pretty hot there Jenny girl."

Jenny gives him a look. "Meggie, hand me a napkin?"

While they eat Gene talks about getting the hell out of there, finding a decent place to live, buying a car. Jenny listens and looks at them in their new clothes, plenty of food on the table, pictures the three of them walking out of the trailer into a car, their own car, driving away to who knows where. It doesn't matter. What she needs is a fresh start. A new life where she can start all over.

"That's the first thing," Gene says. "A car. Can't do anything without a car. Not something new. A decent one just a couple years old. Only way to go." He's king of the world now and it didn't cost him a goddamn thing. Jenny watches his face as he talks, wishes she didn't love him so much. Right now she just needs to be close to him. Tomorrow she will make a plan to leave him.

After they eat some chicken and listen to the Red Sox beat the Yankees 7-1, Gene looks into Jenny's eyes. "Come here, Jenny girl."

Jenny sits on his lap and lets him hold her, lets him kiss her neck, and when Gene tells Margaret to go outside and play, he puts his fingers in her hair and kisses her and they go into the bedroom. They lie on the bed and he is as gentle as he can be.

Chapter 13

T here is a heavy hand on her shoulder in the middle of the night, Gene's hand and then Gene's voice telling her to wake up. Margaret can't remember what she was dreaming about, but the first thing she thinks of is the baby.

"Come on, sleepy head. Get dressed." His voice is a loud whisper and she can tell he is drunk. He and her mother have been drinking a lot the past five days, sleeping late and staying up late, mostly happy except when they first get up. They talk about what they are going to do, where they will go, California or Florida or Texas, or maybe Colorado. All places they have heard good things about. The biggest thing they talk about is a fresh start, a new beginning. They drink to this and talk about having a nice apartment until they can afford a house, decent furniture, new clothes.

Then at some point her mother gets quiet and angry and asks Gene about the money, how much is left, and he says the same thing he always says, that he will take care of everything and for her not to worry. He buys her pills that make her relax, and most of the time they are happy. And last night he went out and came back with a car.

164

It's too dark to see much, just the outline of Gene, his head and hair and ears, shadow and voice. She feels her heart pounding and wonders where her mother is. There is no way she is going back to Darlene's. They can't. "What happened? Please don't leave me."

"Get dressed. You can sleep in the car." He pulls some of her clothes from the top of the laundry basket and shoves them into a plastic trash bag.

Margaret sits all the way up, swings her legs over the side of the bed, pushes her hair off her face and rubs her eyes. She is all the way awake and Gene pulls her up so she's standing and it makes her afraid. Maybe there is a fire or someone is coming after them. "Where's mama?"

"Just get dressed. Time to go." His words sound funny and his breath smells like whiskey. Margaret wants to tell him he shouldn't drive but she just reaches for her yellow dress from the foot of the bed and steps into it, pulls it up over her underpants and slips her arms through. She pushes her feet into her sneakers then Gene grabs her arm and pulls her towards the door.

She doesn't smell a fire; the air is cool on her bare arms and the trailer still smells like the Chinese food they had for supper. Where is mama? She can barely see and her feet feel like they are moving all on their own. Why doesn't he turn on the light so they can see?

"Where's mama?" Margaret feels tears starting at the back of her eyes, but even her tears are afraid and they don't come out.

"Ssshhh. Come on."

Margaret swallows and looks up at him, then turns as her mother walks out of the bathroom with a plastic grocery bag in one hand and her purse over her shoulder. She hugs a yellow envelope close to her chest and doesn't look happy. Margaret waits for her to say something, to tell her where they are going and to not be afraid, but it's like she isn't there.

"All set?" Gene asks.

"No. I'm not all set. What the hell are we doing?" She spits her words out like when they are fighting. Margaret's eyes have adjusted to the dark and she can make out her mother's face as she looks towards the bedroom. She looks a little scared, too.

"We're getting out of here. I thought that's what you wanted."

"Not like this."

"Like what? We can be a hundred miles away from here before it's even light out. We don't owe them anything. That's what the deposit is for. That's enough." He doesn't sound as drunk now as Margaret thought. He drops Margaret's hand and steps over to her mother and holds her face in his hands. "What happened to the old Jenny girl, always ready for an adventure?"

"I just don't want to always be looking over my shoulder."

He sighs and his hands go from her face down her arms, then her mother pulls away from him and looks around as if she is lost in a place she doesn't want to leave.

"Come on, Jen. We're starting over. Come on, honey."

Margaret never heard him call her honey before; it is almost like he is talking to someone else.

Her mother sits down, sets the bag on the table and holds the envelope to her chest. "Tell me what's going on. I'm not going anywhere until you tell me what we're running away from. I have a right to know."

"Jesus. What's wrong with you?" He sits now, too, and his voice is a little louder. Margaret doesn't know what to do so she just stands next to her mother. "You've been running all your life and you pick now to get all high and mighty. I'm telling you we need to go now. You need to trust me."

Margaret watches his face and hopes he doesn't just walk out, take the car and leave them there, but he moves closer to her mother, puts his hands on her legs. "You need to trust me, okay? How many times have I pulled your ass out of the fire?"

"What? When?" Her mother's voice is louder now, too.

"You know what I'm talking about. You turned our life upside down and I went along with it for you." He glances at Margaret, then back to her mother, his voice a little softer now. "I did a lot for you and you know what I'm talking about. Now you have to do this for me. For us."

Margaret puts her hand on her mother's shoulder, afraid now of what will happen if they don't go. She doesn't know what they are talking about, the things he did for her. Buying clothes and food? Getting her pills and beer and whiskey? He does all that while her mother stays home most of the time.

Finally, her mother gets up without another word and they walk out of the trailer to the beautiful blue car her father brought home. It is so quiet outside, just the sound of crickets and her mother's sigh. It feels like they are the only people awake in the world. *Please, Jesus, don't let him bring me to Darlene's.* But her father opens the back door of the car, puts the bag onto the floor and tells her to lay down and go back to sleep.

167

As Margaret crawls into the back, onto the cool gray vinyl seat, she wonders where they could be going. She is awake now and not even tired, not even afraid now because her mother is in the front seat and Gene has slipped behind the wheel and they are all together, going on an adventure. This is the new start they have been talking about for a long time. She sits up, puts her hands on the back of the front seat between them.

Her father starts the car and her mother turns around. Her voice is tired and even a little sad. "Lay down, Meggie. Go back to sleep."

"I'm not tired. Can I sit up there with you?" Margaret pulls herself forward, looks over the seat. She could just climb over.

"No. Go to sleep. It's still the middle of the night. You'll be tired later if you don't."

"But I'm not tired." She wants to stay up, wants to know where they are going on their adventure. It didn't seem like anything was wrong before, and now Gene is nervous. It's usually her mother who is nervous.

"Just lay down then."

She lays down like she was told, but she doesn't close her eyes and she won't go to sleep. It feels like she is in a dark cave and she doesn't like being there by herself. She feels the road underneath the tires, each hole and bump they ride over, each stick that cracks under the wheels. Her mother asks what the plan is, but Gene doesn't answer. She would give anything to be sitting up front with them, watching the road. They make a sharp turn, then her mother says he better turn on the lights.

When Margaret wakes up it is light but it feels really early. She sits up, rubs her eyes and sees that her mother is sleeping, her head resting on a sweatshirt against the window. She looks out her own window at nothing that looks familiar. She presses her forehead to the cool glass and watches the trees and houses go by, stone walls and fences made of branches that don't look like they would keep anything in or out.

They pass an old barn that has fallen in on itself on one side, the roof gone. She stares at it until it is out of sight and wonders if there were any animals inside that got hurt when the roof caved in, wonders why the people didn't take better care of it. They must be a hundred miles away at least, just like Gene said.

She looks at the back of his head, then at the mirror where she sees he is watching her.

"Hey, sleepyhead." He looks happy to see her. "How ya doin?"

"Good. Where are we?"

Her mother lifts her head and looks around, pushes her hair back behind her ears and asks the same question. "Where are we?"

"About an hour past Concord. Staying on the back roads. No hurry now. You okay?"

"A bathroom would be nice. And some coffee. And aspirin. Did you at least bring the aspirin? It looks like we're in the middle of nowhere."

"I'll pull over if you need to go to the bathroom."

Her mother looks at him and makes a face. "Just get us somewhere. You know where we are? And where we're going? The man with a plan?"

She lights a cigarette and waits for him to say something but he doesn't. "So tell me again why we had to leave like that and couldn't at least take our stuff. Not that we have much."

He sighs. "I told you we couldn't make it look like we took off for good. If they come looking it will seem like we're coming back. No one would leave all their stuff behind like that if they weren't coming back. It will look like we just went out for a while, to a movie or something, and by the time they figure out we're not coming back and decide to look for us, which they won't, there's no way they'll ever find us. Plus, they won't look too hard anyway. Don't worry." He catches Margaret's eye in the mirror again and winks.

Her mother puts her window down, letting in cool, fresh air. "You got it all figured out, huh?"

"Doing my best here."

She shakes her head. "As if we go out to movies. When was the last time we went to the movies? Oh yeah, never."

Margaret reaches up, touches the back of her mother's head, her pretty hair. Her mother doesn't turn around, doesn't say anything, just takes another drag of her cigarette then throws it out the window.

"We'll come to a town soon," Gene says. "First place we see we'll stop and have breakfast, get our bearings and make a plan." He looks over at Margaret's mother but she just looks out the window.

Gene turns on the radio, presses buttons until he finds music. It's not country, but something with loud guitar and no words and her father taps the beat on the steering wheel. Margaret is surprised he has so much energy when he didn't sleep at all last night. She likes when he is like this, though, because after a while her mother gets energy, too and they both are happy.

"So you don't think they'll come after us for the rent?" her mother asks.

"Since when do you worry about things like that?" Gene turns the radio down. "They'll just write it off. What is it? Two months? Twelve hundred? It would cost them more than that for a lawyer, plus they have our deposit. And it wasn't like they did anything to the place. Remember that time we had to wait five days for them to fix the septic? Just forget about it. We're long gone and they are not coming after us."

"Who then? Who is coming after us? There's something you're not telling me."

Gene turns the radio back up, hands her a joint from his pocket and smiles. "We're good. Stop worrying."

He always knows what to do and what to say. He doesn't worry about anything. She knows it's wrong not to pay your rent, but if Gene thought it was the right thing to do, that the landlord owed it to them, then it must be okay. When she grows up she wants to be sure of everything, too.

Her mother shakes her head. "I just wanted to get a clean start."

"That's exactly what we're doing."

"We'll be okay, mama." Margaret puts her hand on her mother's shoulder. She wants her to trust Gene and to be happy. She doesn't understand why it's so hard for her mother to be happy.

"You tell her," Gene says, and Margaret is proud she said something.

"So you don't think they will talk to the neighbors, talk to Darlene, find out about the car? They can find us just by the car, the license plate."

Margaret isn't sure who "they" are. The police? The landlord? Would they put them in jail if they found them?

"Screw the neighbors. Screw Darlene and screw the license plate. We're miles away now and can be in Vermont in less than an hour. We can get new license plates easy. We can be on the other side of New York by tonight if we want. Christ, we can go to Canada. We can do whatever the hell we want. Can you just relax and trust me? Haven't I always taken care of you?" They are silent for a few minutes and Margaret sits back, enjoying the rush of cool air from the open windows and trying to feel like Gene, not afraid of anything.

In just a few minutes Gene slows down as they come upon more houses and a store with a sign in the window written in blue marker. *Bait and tackle. Live crawlers.* Margaret shivers and looks away quickly, wonders what kind of people live here. They pass a hardware store, a small parking lot with weeds growing in it, a little restaurant called *Rosie's*. Gene pulls over and parks the car right in back of a red van. There are no windows in the back of the van, just a lot of stickers: *I climbed Mt. Washington, Chicken Farmer, I still love you.* There is a peace sign, another sticker that says, *Guns don't kill people. People kill people.* On the license plate it says, *Live free or die.* Margaret has heard Gene say that lots of times but she doesn't like it. Dying scares her.

"Who's hungry?" Gene says, and they all get out of the car. As they walk by the van Margaret takes Gene's hand, walks quickly without looking at the van again, not sure why that scares her, too. She needs to stop being such a baby. It feels good to be outside the car, to stretch her legs and walk.

Gene opens the door to Rosie's as if he knew right where they were going all along. A bell jingles and the girl behind the counter looks up and tells them to sit anywhere. There is only one other person there, an old man with gray hair tied back in a ponytail and a beard that reaches the middle of his chest. He is wearing a dirty baseball cap and a green tee-shirt and hardly glances up at them before he goes back to his newspaper.

The three of them stand just inside the door for a few seconds, breathing the smell of coffee and bacon until her mother walks to a booth in front of the window and they follow. The girl comes over with a pot of coffee and menus, turns over two of the thick white mugs and fills them, asks how everyone is doing today.

"You sell maps here?" Gene asks.

The man with the beard looks up at Margaret and smiles, shakes his head and folds his paper. Margaret watches him drink down the rest of his coffee, put some money on the table and walk out, still smiling. She wonders what he is smiling about.

"No," the girl says. "There's a gas station up the road on your left. He might have maps. Are you lost?"

"Just planning." Gene reaches over and takes two sugar packets, opens them both and spills them into his coffee.

"We're on an adventure," Margaret says.

The girl looks at Margaret, then at Gene. "I'll give you a minute to look over the menu."

"Don't tell strangers our business," her mother says.

Margaret feels her face get red, watches the girl walk back behind the counter and set the coffee pot down. She wishes she was old enough to have a job like that, old enough to know the right things to say. "I didn't mean to."

Her mother picks up the menu, then puts it down. "Order me the western with an English muffin and orange juice." She slides towards Margaret. "Come on. Let's go use the bathroom."

The bathroom smells like it has just been cleaned and is barely big enough to fit the two of them. Margaret uses the toilet first while her mother stands at the sink, looks in the mirror and combs her hair, puts on lipstick. When Margaret is through her mother tells her to wash her hands and go back out to the table. "I'll wait for you, mama."

"Go out and wait with Gene. I'd like a little privacy if you don't mind."

There are two old men sitting at the counter now. They look at Margaret when she comes out like she shouldn't be there. She walks to the table with her head down, then sits across from Gene, who is looking outside. The menus are gone and there is a glass of milk in front of her. He must have ordered something special for her, a surprise. The milk is cold and sweet.

"She okay?" he asks, tilting his head in the direction of the bathroom.

Margaret licks her lips and nods. "She'll be right out."

"We're gonna have a whole new life now. She just can't seem to get that through her head."

"I believe you."

"That's a girl."

Margaret smiles, drinks some more milk, looks towards the bathroom and wishes her mother would come out. She watches as Gene takes a small bottle of whiskey out of his jacket and pours some in each of their coffees, then winks at her and puts the bottle back just as her mother walks out of the bathroom.

The waitress is right behind her and sets a plate of pancakes in front of Margaret, omelets with fried potatoes and toast, tall glass of orange juice for mama and Gene. "Short stack, two westerns. Anything else?"

"I wanted an English muffin," her mother says. The waitress looks at her little pad of paper, makes a face. "Did you order me an English muffin?" she says to Gene.

"They only have toast," he says and the waitress walks away without saying anything. "Have some coffee."

When her mother takes a sip her eyes get big, then she almost smiles. "Good coffee."

The three of them are quiet for a few minutes while they eat. Gene reaches over with his fork, takes a bite of Margaret's pancake and smiles. "Mmmm. Wanna swap?" Everything feels good now, different, like they have gotten far enough away from everything that was bad, and now there won't be anything to worry about or fight about.

After the waitress comes back and fills their cups and leaves the check on the table, her mother pushes her plate away without eating her toast and her voice is serious. "So where's the money?" She has been so quiet, and now when she talks she sounds angry again. She glances over towards the men sitting at the counter and lowers her voice. "You're not carrying it all in cash, are you?"

"Come on. I have enough to last us a couple weeks and the rest is in a cashier's check.

"Can't they trace that?"

Gene takes a sip of coffee. "Who?"

"The police. I don't know. Whoever is looking for us. Whoever we owe money to. Don't you have to give your name and everything when you get a cashier's check?"

"Jesus. Will you drop it? I told you we don't owe anybody anything. How many times do I have to say it? Just drop it. We're moving on."

"So how much is it for? And how much cash do you have? I have a right to know."

"Enough. More than enough. We're gonna be fine. When we get where we're going I'll open a bank account and we'll be all set." He softens his voice and puts his hand on hers. "Come on. Where's my Jenny girl?"

Her mother stares at him for a second, finishes her coffee and looks out the window while Gene gets up and walks to the bathroom, nodding to the men at the counter as he walks by. Margaret wonders if he knows them, if he has been here before.

"It'll be okay, mama." Margaret puts her hand on her mother's back and when she turns to her Margaret sees her eyes are wet and can't understand why she would be so sad.

"All I want is a life. He can't seem to understand that. That's all I want. A decent place to live, food on the table, clothes. A normal life like everyone else has." She turns again to stare out the window. "Just a simple goddamn life where we don't have to be looking over our shoulder all the time or wondering if we're going to be homeless or starve to death."

"We will, mama." She rubs her mother's shoulder gently and her mother doesn't turn around. Then Gene is back, happier now, his eyes bright.

Her mother stares at him and shakes her head. "If you piss away this money on drugs I swear I'm done."

Gene sits and looks at Margaret. "So what do you think? Where should we go?"

Margaret is sure it matters what she says. She wishes she had more time to think about it, wishes she knew about different places in the world so she would say the right thing. "Can we go to the ocean?"

"See, Jenny? Margaret wants to go to California, too. It's all settled."

Margaret looks at her mother, who takes her last sip of coffee, leaving pretty red lipstick marks on the rim of her cup. She doesn't say anything right away and Margaret hopes she will say okay and they will go to California and start their new life. Instead, her mother's voice is flat. "We're not going to California."

"Why not? It's as good a place as any. I have a buddy lives just outside San Diego. He says the weather is always sunny, between seventy and eighty."

"It's too expensive for one thing, and way too far away. By the time we get there we'll be broke again."

"But mama," Margaret says. "We're not poor anymore, right?"

"Not right this minute. We'll see how long that lasts."

"Why do you have to be like that?" Gene sounds hurt.

Her mother shakes her head again, takes a deep breath. "You know we're not going to California. We need to save as much of that money as we can and put some away for emergencies. I swear, I'll never, ever be forced into a decision like that again."

The waitress comes back and asks if they're all set and starts clearing the table. "I'll take that up at the register when you're ready," she says.

Margaret looks out to the street, at their very own car sitting right outside. She loves their car, the baby blue color and all the numbers and dials in front. And she loves the smell of the pine tree that hangs from the mirror up front.

The buildings on the other side of the street are still dark inside and quiet, the sun reflecting off the windows. She watches a man wearing a black tee-shirt and baggy camouflage shorts walking on the other side of the street with a girl not much older than Margaret. Her long blonde hair is tied back in a ponytail that swings when she walks. She is staring at the ground and doesn't seem to be listening to the man yelling at her and waving his hands in the air.

"So let's make a real plan. We need to be serious." Her mother sounds like she's not having any fun at all on their adventure. "First we need to find a place to live and we need to get her in school. It's already September."

They all look over when the door jingles open and a young girl with a baby on her hip walks through the door. Her dark curls are pulled back with a headband and she has a diaper bag over one shoulder. She takes a seat at a table and the baby sits on her lap. He is a quiet baby with dark hair. Margaret can tell it's a boy and for a second she thinks it's her brother and the girl is bringing him back to them. She can't help but stare at them. The girl looks so young she could be babysitting, but when Margaret hears her talking to the baby she knows he is hers, just by the way she talks and looks at him and holds him close to her like he is the most important thing in the whole world.

Margaret's mother stops talking and stares at them, too, while Gene drinks the rest of his coffee, sets the mug down hard on the table. Then he looks over at the girl and her baby, rolls his eyes and shakes his head. "Christ." He picks up the check and glances at it, takes out his wallet and pulls out a twenty, leaves it on the table. "Let's go."

Her mother sets her purse on her lap, slips the little white dish with the sugar packets into the side pocket and they all walk out without another word.

The red van is still in front of their car. It must belong to Rosie, or maybe the cook. Margaret reads more stickers: *Niagara Falls. Yellowstone.* Places Margaret has heard of but can't picture.

They drive right past the gas station without a word and without stopping for a map. Gene must know where he is going now. Margaret likes the winding road with trees and rocks on the side, signs that say deer crossing and to watch for falling rocks, mailboxes close to the road. She stares at the shadows between the trees, hoping to see a deer, or even a bear.

She looks up at the back of her mother's head and wonders what she is thinking about. They are running away from their old life and Margaret wonders how far they need to go before no one is chasing them anymore. They pass barns and fences and stone walls that have fallen over in places.

Then she sees two brown and white horses, the first horses she has ever seen. They are beautiful and she wishes they could stop and look at them, touch them. One of them looks up as they pass, his eyes huge and dark and sad, and it feels something like a dream.

"Are we going to just drive all day or what?" her mother says. They have been silent since breakfast and Margaret is sure Gene is thinking about how to give them all a better life. He has been saying it for such a long time. Margaret knows he is the one who will decide where they will go and he will know what they need to do when they get there.

Margaret would be happy to keep driving, stopping at another place like Rosie's for lunch, staying at a hotel when they get tired. They could see the whole country and no one would ever find them.

"We haven't gone that far. Relax. Enjoy the scenery."

"I'm sick of driving. It's not like we're seeing anything interesting."

"Did you see the horses back there, mama?" Maybe Gene will go back.

"Why didn't you go towards the coast? That would have been a lot better than this. We could go to the ocean in Maine. That's supposed to be beautiful. Let's turn east. Can we do that? At least we would see something besides goddamn trees."

Gene sighs. "I need to get gas soon. We'll get a map. You want to be in charge? You pick a place on the map and that's where we'll go. Okay? Will that make you happy?"

Her mother lights a cigarette and doesn't answer him, and when she puts down her window and blows a stream of smoke outside Margaret glances up at the mirror and Gene winks at her. She wishes they would stop fighting. They are supposed to be happy now and Margaret doesn't know how to make that happen. After they stop she will ask again if she can sit up front with them.

They drive in silence for about ten minutes, then they start to slow down. Margaret looks around to see why they are stopping. There is no gas station, only trees. They are going so slow now a car comes up behind them, a red car that swerves around them and the driver presses on his horn for a long time. Then they are parked on the side of the road, halfway in a ditch so the car is tilted and Margaret is afraid.

Gene doesn't say anything; he just turns the key and the car makes a whining noise. He tries it a few more times while Margaret's mother smokes her cigarette and stares at him. He bangs his hand on the steering wheel. "Shit. Shit. Shit." Then there is only the sound of birds. There must be a million birds in those trees.

"Don't tell me," her mother says. "This beautiful luxury car, this great goddamn deal you got. This is as far as it's going to take us. Are we in California yet? How much further to San Diego?" Her voice is as mean as it gets, but Margaret can also hear she is a little happy about it, as if she has won.

"Shut up, Jenny. Just shut up."

Margaret has never heard Gene tell her to shut up before, though she had expected it a million times.

Gene gets out and opens the hood and smoke comes out. He will know how to fix it. He can do anything. Her mother slides over and gets out on the driver's side, slams the door behind her and starts in on him again. She likes to fight.

Margaret listens to her saying how he fucked up again, how he couldn't even buy a car that would last a week. Margaret can't hear what her father says back, but in a minute it is quiet. Margaret can't see anything with the hood up, but her mother stands there on the side of the road next to the car, hands on her hips, shouting at him, asking where the hell he thinks he's going. He must be going to get help.

Her mother leans through the window and grabs her purse and the yellow envelope from the front seat. When she turns and looks in back at Margaret, she stares at her for a minute as if she forgot she was there. "Come on."

181

Margaret gets out and closes the door gently behind her and catches up to her mother. They walk in silence and Margaret knows not to say anything; her mother is too angry right now. She turns around a few times to look at the car. It bothers her to just leave it there and she doesn't feel safe anymore. Their footsteps and breathing are the only sounds as they walk along the side of the road, kicking up sand and pebbles. The space between them and Gene is growing longer but at least she can still see him. Margaret thinks of running ahead to be with him, tell him it's not his fault the car broke down, but she can't leave her mother alone.

After a little while they come to a sign that says *Hayfield Welcomes You*. Gene is leaning against a mailbox smoking a cigarette, waiting for them. He and her mother are still angry, at each other and at the car and probably at the place they ended up. Hayfield? They have only been on their adventure one day and everything is messed up. They aren't anywhere near California or the ocean and they are both madder than Margaret has ever seen them.

"Could you have picked a more perfect place?" Her mother's voice is cold and full of blame. She always blames everything on him.

They are lucky that the first place they come to is a gas station. It has a small garage and the man there seems nice. His name is stitched on his shirt pocket in blue cursive. *Hank.* He gives Margaret a lollipop and they wait about half an hour while they tow the car and bring it into the garage. It still looks beautiful to Margaret, but helpless, too, its front end off the ground like that. *Please, Jesus, let Hank be able to fix it. Please let us get to somewhere nice that mama likes.*

She and her mother wait outside on a bench while Gene talks to the mechanic. Her mother smokes one cigarette after another and gives Margaret two dollars to get cokes from the machine. Margaret can't think of a single thing to say while they wait so they listen to the voices of the men and the sound of metal and drills. Gene walks out but doesn't sit down. He leans against the coke machine and smokes and they wait. At least they are all together. Before too long Hank is walking towards them looking like he has bad news and they all stand in a little circle.

"It's a blown head gasket," Hank says. "You want us to fix it we'll have to order the parts. I can call around to Claremont, Concord. Might take a few days. Probably cost about fifteen, eighteen hundred including labor. Timing belt looks nearly shot, too, and you probably want to look at replacing those tires soon. I'm just saying. I don't want to fix one thing and you break down a day later. Just saying."

"Saying what?" her mother asks. "That our new car is a worthless piece of shit?"

Hank's face gets red and he turns to Gene. "It's up to you. How long have you had it?"

"Less than a week," her mother says. "Less than a goddamn week."

"I was you I'd bring it back to the dealer," Hank says.

"It was a private sale," Gene says.

Margaret's mother laughs. "Oh. A buddy? Did you get it off one of your famous buddies?"

Gene gives her such a hateful look Margaret walks back to the bench and sits, takes a sip of her coke and prays everything will be okay.

"What'll you give me for it?" Gene asks.

"Are you kidding me?" her mother says. "How in the hell are we going to get out of here? I'm not staying here."

"What'd you pay for it if you don't mind me asking," Hank says. They are both ignoring her mother now but her mother doesn't notice or doesn't care.

"Yeah, I'd like to know that, too," she says. "What did you pay for it? How much money of ours did you spend on this worthless piece of shit?"

"Go sit down, Jenny." Gene's voice isn't loud but Margaret can tell he means it. For the first time in her life Margaret thinks he might be mad enough to hit her.

Margaret starts to get up, go to her mother, when her mother takes a step closer to Gene. "How much? I have a right to know."

Gene puts his hands on her shoulders, pushes her away and shakes his head. "I'm telling you, you need to shut up and go sit down."

"Whoa, now," Hank says. "I don't want any trouble here."

Her mother keeps her eyes on Gene as she steps backwards and sits on the bench. She is breathing heavily and when Margaret touches her arm she flinches and moves away. Margaret wishes she could hand her a cold beer.

Gene's voice changes as he talks to Hank. "I paid three thousand. So what'll you give me for it?"

Hank whistles, then says, "It might be worth three hundred in parts. That's about as high as I can go."

Her mother shakes her head, then to Margaret's surprise, she starts crying. Now when Margaret touches her she doesn't flinch. Margaret rubs her back gently and in just a minute she wipes her eyes on her sleeve and walks back over to Gene.

"Three thousand dollars? You paid three thousand dollars for that piece of junk? This is what I sold my baby for? So you could blow it and we end up in goddamn Hayville? Hayville. Jesus."

Chapter 14

"**Y**ou got someone you can call?" Hank looks at Gene when he asks this, taking a step back like he wants to get away from them. Margaret notices how skinny his neck is and how his eyes look a little scared.

Gene looks at Margaret's mother and they stare at each other for a few seconds. Margaret can't imagine anyone they could call, anyone who could help them.

"What about Sam?" her mother asks. "Why don't you call your good friend Sam?" She puts on a sweet voice to cover how mad she is.

Gene shakes his head. "No way. He's already done all he can for us. I can't ask him for any more."

"Oh right. He's done so much for us. And what about all your buddies? There must be at least one good buddy out there you can call."

Hank pulls a dirty rag out of his back pocket and wipes his hands on it. "I'll let you talk. Just let me know if you want to use the phone." He disappears into the garage and the three of them stand there. Margaret wants to say something that will help, something about their adventure, but she can't think of what it would be, plus when Gene and mama are in the middle of a fight she only feels scared.

"What about you, Jen? Why don't you call someone?"

The last thing Margaret expects is for her mother to laugh but that's what she does, then it stops as fast as it started. "Who? My parents? You know I'm not calling them. As far as they're concerned I might as well be dead."

"Just call your father. Your mother's the one disowned you. You were daddy's little girl, right?"

Margaret sees her mother's eyes fill up with tears and she is shaking as if it is cold outside. "You have no idea who I was," she says.

"I know he'd want to hear from you and he would be more than happy to help us out here, help us get back on our feet. Tell them I'm not in the picture anymore. That'd make them happy, right? It doesn't matter what you tell them, but it's all we got right now. We're out of options here."

"We're always out of options and it's always up to me to fix everything, always me who makes the sacrifices. And for what? So you can have a good time for yourself. That's all I've been doing, making sure you have a good time. That's what I sold our son for. Are you having fun now? I'm not."

She's crying hard now and Margaret puts her hand on her arm and gently leads her back to the bench. Gene walks with them but doesn't sit.

"They owe you, Jen, and I bet they realize that now. The way they treated you back then. I bet they feel bad, and I bet if you told them about Margaret, that we have a kid to provide for they would give you whatever you needed. If you just do this one thing I promise we'll make it work."

"What about the money? How much is left?"

Gene hesitates for a few seconds. "A little over eight."

Her mother jumps up. "Are you kidding me? You blew twelve thousand dollars? Jesus. How do you even do that?" She stares at him, her arms by her side and her hands in tight fists like she is going to punch him.

"I owed some, okay? But we're all square now. We can still have a new start. Just call them and tell them our car broke down. I bet they have extra cars they don't even use. We can get on our feet and get far away from here. We'll be smarter this time. I promise."

"You actually think I'm going to call them. There isn't a chance in hell they're going to help us. I burned that bridge a long time ago."

"Exactly. It was a long time ago. They've had enough time to get over it, don't you think? It's worth a shot."

"It's worth shit."

Gene pulls his wallet out of his back pocket, takes out a dollar and gets a soda from the machine, drinks half of it down, then sits next to Margaret but doesn't say anything. Margaret wonders if he is getting his words just right before he talks again.

"I already called them." Her mother's voice is soft and sad. Margaret and Gene both look up at her.

"When?" Gene's voice is soft, too.

"After you and Sam left. That day I signed those papers." Her mother is looking at her hands as she talks. "I thought if I told them they were going to have a grandchild." She looks down at Gene. "I was going to leave you then, go home and have my baby and be a new person."

Gene just stares at her. He looks a little surprised and a little hurt, but he doesn't say anything and no one looks at Margaret. It's like she isn't even there.

"She answered the phone and when she heard my voice she said she couldn't believe I had the nerve to call and before she could hang up on me I told her she was going to be a grandmother. I thought that would make all the difference, that she could put what happened behind us but she said she had no daughter and that she certainly wouldn't have anything to do with some bastard grandchild."

"What happened, mama?" Margaret asks. What could have happened to make her own mother say such awful things to her?

"Nothing," her mother says, then she stands up just as Hank walks out of the garage. "Where's the ladies' room?"

"I'll get you the key. It's around the other side." He turns and walks into the little office, takes a key attached to a piece of wood with a W on it and holds it out to her, and as soon as she is around the corner, Hank says, "I'll help you get your stuff from the car if you want, give you a ride somewhere, unless you have someone you can call. There's a motel up the road if you're looking for a place to stay the night. They'll have good rates now that it's after Labor Day."

It only takes a couple of minutes to get to the hotel. Margaret sits in Hank's back seat with her mother, while Gene and Hank sit up front and talk about the area, how peaceful it is, how off the beaten path. "People from here tend to stay here," Hank says. "Don't have a lot of new people moving in. It's a nice area, though."

Margaret and her mother don't say anything on the ride; they just look out their windows and Margaret wonders if this is where their new life will be. They pass a few houses, a pizza place with a bank next to it, a general store, then Hank turns left into a long driveway that goes up the side of a hill. Margaret sees the sign, *Hillside Motel. Vacancy. Pool. Cable.*

The hotel is a long white building with dark green doors in the front with numbers on them. There is one other car there and a red truck with a dog in back. The dog looks hot and tired as he lifts his head a few inches to see them, then puts it back down and closes his eyes. The four of them get out and Hank opens the trunk where they put Gene's duffle bag and a black trash bag with some of their clothes in it. That's all they have of their whole other life.

Once their things are on the walkway outside the hotel Hank says good luck and shakes Gene's hand. The only time Margaret ever saw Gene shake hands was with Sam, and it seems like she is looking at someone else, someone on a television show.

"I'll be right back." Gene walks into the hotel office while Margaret and her mother wait outside with their bags. They stand in the shade, her mother holding the envelope to her chest, looking at Margaret like she wants to say something. Margaret wants to say something, too, but all she has are questions, probably the same questions her mother has.

Gene is back in just a couple of minutes, holding a key on a yellow plastic keychain with the number 9 on it. "We have the room for a week. That should give us enough time to figure things out."

They walk almost to the end of the building and when Gene opens the door everything looks so neat and welcoming to Margaret – the orange and brown plaid curtains and bedspread, the brown carpet. There are two beds, bigger than their beds in the trailer, and even Margaret's mother seems to like it. She walks around, touching the dresser, the television, then she sits on the edge of one of the beds and sighs, bounces a little then goes to the window and opens the curtains.

"There's a pool." Her mother's voice is flat, almost like she is talking to herself. It seems like her mother has forgotten all about the car and the money for now, or she is just too tired to fight anymore.

Gene sets the bags down by the bed, walks to the window and puts his arms around Margaret's mother. "Let's go down," Gene says. "Check it out."

Her mother pulls away and turns to Margaret. "Meggie, are you hungry? I'm starved."

"We passed a pizza place down the road," Gene says, as if she had asked him, and Margaret hopes they can all walk down together and get pizza. If they just stay together things will be okay again. But still her mother ignores him.

"Come on, Meggie," she says. "Let's get something to eat." Before Margaret can answer or move, her mother turns to Gene then. "I want half that money. I want you to go to the bank and cash that check and give me half. Today. I mean it."

"Let's get some pizza," he says, walking out the door before her mother can say another word. Her mother picks up her purse and they follow him outside. The sun is hot, but not as hot as it always felt at the trailer.

Margaret looks up at the bright blue sky, the pine trees pointing to heaven and says a little prayer to the Blessed Virgin Mary that everything will be okay. She remembers her mother telling her about Mary, the mother of Jesus and how she will answer your prayers. This seems like a good time to pray to her. Praying is always good. When her mother told her about Blessed Virgin Mary, Margaret had asked, *What's a virgin, mama?* She said *Never mind Just*

191

*make sure you stay one as long as you can. Once you
give it up you're never the same.*

Margaret is glad when she sees the beer signs
at the pizza place; it will put her mother in a good
mood. It's called *The Pizza Palace*, though they didn't
even try to make it look like a palace. It's small and
the walls are wood, and the floor is white and black
squares. She looks around at the tables, all empty
except for one, where four guys sit with their table
full of beer bottles and paper plates and little red
plastic baskets.

They walk up to the counter and Gene and
Margaret stare up at the menu on the wall while her
mother sits at a table by the window. Margaret
watches her mother looking at nothing, glances over
at the men who don't seem to notice them. They are
laughing at something and one of them says
something about Jack and they all laugh even louder.

Gene doesn't ask her what she wants, but
orders a large pepperoni and mushroom and a small
cheese, two bottles of beer and a ginger ale. Her
mother hasn't said anything, not on their walk here
and not to tell him what she wanted. He pays with a
credit card, takes the receipt and the two beers and
they walk over to the table, where he sets the beers
down and tells her what he ordered and says how
good it smells, but Margaret's mother looks away and
doesn't say anything.

It's bad when her mother is this quiet.
Margaret can't tell what her mother is thinking or
what she might do. When Gene pushes her beer
towards her mother he touches her hand and she
pulls it away, so he makes a face and shakes his head,
leans back in his chair and drinks his beer, tries to
act like he doesn't care.

When she finally speaks, her voice is calm and strong. "You should probably go over to the bank now to cash that check, before it closes."

"I'm not about to walk around with all that cash. We'll take care of it when we decide where we're going and how we're gonna get there."

She laughs, a short, mean laugh. "We're not getting anywhere. There's nowhere to get and there's no way to get there if there was." She says it like she has been thinking about it, then picks up her bottle of beer and takes a swallow. For a second she looks like she's going to cry again, but her eyes stay dry.

"Okay, then. If that's what you want, we'll stay here for a while. Whatever you want." He tries to take her hand and she pulls it away again.

"What I want is for you to cash that check and give me half. After you get me another beer."

Gene pushes his chair back and walks back up to the counter, gets two more bottles of beer. Then a man comes out of the kitchen and brings the pizzas to their table, asks if there is anything else they need.

"What time does the bank close?" her mother asks.

The man looks at her and doesn't answer right away, like he didn't understand the question, then he says, "It's Wednesday. Closed at one."

While they eat their pizza Gene tries to make it seem like nothing has happened, as if he had planned all along to be right where they are. He says it isn't a bad idea to be out in the boonies for a while. "There's always some kind of work up here. Plus the cost of living is a lot less. I could even ask Hank if he needs a hand if you really want to stay. It's not a bad idea."

Her mother says nothing.

"Mama? Do you like the pizza?"

"I'm not hungry."

"Did you see the leaves changing near the hotel?"

It's like her mother has disappeared inside herself and isn't coming out. Even Gene gives up trying to make her talk, trying to make things seem okay. Margaret decides she likes it better when her mother is talking, even when she talks crazy, even when she says mean things it's better than this. At least then they know what she is thinking. Her silence is scary.

Margaret's mother stops on the street outside the bank, her arms crossed, just staring at it like she is trying to decide whether or not to go in. She looks at the closed sign, then at Gene like it is his fault. "Tomorrow," she says, then she leads them down the street towards the Hillside Motel. "I want my money tomorrow."

It's dark by the time they get to their room. As soon as Gene opens the door Margaret's mother grabs the bag with their clothes and walks straight into the bathroom. Gene turns on the lamp, sits on the side of the bed and opens his duffle bag, takes out a bottle of whiskey.

Margaret goes to the window and looks down at the pool. In a minute she hears the shower and hopes her mother isn't crying, hopes she is taking a shower and that it will help her feel better. She stares at the water in the pool, so still and cool and dangerous looking. Some day she will learn how to swim.

"She'll be okay," Gene says.

Margaret flinches. She didn't hear him come up behind her. "I know," she says, even though she doesn't know, not really. She never knows what her mother will do or how she will react to something, but she seems different this time. Maybe it's because they are in a strange place, maybe it's because her mother has been so quiet, but Margaret knows something bad is going to happen and there is nothing she can do to stop it.

"How 'bout you? You okay?" He puts his arm around her and she smells the whiskey.

"I'm okay."

"She'll come around. She'll be okay. It was bad luck about the car. That's the thing about buying used. You never really know what you're getting." He stares at Margaret like he is remembering something. He smiles, then laughs a little.

"What?" she says.

"Nothing." He still stares at her. "Just remembering a day." He takes a swig of whiskey and they both stare down at the pool.

They listen to the shower, and because her mother isn't there Margaret has the courage to ask, "What day?"

He smiles again and his eyes change like they do when he is glad to be home. "I guess it turned out just the way it was supposed to. I didn't know it at the time, but she did." He glances over at the bathroom door. "Things happen when you just follow your instincts and do things. You don't think about right or wrong, you just do it. She did what she thought she had to do. I'll give her credit for that. She operates on pure instinct most of the time. No thinking."

Margaret never heard him talk like this before, not to her. She has no idea what he is talking about, but he is talking to her like an adult, and she tries to figure out what he means. Something her mother did, probably something she stole, something big and now she might get caught? She doesn't want to say

195

anything stupid, anything that would make him stop talking to her, so she just looks up into his face then leans into him.

"You're the best thing that ever happened to her." He laughs. "I used to think it was me, because she kept saying it. Tried to convince herself and anyone who'd listen. She put all her hopes and dreams for the future on me like I was some knight in shining armor. I tried to make her happy. You know that, right?"

He stands and looks out the window, then sits on the bed and she turns to face him. She watches him drink from the bottle and waits. "She likes to say how she saved you, but I think it's the other way around."

"Saved me from what?"

Even though he looks right into her face, his eyes seem far away. "From anything that would hurt you. That's what she said."

Margaret doesn't know what to say. She wants him to explain more, wants to know what he means, what her mother did, but he takes another drink of whiskey and says the worst thing he could ever say." I think both of you would be better off without me."

"No, we wouldn't. We never are." She has never asked him not to leave, never said a word all those times he left them after their fights. When her mother comes out she will be in a better mood and everything will be okay. They will get another car or they will stay there and find a place to live. She watches him as he looks towards the bathroom door and nods like someone has asked him a question.

Margaret steps over and sits next to him, puts her hand on his arm. "You're not leaving us here, right?" If they were still in their trailer it would be different. They are in a strange place, in a motel, with nothing of their own. When he doesn't say anything, she holds his arm with both hands. "We don't have any place to live." His eyes are focused on something out the window and Margaret wonders where he went.

"I can't make her happy anymore. It wouldn't matter if I gave her a mansion, she still wouldn't be happy. I don't want to live like this anymore. Life's too short."

"Then let's all go somewhere else."

Gene laughs and Margaret looks over at the bathroom door, pictures her mother coming out and Gene gone. Then what? She holds onto his arm tighter.

"That's all I wanted in the first place. A new start. Right? Isn't that what I kept saying? She's been against everything. *Too far. Too expensive.* She has no faith in me whatsoever."

His voice is angry and drunk and there is nowhere for Margaret to go when her mother opens the bathroom door, steam and shampoo smells coming with her. She has a towel wrapped around her, another in her hair, and she looks angry, too.

"What?" she says. "What are you two talking about? Me?"

"Nothing. We were just saying how nice it is around here," Gene winks at Margaret.

Her mother drops the towel, walks over to the dresser and opens the plastic bag. She puts on a pair of underpants and a tee-shirt, walks over to the other bed and slips under the sheet with her back to them.

Margaret wakes in the middle of the night. She and her mother are lying back to back and she can make out Gene's shape in the other bed. She closes her eyes and turns onto her back, thanks Jesus and Mary that he is still there, and after a few minutes she is asleep again. When she wakes up the room is bright and she is alone in the bed. She looks over at the other bed and sees it is empty, jumps up, looks in the bathroom. Her heart is beating fast. They wouldn't have left her. They wouldn't.

She looks everywhere for a note, but there is nothing. Then she looks out the window and sees Gene and her mother sitting on the side of the pool with their feet in the water. Her mother has her face tilted up to the sun and Gene is talking to her. She wonders what he is saying and if she is even listening. He must be telling her their plan. He will figure things out and they will be happy. This is their new life.

She tries to get back the good feeling she felt yesterday as they drove and Gene was so sure of himself, before the car died. Maybe they don't need a car.

Margaret looks through the plastic bag and finds some of her clothes mixed in with her mother's. She takes clean clothes into the bathroom, uses a facecloth to wash her face, then her whole body before she gets dressed. When she opens the door her mother is right there.

"Meggie we're going out to do a few things. You be a good girl. We won't be long."

"Can't I come, too?"

"We have some things to do. There's a nice television right here. And the A.C. Be a good girl and we won't be long." Her mother turns and then she and Gene are gone, the door clicking behind them, and Margaret stands there, hugging herself.

While Margaret waits she fights the panic that they won't come back. She tries to imagine what would happen, what she would do, who she could call. There is really no one. The police would come

and take her away and make her live with other
homeless girls, or put her with some strangers
somewhere.

She turns on the television and walks around,
opens empty drawers, flips through the Gideon's
Bible, then sets it next to the bed for later. The corner
of her mother's yellow envelope sticks out from
under Gene's bag and Margaret slides it out and
holds it. It isn't sealed, just held closed by a little
metal tab. She wonders if it would be bad to look
inside, if it would be a sin. Her mother never said
anything about it, never told her not to look in it, so
it wouldn't be like she was disobeying her mother.
It's probably just boring papers anyway.

She sits on the side of the bed with the
envelope on her lap, turns towards the television to
see the mean lady from General Hospital, the old one
with all the wrinkles and jewelry. She is standing on
a boat talking to herself about taking care of
someone, how they will never know what happened
until it's too late. Darlene hated her. She called her
the old bitch.

Margaret turns away from the television,
opens the envelope and peeks in to see what looks
like stories cut out of a newspaper. She closes the
envelope and slips it right back where it was, with
just the corner sticking out, sits on the other bed
with the remote. She wishes she didn't open the
envelope. Even though she really didn't see anything
she still did something bad, something sneaky, like a
lie. *I'm sorry, Jesus.*

They are gone most of the day. Margaret eats a
slice of the leftover pizza and tries not to cry. The
only thing to read is the Gideon's Bible.

When her mother walks in she isn't any
happier than when she left. She walks straight into

the bathroom and slams the door. Gene is right
behind her but stops and looks over at Margaret,
takes a deep breath. "You take care of her now. I'm
done."

Margaret stays where she is and doesn't say
anything. Her mother is in the bathroom and Gene is
leaving and Margaret wishes she were older than
eight. The news has just started on television and
Margaret turns down the sound, then turns to face
Gene but still doesn't get up or say anything.

Gene looks around the room like he has lost
something, but they never unpacked anything and he
just picks up his duffle bag and stands there, then
puts it down and walks around the bed to Margaret.
"You be good. Take care of her, but take care of
yourself, too, okay? I'm done."

"But you're coming back, right?" He has to
come back.

He shakes his head. "Don't count on it."

In her head she thinks, *But what about me?* She
can't say it out loud or even think it; it would sound
too selfish.

Her mother flings open the bathroom door so
it bangs against the wall. "Go," she says. "Go ahead.
We don't need you. Goddamn three thousand dollars.
Goddamn you."

Gene stares at her, his face sad and mad at the
same time. "What do you think I used for all the food
and the clothes I bought you? The pot and speed and
beer? And the car? You think people just gave me all
that? You have no idea what things cost." He kisses
Margaret on the top of her head then pats her hair
down. "Be good."

Then he is gone and the room feels empty. She
wants to ask her mother what happened but her

mother just steps over to the bed and lays down facing the window with her back to Margaret.

"Mama? Are you okay?"

"Leave me alone."

Margaret stands there for a few minutes, staring at her mother's back, her hair all wavy and pretty on the pillow. She isn't sure what to do but then her mother's shoulders are shaking and Margaret lays down next to her, puts her arm around her and smells her hair, smoky but sweet, too. Her mother puts her arm on Margaret's and cries quietly and after a while they both fall asleep.

Chapter 15

The first day of summer falls on Margaret's fifteenth birthday, hot and boring like every other Sunday. The window is open to the sounds on the street, quieter than a weekday, just a few cars and trucks, sometimes a motorcycle. She likes how they sound so powerful. She listens to a far-away train whistle and wishes she were on it, going somewhere. Anywhere she has never been, like Portland or Providence or Boston. A boy with a high voice yells, *hey wait*! and she listens to his sneakers hitting the pavement as he runs to catch up.

Today is her birthday and she tries not to want or expect anything. For some stupid reason, though, she thinks of Gene. She doesn't think of him constantly like she used to, but for some reason on her birthday he sneaks back into her thoughts. If he comes back at all, it will be on her birthday, or at least near it, and he will have something special for her. When he first left she thought he would be gone only a few days, then after her mother told her a million times he wasn't coming back it finally sank in. She can still hear him telling her not to count on it. But she did. She always counted on it. She expected him to come back and she waited for so long. She doesn't count on it anymore, not really, just sometimes on her birthday and she has no idea why.

When her mother got an apartment a few miles from Hayfield Margaret had asked her, *What about Gene?*

What about him?

How will he find us?

Grow up.

That was it. *Grow up.*

Margaret didn't ask again, but for a long time she prayed that he would either come back and find them or she would get a letter or phone call asking her to come live with him in California or Florida or maybe Canada. When he does come back it will be for her.

Margaret lies on her stomach on her unmade bed, her notebook in front of her, working on an ad to tack up on the bulletin board downstairs, where people post ads for everything. Landscaping jobs and tree services and plowing, picnic tables and firewood for sale, free kittens to a good home. She begged her mother for one of those kittens, but of course she said no.

She looks at what she has written so far: *Responsible girl willing to babysit full-time in summer and after school during school year.* She crosses out *girl* and writes *woman.* She isn't a kid anymore. *Young woman.* Then she crosses out everything and starts over. *Looking for a responsible person to babysit? I am available immediately.* Keep it simple. She adds *experienced* and rewrites it, decides to go to the library tomorrow and type it, make it look more professional. Maybe she could even put it in the newspaper if it doesn't cost much. As she rolls onto her back, ready to swing her legs over the side of the bed, her mother appears in the doorway.

"Let's take a walk, Meggie. Let's get out of here. It's too nice to stay in."

Margaret looks up at her mother. Her hair is brushed back into a high ponytail and she has pink lipstick on, the bright pink Gene used to like. Her eyes are done with pale blue shadow and mascara. She looks like she is a teenager going out on a date, so why would she want Margaret to tag along? Unless she has a surprise for her birthday. Last year she didn't even remember until a week later, telling Margaret she should have reminded her.

She closes her notebook, slides off her bed and stands. She is almost as tall as her mother.

"Here." Her mother holds out an envelope. "Happy birthday."

Margaret takes it and hugs her mother. "You remembered."

"What does that mean? I always remember."

On the front of the card is a birthday cake, pink and white, with one candle. It says, *Wishing you . . . the best birthday ever!* Her mother signed it, *Love, mama,* and there is a five-dollar bill in it.

"I wish it could be more."

"It's plenty. Thanks, mama." She will add the five dollars to what she has in the bank, almost two hundred from her babysitting money. She was counting on watching the twins at least another year until all of a sudden Nancy said they were moving and they were gone within a week.

"I want you to buy something nice with that."

Margaret smiles. "I will." As if she could buy anything nice for five dollars.

"Change your clothes and brush your hair and we'll go out and celebrate, get a little something to eat." She walks over to Margaret's dresser, opens the top drawer and lifts underwear, bras, a thin cotton nightgown that barely fits her anymore. She closes that one and opens the next one down.

"What are you looking for?" Margaret watches her mother fish through her tee-shirts and shorts. There is nothing to find.

"Where are all your clothes?"

"That *is* all my clothes." I don't have a ton of clothes like you. It's not like I go anywhere."

"And that's my fault? What do you do with all your babysitting money? I thought you were buying what you need. You're old enough to buy your own clothes. You're old enough to know what you need."

"I don't need anything." She looks down at her wrinkled tee-shirt and cut-offs, the same clothes she wore yesterday, which is pretty much her summer wardrobe. It's not like she has a boyfriend or someone she wants to impress. No one ever gets dressed up anyway.

Her mother is wearing white capris, a blue tank top, silver earrings and a silver chain, and she probably didn't pay for any of it.

"Hold on." Her mother goes to her room and comes back with a pink tank top with the tags still on it. Another present?

"Here, you can borrow this. Do you have anything besides shorts and jeans?"

"Like what? Why? Where are we going?"

"Then wear this and your jeans. There aren't any holes in them I hope. You're not wearing those jeans that are all ripped, are you?

"No. They're too expensive." Her mother has no idea what she wears, what she looks like when she leaves the house. No idea. "It's too hot out for jeans."

"You'll be fine. It'll be air conditioned."

"What will?"

"Wherever we go. Get ready." Her mother walks away, into the kitchen where she opens the refrigerator, and Margaret hears her pull the top off a can of beer.

Margaret sighs and takes the tank top, pulls out her best jeans from the bottom drawer and changes in the bathroom. She brushes her hair and teeth, splashes cold water on her face and pats it dry. Then she uses a little of her mother's mascara and looks at herself in the mirror. The tank top is a little big, but it is a good color on her. She opens the door and calls, "Mama? Can I use some of your lipstick?"

Her mother comes to the door, looks at her. "I guess it won't hurt. Not too much. Then her voice gets soft. "I can't believe you're 15." The way her mother looks at her makes Margaret feel like a grownup and a kid at the same time. She can't wait to be older, to be old enough so she doesn't need her mother anymore, doesn't need to ask for every little thing.

It's not as hot as Margaret had thought; there's a gentle breeze as they walk the few blocks into town, past the salon where her mother has worked for five straight weeks now without a problem, past the Asian market and the bank. Margaret makes a point to look away when they pass the bank like it doesn't exist. If her mother had any idea she had all that money in there she'd take it in a heartbeat.

They pass the laundromat and Margaret's mother asks her if she has any plans for the summer, as if they are friends. It's like all of a sudden her mother is interested in her, in her clothes and her plans, and Margaret forgets for a minute that her mother really doesn't care and actually starts to tell her things. She tells her how she is trying to get a new babysitting job and says how weird it was that

Nancy left like that and how she was counting on that babysitting job for the summer. "I want to start saving for my license."

When she looks at her mother to see her reaction, it's obvious she isn't even listening. Her mother nods and smiles, but there is nothing behind it and Margaret stops talking. At least she is trying to do something nice to celebrate her birthday and make it special. Doing the best she can.

Her mother looks into the windows of a store that sells all kinds of junk collecting dust. She has some salt and pepper shakers from there, two little ducks. Her mother is in her own little world. At least today her world is pretty calm, even happy.

They turn down a side street and it is clear to Margaret that her mother knows exactly where they are going, even though she makes it seem they are just out walking around. Margaret can tell they will end up in a place her mother is heading for all along. There must be a surprise, something for her birthday. It can't be a party because who would they invite? Still, Margaret knows something is going on. She can't remember her mother ever having a surprise for her before; Gene was the one who surprised her. It couldn't be that. No way Gene is coming. Don't even think it.

She has a vague memory of being a kid and walking with her mother on a hot day just like this, sunny and hot and they were both as happy as they ever were, on their way for sneakers. Her mother was young and told Margaret she was going to have a baby and it was a secret. Margaret understands now why she wanted to keep it a secret, so Gene wouldn't tell her to get an abortion, but would he? She lost the baby anyway, Margaret's brother. They sold him to strangers.

When Margaret feels most alone she thinks about him, wonders where he is, what he looks like, if he looks like her. She wonders what his new family is like and what they told him, if he even knows he has a big sister, and she hopes he's either an only child or he only has brothers. It's strange how she can love someone so much that she never even met, but just knowing he exists makes her know she is not alone in the world.

She started writing to him last year, telling him about herself, how she liked to run and was thinking about trying out for track in the fall. About Gene leaving and her life with their mother. She can tell him anything – about her mother's moods and her stealing and how she can be crazy sometimes but deep down she is a good person. Mostly Margaret feels sorry for her mother, but she could never tell her that. Tonight she will write to him about her day, and some day if she ever meets him she will give him the letters and he will know she never forgot him, that he has always been with her.

They come to a place on the corner with a sign hanging over the door. *The Green Lantern.* The sign looks about a hundred years old, with a guy who is probably supposed to be Paul Revere or something, holding a lantern. Her mother stops, looks it over like she has never seen it before. "Let's try this place." She opens the door and steps back so Margaret has to go in first.

Margaret isn't sure what to do once she steps into the cool darkness, so she stops and lets her eyes adjust. There is something almost familiar about the place, the smell of beer and the faint smell of cigarettes, a smell like home. The few guys sitting at the bar glance up at them for just a few seconds and the woman behind the bar looks up at them but doesn't say anything right away. All kinds and colors of bottles are lined up on shelves in front of a lighted mirror in the back of the bar. It looks just like a scene in a movie but it feels like an actual memory of being here before, or at least a place like this.

Margaret follows her mother to a table against the wall. The air conditioning hums in the background and she is glad she wore jeans instead of shorts. The baseball game is on and her mother smiles as she looks around, then sits.

She seems so happy and content and beautiful, Margaret begins to think it's possible Gene is meeting them there. After almost seven years maybe he is coming home, walking in here like it's an accident. *Hey, what are you two doing here? I've been looking for you for a long time. How's my girls?* He won't believe how grown up Margaret is now.

Then the waitress is standing there asking them what they would like. She's an older woman, sixty at least, and seems genuinely happy to see them. She looks at Margaret first.

"A coke?"

"Make it two," her mother says. "And put a shot of rum in mine."

"You got it. You want menus?"

"Sure."

Everything will be perfect when Gene walks in. Margaret imagines him stepping through the door, looking around and acting surprised to see them. Her mother will sit there and at first she will act like she isn't glad to see him. She will have that mad look on her face, but not for long. Or maybe she won't act mad at all or surprised because they have planned this together. Margaret will run up to him and hug him right away so he will know she isn't mad, either, and he will say how much she has changed, how she has grown into such a beautiful young woman. And he will tell them how sorry he is for being gone so long but he made a lot of money and has a nice house and a car and a dog all waiting for them. All he wants is for them to be a family again.

They sit quietly for a few minutes, sip their drinks and look at the menus, though Margaret can barely concentrate now. They both look up when someone walks in. Not Gene. She tries to decide what to order that he would like, but he was never picky. Her mother drinks down her rum and coke and asks for another one, and when she orders buffalo wings with extra hot sauce on the side, his favorite, Margaret can't keep it in another second. She will show her mother how smart she is, how she isn't a little kid anymore that has no clue.

"So what time is he coming?" She tries to sound like it's no big deal, instead of like an excited little kid.

Her mother sets her drink down, frowns. "Who?"

"Gene." She hasn't said his name out loud in such a long time.

Her mother's face changes from calm to surprise to anger in just a few seconds, anger that comes from somewhere deep. "What the hell are you talking about?"

Margaret feels about five years old again, her face hot and her eyes getting watery so things are blurry. She doesn't say anything, waiting for things to change, waiting for something else to happen, waiting for her mother to smile and say how she wanted it to be a surprise or else for Gene to just walk in and make everything special and right. But there is just the sound of the baseball announcer telling them the Sox leave men on first and third and after six innings are down by two. Even the guys at the bar are quiet, as if they are waiting, too, to find out what the hell she is talking about.

She wipes the one tear that escapes and looks around and there is nothing. No Gene. No nothing. She tries to smile but knows it must look fake and all she can think of to say is the truth. "I thought there was something special. For my birthday. You got all dressed up and made it seem like you had a big surprise so I thought Gene was coming." All her words come out in a rush that make no sense even to her and with each word she knows how wrong she is, how stupid. She always says the wrong thing, always thinks the wrong thing. She never knows what to think about anything.

Her mother stares at her like she's an alien or something, shakes her head and gives her such a hateful look. "What's wrong with you?" Her words come out in a slow, angry, loud whisper and Margaret can't think of an answer. She has been asking herself the same question since forever. All she can do is take a sip of her coke and blink back the tears.

"You never appreciate anything. Always want more. This isn't special enough? And what in the world would ever make you think for one second that he would be coming? Has he ever called you? Has he written a letter or even sent a postcard?" She looks at Margaret closely now. "Has he? It would be just like him to get in touch with you and not me, you two keeping it a secret."

The buffalo wings come and her mother's face and voice change to sweet as she orders another round.

"I haven't heard from him," Margaret says. "How could I? We keep moving." She wipes the tears that have spilled down her cheeks. "How could he even find us? We moved like five times since he left."

"If he wanted to find us he'd find us. Like an idiot I left forwarding addresses the first three times we moved, even at that shitty motel. After all this time, not even calling to see if we're okay. Not even a goddamn postcard? Screw him." She picks up a buffalo wing, dips it into the sauce and takes a big bite. "Boy you know how to ruin things."

They both look up as the door swings open and a group of guys come in, sweaty and excited, looking like they just finished a game of baseball or basketball or something. They look around, at the bar, at Margaret and her mother like they are uninvited guests, laughing the whole time about some catch one of them missed, their deep happy voices filling the whole place. They push two tables together and scrape chairs around it, then the waitress is there with two pitchers of beer and plastic cups before they even ask. She asks what the score was, which makes the guys laugh and talk at once.

Margaret looks up at her mother. "I'm sorry." Then she turns away so her mother won't see another tear escape. She brushes it away, reads the blackboard with the specials printed in chalk. *Fish 'n Chips. Reuben. Chicken Caesar Salad.* There is nothing her mother hates more than to see Margaret cry. Gene, too. Maybe they weren't allowed to cry when they were kids, either.

She pushes back her hair and turns back to her mother, hoping she hasn't ruined the whole day. She wishes she could explain how she feels, how she didn't realize until today how much she missed him. Her mother must miss him, too, but she would never admit it and she doesn't want to hear about it.

212

Margaret pulls the strap of her purse from the back of the chair, slips it over her shoulder. "I'm going to the bathroom." She walks past the men hunched over their drinks and bottles, Gene's age or older, who glance at her for less than a second, then turn their attention back to the game.

When she is in the bathroom she tries to think of what she can say that will make everything all right. She just made a mistake. Anyone would have thought the same thing, the way her mother got all fixed up and acted so secretive and took her out to a bar and ordered buffalo wings. She won't say anything else about Gene, and hopefully her mother will forget about it by the time she gets back. She combs her hair and tries to fluff it up a little, puts on a smile. Act like nothing happened.

When Margaret walks back to their table there is a new coke in front of her with a cherry in it and a buffalo wing on her plate, drenched in hot sauce. Her mother watches as Margaret takes a sip of her coke and chokes on it, totally not expecting the rum. Her mother winks at her and smiles. It's not like Margaret has never tasted a rum and coke before, but her mother could have warned her. This is her way of getting back at her. When her mother laughs, Margaret laughs, too, even though she doesn't think it's funny. She doesn't like the taste very much; she likes beer better, but she takes another big sip to show her mother it doesn't bother her. It's strong and it burns going down, but in only a couple of minutes Margaret feels the alcohol and it softens things.

It doesn't matter anymore what she said and what she thought. Everyone says stupid things sometimes and anyway it's partly her mother's fault for setting her up to think there was this huge birthday surprise, and what else could it have been? She probably did it on purpose.

Before they leave, Margaret's mother goes to the ladies' room and Margaret turns towards the television. The game is over. The Red Sox lost five to three and who cares. The guys at the bar are talking about the lousy pitching but Margaret focuses on the screen where they are showing a picture of a little girl, only three, who disappeared twelve years ago.

The girl's name is Adeline Jenkins and they believe she was abducted from the back seat of a car while her foster father was in a convenience store. They are saying she is only one of hundreds of children who have simply vanished from foster care. The woman tells them to tune in tonight at eleven to see the special investigative report, part of a three-part series focusing on the challenges and failures of the child welfare system. *The Forgotten Victims.*

Margaret turns as her mother comes out of the ladies' room, the door squealing then closing behind her, and when Margaret glances back at the television the little girl's picture is on the screen again, next to an age-enhanced picture of what she may look like now. Her mother stops and stands next to her, looks at the faces on the screen and Margaret sees the surprise in her mother's eyes. The girls face is thin and pale and she looks so scared.

Her mother turns away. "Let's go."

"Wait. Look at that girl."

"Come on." Her mother takes her arm, then their eyes go back to the television when the news lady says it was a tragic ending to a tragic young life. *Be sure to tune in at eleven for this provocative and eye-opening program.*

One of the men at the bar turns around, his bloodshot eyes roaming over Margaret's face, then her mother's, then he turns back around and picks up his empty bottle, holds it out to the waitress.

"Let's go," her mother says again, walking out ahead of her without another word. It takes Margaret a few seconds to turn away from the television and she has to practically run to catch up to her mother, the girl's image still in her brain. That little face looking so innocent and scared. How can a computer figure out what a person would look like from a baby to a teenager? And how could she look so much like her? It feels like she just saw herself on television.

They are the same age and Margaret knows it can't be her, but maybe she is related to her somehow. She has heard of twins being separated at birth. Maybe her mother gave her twin away. Or sold her, just like she sold Margaret's brother as soon as he was born. It could be possible. Anything could be possible in her life. How else could she explain the weird connection she feels to that girl?

Chapter 16

Jenny walks as quickly as she can and Margaret keeps right up with her, just like Gene kept up with her twelve years ago as she hurried away with Margaret in her arms. But now Margaret isn't in her arms and she isn't some stranger's child anymore. It wasn't quite real at the time, but it sure as hell is real now. After all this time.

She looks over at Margaret, thinking her own thoughts, trying to figure things out. Twelve years. And now these people have nothing better to do than dig up something from twelve years ago that no one cared about when it happened. A little girl goes missing and they do nothing to find her but point fingers and say how awful it is, but at the end of the day they do nothing. It's on the news for a few days, then who cares? Only Jenny. Where were they then with all their concern? And now after all this time someone is going to recognize Margaret and Jenny is going to get caught, as if she did something wrong. They wouldn't understand. No one would. They wouldn't even try to. She can't go to jail. She won't.

She looks over at Margaret again, her Meggie. She must be wondering why some girl who has been missing for twelve years looks just like her. Is that what she's thinking about? Or is she still thinking about Gene? It's amazing how a computer can make a picture like that, so close to how she looks after all these years. That was one of the things that made Jenny feel safe, that no one could possibly recognize her now, practically all grown up.

Jenny finds herself thinking about Gene, wanting him to take over for a while. He would open a beer, lean back in his chair and tell her not to worry. He would know exactly what they should do, which is probably nothing. *Just lay low* he would say. *There's nothing to worry about.* He would call her *Jenny girl* and hand her a beer and a joint or whatever he could get his hands on and everything would be right with the world. Their world. She can hear him now, his laugh, his calm voice. *Just relax. Lay low.* They could go back to Ray's. She liked that house.

If he were here he would be as surprised as she is that they dug this up after all this time, that they have Margaret's face on the television, but he wouldn't panic. *It's about time* he would say. And he would laugh. *Took them long enough.* Then he would figure some angle, some plan to get something out of this. He would think they deserved something for taking care of Margaret all these years, and he would probably not think twice about giving her back if they were willing to pay. She looks over at Margaret, staring down at her feet, still lost in her own thoughts.

"You're awful quiet."

Margaret looks up. "Did you see that girl on television?"

"Just for a second. I'm sure she's fine. What do you want for supper?" All of a sudden she is starving.

217

Margaret shrugs. "I don't know. It's weird. I thought she looked just like me. Don't you think that girl looked like me?"

Jenny slows down a little and turns to her, then stops and forces a laugh. "Do I think she looked like you? I wasn't paying that much attention." Margaret's face is so serious, so concerned. "I don't know. Maybe a little, okay? So what? They can do anything they want with computers. It's not real. You know that."

Margaret stares at her but it doesn't seem like she is listening. Jenny stops and puts her hands on Margaret's shoulders, looks her in the eye. "What? You see a picture of some girl on television and all of a sudden you think you're some orphan? You think you're someone else and I'm not your mother?" Jenny steps away and turns around, starts walking again.

"No." She doesn't sound so sure. "I didn't say that. That's not even what I was thinking."

Jenny stops again, touches Margaret's hair, that sorry looking hair, and makes herself smile. "Did you have a good time today? Did you have a good birthday? I can't believe you're fifteen. Are you hungry? I'm starved. Let's stop at the store and get something for dinner."

She puts her hand on Margaret's arm and together they walk to the grocery store. She will get something good and they will watch television – not the news – and forget all about that girl. She's not that girl. She's her Meggie. "She probably doesn't even exist you know. They even admitted they made that picture with a computer. You know you can't believe what you see on television."

Margaret nods. "I know." She smiles but her eyes are still serious.

In a few days there will be some other big story on the news, and by the time Margaret goes back to school in a couple months it will be history again. No one cares and no one wants to get involved. Just act normal, act like it is nothing and it will all go away.

There are only a few people in the store, mostly women and kids who look like they had a busy weekend of family dinners and parties and sports. All the things normal people do. Now they are tired, in a hurry to get what they need and go home. Jenny pulls out a cart and they walk down the dairy aisle where she grabs a dozen eggs, a half-gallon of milk. She likes the music, *Hotel California*, and sings along. If Margaret asks for anything she will say yes, no matter what it is. "Why don't you go pick out some snacks and I'll catch up with you?"

"What do you want me to get?" Margaret asks.

"Whatever you want. It's your birthday." She is sick of being careful with money all the time. Not today. She thinks again of Gene, always the big shot spending money they didn't have.

Jenny walks over to the meat department, picks up a package of cut-up chicken, then pork chops, ribs, putting each one back before she comes to the steaks, the t-bones and filets and sirloins. She loves a good steak. Too bad they don't have a grill. She looks at the prices and shakes her head, wonders how they have the nerve to charge so much.

"Can I help you, ma'am?"

Jenny looks into the face of a man not much older than her. He has pale blue eyes and thin blonde hair and probably a wife and two kids and a nice house and a yard and a dog, all waiting for him at home where they can have all the steak they want because he has a good job and goes to work every day. She gives him a little smile, looks in his eyes and wonders if he cheats on his wife. "I'm not sure what I want."

He stands there for a minute, nods. "Well just ring the bell if you want something you don't see." He smiles and turns away, walks through a swinging door, and after a few more minutes Jenny walks back the way she came, chooses a package of chicken thighs, then finds Margaret in the produce section, looking at the grapes.

There is a package of potato chips in the cart and some chocolate chip cookies, both the store brand like they always get. "All set?"

"Can we get grapes?"

Jenny grabs a bag of green grapes and adds them to the cart, anxious now to get out of there. "All set?"

As they walk to the checkout the man from the meat counter and another man in a red coat stop them. "Excuse me, ma'am?" Red Coat says. He doesn't look as nice as the meat guy. He has short dark hair and even darker eyes that look right through her.

"Yes?" Jenny looks over at the meat guy who looks upset. At her?

"Leave the cart here and come with us please."

"What do you want?" She puts on her innocent face. Margaret looks at her, fear in her eyes. They are all looking at her, waiting. She holds the strap of her purse tighter as they wait.

Red Coat says, "I think you know exactly what we want, ma'am." The people in the checkout turn and stare at them as if they have a right to judge. Her heart is pounding and her face feels hot. She hasn't gotten caught in such a long time. If Margaret wasn't here she would run.

"We can do this quietly in the back or we can stay here. It's up to you." His voice is louder than it needs to be.

Margaret grabs Jenny's arm. "Mama?"

"Wait here. I'll be right back." She is so tired she is close to tears, which is a good thing. The meat guy stands next to Margaret while Jenny follows Red Coat to a door marked *Employees Only.*

Inside are two gray metal desks, file cabinets along the wall, stacks of folders and papers everywhere, three different bulletin boards overloaded with notices and schedules. A small television is attached to the wall in the corner like in a hospital. No windows. What a shitty place to work. "Let's not drag this out," he says. "Take the steaks out of your purse, then I'm calling the police. We take shoplifting very seriously."

Jenny blinks and tries to look confused and angry. "What are you talking about?"

"Okay, fine. Have it your way." He punches in a phone number he knows by heart. "Joe Sweeney, please."

"Okay, for Christ sake. Here." Jenny opens her purse and stops herself from hurling the steaks at this smug son of a bitch. "Here's your precious steak, okay?" She tosses the package of steaks onto his desk. "I'm going now. My daughter is waiting for me and is probably scared to death. It's her birthday. She just turned fifteen and all I wanted was to have a nice dinner for her." She looks into his eyes, gives him her best victim face. "My husband left us and took everything. I'm doing the best I can, but it's hard."

The tears are there now, right on cue. He still has the phone in his hand, but he has been looking at her and she knows she looks good. "Please don't call the police. At least do it for my daughter. I'm all she has." That's the truth.

"Is there someone you can call to come get her?"

"I just said there's no one. I'm it. I swear I've never done anything like this before in my life." *Come on you asshole. Give me a break.*

He stands there and watches her cry, makes her sweat it out for a minute, then his face relaxes a little and he almost smiles. "Hey, Joe. Good. Good. Sorry to bother you. Just had a misunderstanding. I know. I know. Yeah, you, too." He keeps his mean eyes on her the whole time he is talking. After he hangs up he picks up the steaks, examines them. Two nice filets. She doesn't even want them anymore.

"Let's go." He puts his hand on her arm as if she is going to make a run for it and they walk out together. Margaret and the meat guy are sitting on two plastic chairs outside the office, talking like they are old friends. Margaret is even smiling. No one gives a damn about what she is going through.

Red Coat's voice is mean. "You can leave. Take your daughter and don't ever come back in here. If I see you in my store again I will have you arrested." Jenny starts to say something, but as soon as she opens her mouth he says, "Go before I change my mind."

Margaret stands and the meat guy looks at her then at Jenny, shakes his head and walks away.

The day started out so good. Not just today but she had been on a good run, finally things turning around a little. A job she doesn't mind, checking people in, making appointments. She likes when people leave, feeling good about their new hairdos and colors. She might go lighter. And Michael has been showing interest lately, showing up in the back whenever she is there, leaning over her when she is using the computer. So what if he is her boss? It's not against the law. She has begun to believe she could actually have a life. And now she almost lost everything, just because she was trying to be a good mother and this guy wanted to be an asshole. He could have at least given her the steaks.

They walk silently and Jenny looks down at the sidewalk. She has nothing to say to Margaret, not right now, and Meggie being Meggie knows this and leaves her alone.

Jenny hasn't prayed in a long time, but finds herself asking Jesus for the impossible, that Gene sees the television show and comes back. Not the old Gene, though – a new and improved Gene, a responsible Gene who has missed them and wants to make it right. She imagines him at least getting in touch. Saving Margaret was the biggest thing in their lives. Having a child bonds two people forever. Now she can understand her parents staying together through everything. They had that unbreakable bond. Jenny gave them that. Why did they find it so easy to throw her away?

They stop at the corner, wait for a few cars to go by so they can cross. If he does see the story on the news, would he come back? He wouldn't let her go through this alone. They were in this together. What he should do is send tickets for them, one-way to California or Canada or wherever the hell he ended up.

Now she's being as stupid and naïve as Margaret. And she's assuming the worst, that the police are going to be pounding on the door, that they would somehow be able to track her down after all this time. Stupid. Stay calm. You have her birth certificate, courtesy of Sam. Hopefully it will hold up.

But it won't even come to that. Don't assume anything is going to happen; no one has any reason to question her or Margaret. She is worrying for nothing. If they couldn't put anything together twelve years ago; they sure as hell aren't going to figure it out now.

All they want is to blame someone so they do a story to get people all outraged for a little while about the system, but they never do anything about it. They get big ratings, then it dies down and the next crisis happens.

They go straight home. No more stores. She needs to think, needs to decide if she should do something or do nothing. Twelve years ago she was sure the police or the FBI would be at her door looking for Margaret, but they didn't know anything then and they don't know anything now. Should they move? They should have moved a long time ago when Gene wanted to go to California or Wyoming. Who knows? Maybe they would even be happy.

This is when she misses him, even after everything he did, even after he abandoned them like that. He would know what they should do and he would make her feel safe, at least for a little while. It was better than nothing.

"Why're you so quiet?" They are home now and neither has said a word. Margaret walks right past her toward the living room, so Jenny raises her voice a little. "Hey. I asked you a question." She doesn't mean to sound so bitchy.

Margaret turns to her. "I don't know why you have to do stuff like that." She looks Jenny in the eye then looks down at the floor.

It takes Jenny a few seconds to realize she is talking about the steaks. Even though she knows she was lucky they let her go, the guy was still an asshole.

Margaret should be able to see that. "Did it even cross your mind for one second that I might have done it for you?"

"How is it for me if you go to jail? What would I do?"

"I'm not going to jail for a piece of meat. They're not going to send me to jail for trying to feed my daughter."

Margaret frowns and turns away, drops herself onto the couch and picks up the remote.

That's all she needs right now, Margaret seeing that story again and being suspicious, or at least curious, asking a million questions. She is so sick and tired of always having to explain herself. "I don't need an attitude right now. Come help me make dinner." Margaret doesn't need to see her face again on television, doesn't need to hear their lies and start doubting herself, doubting who she is. She wouldn't understand. She would probably hate her. It's so easy to hate your life when you're fifteen.

"I'm not hungry."

"Well maybe I am." She opens the refrigerator, knowing already what's in there, or rather what's not. Just like old times. What she needs is a cold beer and a joint. It's been so long since she had any weed.

Why in hell did Margaret have to bring up Gene, so sure he was actually going to show up today? It would be just like him to walk right in, assuming he would get back their old life. That's what started ruining the day, all the talk about Gene. Now she pictures him opening the door, standing there with beer and pizza, acting like everything is fine. It's been a while since she missed him this bad, thanks to Margaret and her goddamn birthday.

Jenny takes out the cheese, bread and margarine and the last beer. She pulls out the frying pan, puts a scoop of margarine in the pan and turns the burner on low. "Shut off the television, Meggie. Come out here."

Margaret gives her a loud sigh, clicks off the television, stands in the doorway with her arms folded across her chest. She looks upset, as if she is the one who has a right to be.

"What's wrong with you? Are you mad at me because Gene isn't here? Are you blaming me for that?"

"It's not that. I wasn't even thinking about him. Anyway, he's not here because of you, not me. You're the one he left."

For the first time in a long time Jenny wants to slap her. "He's not here because he's a selfish bastard who only cares about himself. You don't remember him taking off for weeks at a time whenever he felt like it? Leaving us with no food, no money? Just me to take care of you?"

Jenny spreads margarine on the bread and sets it in the pan, then adds a slice of cheese on each one, then the other piece of bread. Her hands are shaking a little. "You watch the sandwiches. I'll be right back."

The store around the corner is closed, so she walks a little further to the 7-11. The teenager behind the counter glances at her then goes back to her phone. There are no other customers and the nearly empty place feels a little creepy. They couldn't pay her enough to work here at night. When she walks back into their apartment with beer and a cake and some candles, Margaret is standing at the stove, spatula in hand. There are two plates at the table, a napkin folded next to each one.

"I thought you didn't have any money." Margaret's voice is flat, still angry underneath.

"I have plastic. Since when do you think about money?"

Margaret laughs and slides the grilled cheeses onto the plates. It's almost a grownup laugh, something Jenny has never heard from her before. Gene laughed like that.

They eat their sandwiches and Jenny gives Margaret her own beer, in honor of her birthday. She will remember how special Jenny made it and forget about everything else. And maybe it will put her to sleep before that show comes on.

"Can I stay up and watch that news show?"

"Since when do you watch the news?" Jenny looks at her closely, tries to get into her head. If she doesn't know now she will for sure when she watches the show. She's not old enough or ready to know the truth. Her sensitive girl.

"I want to see that story, about the kids."

"You don't need to watch stuff like that. It's depressing. These kids in foster care. No one cares about them. Unless they're really lucky, they end up in places worse than where they came from." Jenny knows this is true. Maybe Margaret would understand.

After her third beer, it hits Jenny that if Margaret is going to find out, she should be the one to tell her. She pictures the man from the bar, the one who turned around and stared at them when Margaret's face came onto the screen. It was funny seeing her little Meggie. She has no pictures from when she was that little.

Margaret shrugs. "It looks interesting. And I want to see who that girl was that looks like me."

Jenny lights a cigarette, blows smoke up towards the ceiling. "Is that all?" Maybe it is time Margaret knew the truth, coming from her, the real truth. That thought fills her, comes from somewhere in her soul, from Jesus or Mary, and she knows it is time, the perfect time. The only time. She opens another beer, picks up their plates, sets them in the sink then turns back to Margaret.

Margaret shrugs again. "I don't know. When I saw that girl I thought she looked like me. I know it sounds crazy, but did I have a twin? You can tell me." She looks at her hands as she talks.

"A twin?" Jenny laughs but stops when she sees how serious Margaret is, how upset. She never thought of a twin.

"Well she did look like me, right?"

"You don't have a twin. Where do you come up with this stuff? You think you have a twin and I lost her? You think I would put my own child in foster care?" Why does everyone think the worst about her?

"I was thinking maybe you had to give her up or something, that maybe you couldn't afford to keep two kids. That's what you and Gene fought about when you were having my brother, right? That you couldn't afford two kids?"

Where the hell did that come from? "Your brother? What brother?"

Margaret scrapes her chair back, puts her empty beer can on the counter. She turns and stands there, looking at Jenny. "My brother. The baby you gave away because we were so poor." She looks away now.

Jenny takes another drag of her cigarette, a swallow of beer. In all these years they have never talked about him and Margaret's words cut right into Jenny's heart. The day wasn't bad enough that they have to talk about this now, too. Jesus. "He's not in foster care." She stands up and rinses the plates in the sink, sets them in the strainer. "And I didn't sell him. He was adopted by a good family, a rich family who could give him all the things he deserves. He's almost seven now and I have to believe he is happier and healthier than he would ever be with us. That's it. I don't want to talk about it. I was hoping you'd forgotten all about it."

"How could I? He was my brother." Margaret's voice is shaky, but she goes on. "He was a person. I still can't believe you gave him to strangers. It seems so wrong."

Jenny takes a deep breath, tries to hold in the anger and sadness building up inside. "Don't you judge me. It was an adoption. We got money, but that wasn't the reason I did it. That was all Gene. Your wonderful, precious hero only wanted the money. I did it for the baby. And for you. Stupid me. I thought we would all have a chance for a better life."

"But he was my brother."

"And he was my son. And in case you don't know, it was the hardest thing, the most awful thing I've ever done in my life and I have to live with it every day. Now drop it, okay?"

Jenny picks up her beer, surprised it is empty, pulls another one from the fridge and sets it on the table, then gets the cake out of the box and starts shoving all twelve candles into the top. It is a pound cake and only now does she think of ice cream. She lights the candles and sets the cake down in front of Margaret, shuts off the overhead light. "Make a wish."

Margaret looks so sad as she closes her eyes for a second, then blows out all the candles.

"Let me guess. You wished Gene would just waltz through that door."

Jenny pulls out the candles, cuts a slice of cake for each of them and sets them on napkins. *Good old Gene will come back and save the day.* They eat their cake in shadows and silence, the light seeping in from the lamp in the living room just enough.

"No. I didn't."

"Good. Because he's not. Get it out of your head that he is ever coming back. He has a new life now with no room for us. "

"How do you know?"

"Because I know. It's been seven years. No one comes back after seven years and if he did he wouldn't be welcome here. You can't just desert your family all that time and expect them to be waiting for you when you decide to come back."

There was a time she considered going back to her parents, even after what happened, even after what her mother said. Could she turn her and Margaret away if they just showed up on their doorstep with nowhere else to go?

But the more time that passes the more she knows it couldn't happen. Ever. Same with Gene. Too much time has gone by. Her parents used to talk about burning bridges. That's what she did and that's what Gene did and there is no going back for anyone.

"Why did I always call him Gene instead of dad?"

"Where the hell are all these questions coming from? He wanted you to call him Gene, that's all."

"But he was my father, right?"

Jenny shakes her head slowly. Her Meggie seems so grown up all of a sudden. Looking for answers she might not want to hear. "He was as close to a real father as you ever had."

"But what does that mean? He's not my real father, then, right? I'm fifteen. I should know who my real father is."

Such drama. Jesus. Jenny breaks off a square of cake and puts it in her mouth. It's dry. Ice cream would be good. "All I know is he loved you as much as he loved anyone. Anyway, you always had me, right? A little gratitude would be nice."

"So you're not gonna tell me? Does that mean you don't even know?"

Jenny drinks the rest of her beer, takes a last drag of her cigarette and drops it into the beer can. It's now or never. She takes a deep breath. "You know what? You're right. You should know. You're old enough to know where you came from. But I want you to remember I have always been the only mother you ever had, the only one who ever cared about you."

"I know."

"That show you want to see so bad? They're going to say someone kidnapped you. But I didn't. I saved you, and that's the truth. That's what really happened, but they don't know that so they make stuff up, make me sound evil instead of someone who saved a little girl from dying in the back seat of a car." It all comes out in a rush and Margaret stares at her, her mouth open a little, her eyes full of confusion and disbelief.

She sits down and puts her arms on the table, gives Jenny all her attention. "Why would anyone say you kidnapped me?"

"These people who think they know everything? They don't. No one knows what really happened except me and Gene and I'm telling you I saved you. I saw you in the back of that car, all alone. We found out later these foster parents had you and they never even reported you missing until more than a month later when the so-called social worker went to check on you. They wanted to keep getting the money. And they got it. They didn't even have you; we did. And they got paid." She shakes her head.

The more she tries to explain the more fear she sees in Margaret's eyes. She just stares at Jenny like she is a stranger. She has to understand. Jenny has to make her understand.

But Margaret shakes her head, looks confused. "What are you talking about? You're talking about me? You're saying I was in the back seat of a car and you kidnapped me?" Her voice is getting way too loud.

"Don't use that word. And keep your voice down, You would have died if I didn't save you. Do you understand that? If I left you in that car you would have died."

Margaret stares at her, tears quietly spilling out of her eyes.

Jenny lights a cigarette, takes a puff and blows it towards the ceiling. "You were just a tiny thing. Strapped into a car seat all alone in a hot car on a hot summer day. You could have died. You would have died. But I went right in and took you out and carried you down the street." She smiles at the memory, at her courage. "No one even looked for you. No one wanted you. It was the best thing that ever happened to you when Gene and I came along. You believe that, right? I'm the only one who wanted you. Now they just want to make up a news story with absolutely no facts."

"So you're telling me you took me out of a car and kept me, told me you were my mother?" She shakes her head and looks at Jenny in amazement. "How old was I?"

"You were about three. Not even." Jenny has an image of looking at the tag on her shirt. 3T. "Wait a second." She gets up and walks to her bedroom, comes out with a manila envelope. All the proof she needs. "Here, look at these and tell me I didn't do the right thing."

Margaret stares at the envelope. Her eyes are focused on it as Jenny opens it and takes out the newspaper clippings she has saved over the years, pushes them in front of her. Now Jenny is the one who watches. Margaret glances at them at first, scans the headlines Jenny knows by heart. *Infant found dead in vehicle; 9-month-old boy found dead; Mother charged in death of toddler; Toddler dies after being left in car.* Margaret looks up at her. "These aren't about me."

"No, but any one of them could have been you. You were lucky. These kids weren't so lucky. Look at the date on this one. Exactly a month from the day I saved you this little boy died because his own father left him in a hot car. If that's not a sign I did the right thing I don't know what is. I kept them just in case I had to prove to anyone that I saved your life, that I didn't do anything wrong."

Margaret starts reading one of the articles, the one about the little boy who died when his father forgot he was there and went in the house, remembering him about three hours later, when it was too late. Then the one about the mother who went to Foxwoods to gamble, leaving her daughter in the car for four hours, windows open just a crack, not enough when it gets over a hundred degrees in the car. And there is the father who forgot to drop his son off at child care and just went to work, found him dead at the end of the day.

Margaret swallows as she reads. The tears are gone. "So you're saying you found me in a car and took me so I wouldn't die? So I would be okay? But then when I was okay, why didn't you give me back or tell the police or something?"

233

"Are you serious? Give you back to who? The people who left you in the car? Why? So it could happen again?"

"But what about my real parents? They must have been worried. They must think I'm dead."

"Your *real* parents? What do you mean your *real* parents? What the hell am I? What have I been doing all these years? Being your mother, that's what. Your *real* mother." Jenny gets up and goes to the sink, turns on the water and rinses the sponge.

"But I mean my birth mother."

"Your birth mother didn't want you. Don't you get it? You were in foster care. Your so-called real mother either didn't want you or didn't take care of you so they took you away, put you in the system. You see how that was working out for you."

She sits back down, drinks her beer and glances at the clock. She's curious now about what they will say on this program, how they paint her. A villain of course. A kidnapper. A bad guy. Surely Margaret can't think that. She reaches out and puts her hand on Margaret's. She can't really blame her for being upset, but if she just thinks about it she will understand that Jenny saved her.

Margaret's face, her eyes, look about ten years older now, but her voice is so small. "Was there anything in the newspaper about me?"

Jenny shakes her head. "Not really. No. A little. But not much, and it wasn't even until months later. They didn't even report you missing until months later, and then most of the story was about how bad the foster care system was, how overworked they are and what a bad place it is. Same old story. Maybe we should watch that show tonight. You'll see."

"So they left me alone in a car. You saw me and you just took me? You took me out of a car, then you kept me and pretended I was your daughter? That's sick."

"Sick? You are my daughter. I raised you. For twelve years now. Don't you think I earned it? Being your mother?"

"Did you ever adopt me?"

She just doesn't get it. Jenny grabs another beer and a shot glass, pours some in the glass and puts it in front of Margaret. "Not legally. How could I? Do you know what they would do if they ever knew what really happened?"

Margaret stares at her, waiting. Still such a kid. Jenny remembers how much more mature she was when she was fifteen. The age she seduced her father. Jesus.

"Nothing would happen to the people who were supposed to take care of you. The people who were getting paid to take care of you. And me? I'd go to jail. For a really long time. You think that's what should happen? That's what they want. Whatever they have on this so-called news report is what someone made up to make a story. They don't know and they don't care about real people or what really happened and why, and they would never, ever admit it was the right thing to do."

Margaret is crying again and Jenny pushes the shot glass closer. "Have this. It will make you feel better. And then if you want, we can watch this show together. As long as you remember, they weren't there. I was. And if Gene was here he would tell you exactly the same thing I'm telling you."

"What, though? Tell me what happened."

"I told you. We were walking by this car. I could feel something was wrong so I looked inside. You were in the back, strapped into a car seat, sound asleep. It was really, really hot and all the windows were up. It must have been a hundred degrees in that car, but luckily it was unlocked. All I could think of was getting you out of there. I opened the car door and unbuckled you, held you in my arms and you didn't even wake up. I stood there for a few minutes, thinking someone would come. I looked around and there was no one. So I started walking with you. I thought it would help get you cooled off. Then Gene came and said we should bring you home and make sure you were okay, so that's what we did. We thought someone would be looking for you right away so we watched the news."

"Why didn't you call the police?"

"Because we couldn't. They would throw us in jail and throw you right back in the system. And next time you wouldn't be so lucky."

Margaret looks at the shot glass and picks it up, drinks down the beer, pushes her chair back and walks into the bathroom.

Jenny wishes she had gotten a bottle when she got the beer, just a little something to take the edge off. But the more she thinks about telling Margaret the truth, the better she feels. It was the right thing to do, and once it all sinks in Margaret will understand. How could she not understand that Jenny is her mother and did the best she could in a bad situation? She has taken care of her for all these years, done the best she could, and now she doesn't have that secret hanging over her head.

She finds herself smiling as she walks into the living room and sits on the couch, picks up the remote and turns on the television just as Margaret comes out of the bathroom and sits next to her.

Chapter 17

*L*ittle is known about Adeline Jenkins, and *even less is known about what happened the day she disappeared. Twelve years ago today. What we do know, however, is that little Adeline was an innocent victim. She began her life as the victim of unfit parents, then became the victim of a foster care system that was, and unfortunately still is, badly in need of improvement. And lastly, little Adeline Jenkins became the victim of unimaginable horror, being snatched from the backseat of a car by what police believe can only be a dangerous predator. Stay tuned for this provocative investigative report.*

Margaret leans in towards the screen and watches closely, trying to imagine, trying to remember something from when she was little. Something.

They said she had unfit parents. Her earliest memories are in the trailer, the fights, Gene leaving time after time and how empty and afraid she felt. And it seemed like she was always hungry. She and her mother barely got through each day when Gene was gone. He left such a hole in their lives. It felt like everything slowly fell apart, then he would appear again with food, filling the trailer with his stories and music, and it seemed like he put them back together again. *Where's my girls?* She would give anything right now for that to happen, for him to walk in and change everything. Would he be able to put things back together this time?

Her mother sits beside her watching, smoking and drinking probably her tenth beer. Margaret can feel the beer she drank and wonders if that is what's making her so sad.

"Oh for Christ sake," her mother says. "See? They think it can only be a predator. They only think the worst. It would never cross their mind that someone would actually be doing a good thing. Jesus. Talk about hype. Oh, the horror. The unimaginable horror. Is that what it's like living with me?" She laughs and Margaret wonders what is so funny about missing children, what is so funny about children put in foster care then disappearing. Or what could possibly be so funny about her life.

"It's not funny." Margaret says. She doesn't look at her mother. She can't. She's not even her mother. She is some random person who kidnapped her. No matter what she says, that's what she did. She had no right to just take her and keep her. People can't just take children like that.

Margaret feels the tears again, angry tears filling her eyes and spilling over and she doesn't care. If she could, she would go back and start this day all over again. No wonder she always felt different. She knew something wasn't right. She should have known her mother did something.

She flinches when her mother touches the back of her head, smooths her hair like she's a little kid. "I know you must be surprised. I know it's kind of a shock, but there's nothing to be upset about. You can see that, right?"

She put her arms around Margaret's shoulders, pulls her close. "I feel so much better now that you know the truth. It was awful keeping such a secret all this time." Margaret watches the commercial as her mother talks. Jewelry she will never have. Insurance. "We'll watch the show and you'll see how much better off you are than if I left you in that car. Okay?"

"I don't even know who I am." She still can't look at her. "Is that my real name? Adeline? Is that who I really am?"

Her mother's voice has that edge now, as if any of this is Margaret's fault, as if Margaret should just accept it all like it's nothing like she always has. "You know who you really are. And it's not that foster kid. You're my Meggie. I have been your mother for almost your whole life. I named you after my grandmother. I told you that, right?"

Margaret turns to her, not even sure what she feels beyond being angry, except she realizes that even though she wants to, she doesn't hate her. "You know what I mean. I mean *really*."

The show comes back on with the blonde woman who acts like she knows everything. *If you're just joining us, prepare to be shocked, and, hopefully, outraged, at what you are about to see.* The screen fills with pictures of children - babies and little kids, teenagers. They all have the same expressions, like they are lost, looking for someone to tell them where they belong. Someone to care about them and help them. The screen changes four times, the faces getting smaller and smaller as they add more and more until there must be over a hundred faces staring out from the television. *Every one of these children was entrusted to our country's child welfare system, and every one of these children is missing. Vanished. And virtually forgotten.*

239

Margaret watches closely as they talk about teenagers running away from foster homes only to be caught up in prostitution. They show babies and little kids missing for years, including the girl who is supposedly her, Adeline Jenkins. The name means nothing to her. If that was really her wouldn't she know? They show computer-enhanced pictures of what she would look like now, and there is the same picture she saw earlier. Margaret tries to put it together with her mother's story, like pieces of a puzzle. God.

They put a number across the bottom of the screen telling people to call if they recognize any of the faces they have seen or have any information that might help locate and possibly rescue these innocent victims. Margaret wonders if anyone will recognize her, any neighbors or anyone from school or the library. Or what about the guys from the grocery store today? And if someone did call and they came to investigate, what would happen to her? It seems impossible and awful that the police or some agency would come looking for her. And then what? Take her away and put her in a foster family?

"What if someone recognizes me?" Her mother is the one who should be nervous. "What if someone calls the police?"

"Who? No one is going to call the police. People around here mind their own business. And even if they did, I have your birth certificate that proves you're you."

"How can you have my birth certificate?" Maybe she actually did something right. Maybe it's not as crazy as she thinks.

Her mother laughs again. She looks like she is enjoying this. She goes to the kitchen and returns with the manila envelope and Margaret isn't sure what she is going to pull out of there now, but then she is handing her a birth certificate with her name on it and today's date 15 years ago. It says she was born at 5:13 a.m. There is her mother's name and Gene's name as the father. Lawrence General Hospital. It is signed by a doctor and there is a seal and everything. It looks real, but Margaret knows she can't be two different people. She hands it back to her mother. "Is this even real?"

Her mother takes it and holds it up, studies it and smiles. "Looks real to me."

The rest of the show is about other kids missing from foster care, older than Margaret though, who have run away from foster homes. They make it seem like foster care is the worst thing that can happen to someone, even worse than being homeless. Maybe her mother is right. Maybe she did save her. She wants to believe that.

When her mother turns off the television they stare at each other, both waiting for something – her mother for gratitude, maybe, and Margaret for the real truth, something that makes sense. She thinks about the newspaper articles about kids left in cars. She could have actually been one of those kids and in her mother's own perverted way she did something good. In her mind she saved her.

"I'm going to bed." Margaret feels more tired than she has ever been. Empty. She closes the door to her room gently behind her, pulls off her mother's tank top and her jeans and slips on a tee shirt, then lies down on her bed. Her stomach feels sick and the day feels like it was about a hundred hours long. It doesn't seem possible that it was only this morning she woke up all happy to be turning fifteen, and now she doesn't even know who she is. She isn't even sure if she's really that girl on television anymore. Just because she looks something like a computer picture doesn't mean it's her. Maybe her first idea was right, that she has a twin her mother gave away or sold.

It takes Margaret a long time to fall asleep, and when she wakes before it's even light, her dream is still vivid and real. She was in a bar with her mother. They sat at a table in the corner drinking tall glasses of beer that left white circles on the table. It was dark and smoky and Margaret's mother put a cigarette between her bright pink lips and lit it. Margaret tried to grab it, but her mother smiled and turned her head away, out of Margaret's reach. *Please don't smoke, mama. It's not good for you.*

Then Gene walked in, sat next to Margaret and lit a cigarette. His face was dirty and his clothes and the backs of his hands were speckled with baby blue paint. Margaret's mother gave him a half smile as she tapped the edge of her cigarette on the ashtray. *So you're working again.* Gene tossed a roll of cash onto the table and her mother picked it up, studied it and shoved it in her purse. Then they picked up their glasses and had a silent toast, smiled at each other as if Margaret wasn't there.

I wish you wouldn't smoke. Please stop.

They both looked at her at the same time and said, *You stop. Stop being such a baby*

They laughed and touched glasses again, finished their beer and got up, walked out holding hands, leaving Margaret sitting alone. The bartender, a big man wearing a dirty white apron, came over with a tray and picked up the empty glasses.

She lays there for a few minutes, looks at the clock on the table next to her bed and sees it is only 4:10. There's no way she can go back to sleep now. In all these years it is the first time she has had a dream about Gene, at least one she can remember.

Maybe it is a sign that he is coming back or that he's not coming back, or maybe it is a sign he is looking for them. He would give her the real story or just laugh and say there isn't any story.

She slips out of bed and stands at the window, stares down at the empty street and pictures Gene pulling up out front to take her away. If he did she would run down and get in and they would drive away together. It wouldn't matter where they went; anywhere else would be so much better than this.

She remembers him talking to her before he left, saying things she didn't understand then. About her mother saving her. Just what her mother said. Same words. Maybe everything she said really is true. If she heard it from Gene, though, she could accept it, plus he would tell her the whole truth about what happened.

In her heart she knows she is that girl. Adeline. Oh God. She just wants to know who she really is.

"Are you okay?" her mother asks. Margaret is sitting at the kitchen table eating a bowl of cereal. It is almost eight and her mother looks like she didn't sleep very well either.

"Did they ever say who I really was? I mean not my foster family but whoever gave me away? Do you know where I came from? Did they ever say who my biological parents were?" She is careful not to say "real" so her mother doesn't go ballistic again.

Her mother takes a mug from the shelf, fills it with coffee and adds sugar. Her voice is soft but mad. "Do you know what it means to be a foster child? It means whoever had you didn't want you. They either gave you away or you were taken away because of neglect or abuse. That's what it means when you're in the system. So why would you want to know who your *biological parents* were? You planning on having some kind of reunion or something? For Christ sake." She takes a sip of coffee. "Can we just drop it for now? I have a splitting headache and I have to get ready for work."

"I just want to know. You'd want to know if you were me."

"If I were you I'd be thankful. Why do you care who those people were? They were terrible people you're better off away from. Do you realize how lucky you are?" Her mother doesn't wait for an answer, but she picks up her coffee and walks into the bathroom and in a minute Margaret hears the shower. That's it. She's done. So typical. Make a mess, then act like it's nothing.

When her mother leaves for work she will go to the library and try to find out who she is. There might be someone out there looking for her. No wonder all her life she has felt like she didn't belong, like she was this stranger in her own skin. It makes a twisted kind of sense now.

Her mother comes back looking like she is going on a date instead of work. She has her hair twisted up in back and is wearing a new black jersey and a silver chain with a cross Margaret has never seen before. "I want you to stick around here today, okay? I think we should still stay out of sight for a while. Not that I'm afraid of someone recognizing you anymore. Now that you know the truth, if anyone says anything, which they won't, you can tell them they're crazy, that you're not that girl. You are who you are, right?"

Margaret laughs. "Wrong. I don't know who I am."

"What's that supposed to mean?" Her mother really doesn't get it. She stares at Margaret for a

244

minute, touches her face. "I never should have told you."

"Why did you?"

"Because of that stupid show. I got nervous when you saw that picture of yourself. I thought you knew or were at least suspicious. You should've seen the look on your face. I guess I just wanted you to hear it from me. Now I think it was a mistake. We could have just gone on forever the way things were. You didn't really need to know, did you?"

She takes a deep breath, sighs it out. "Well, what's done is done, right? Just remember I'm still your mother and I have taken care of you for almost your whole life. Can you do that?"

Margaret doesn't answer. She can't just forget everything her mother told her, forget she isn't really her mother.

"What? Doesn't that mean anything?"

"But I don't *belong* to you."

"Belong? No. You're right. You don't belong to me. You belong to the state. So if anyone finds out about who you were all those years ago they will want you back so they can put you back into their system and lose you again. Is that what you want?"

"I just want to know who I really am."

"I don't know how you could possibly find out, but I do know one thing for sure. If you tell anyone the truth two things will happen. I'll go to jail and you'll go back in the system and wind up in some foster home. That's what'll happen. Is that what you want?" She stares at Margaret, trying to get inside her head and figure out what she's thinking. "Don't do anything stupid. Promise me."

"I won't do anything stupid." *I'm not you.*

It takes Margaret about fifteen minutes to walk to the library, a cool stone building, a place she loves to be, though she would never admit that to anyone. She loves the books stacked on the shelves all in order, not messing with anyone, just waiting. If someone wants to look at them or borrow them for a while that's fine, then they will be returned and put right back where they belong. And if no one touches them or wants them for a week or a month or even years, that's okay, too. It doesn't matter. They have a place they belong.

"Hi Margaret." Mrs. Stewart is behind the counter, as always. Kids joke about her living there. She looks up from the open book in front of her, a thick, hard-cover that stays open by itself. Mrs. Stewart told her once how she loves reading about the church. It sounds boring to Margaret but she doesn't say so.

They are the only two people in there today, except for the guy with the thick glasses who reads his newspaper every morning by the window. He always wears jeans and a white shirt and never speaks to anyone. He makes Margaret think of Gene, maybe because he is a man alone, a silent man who only wants a peaceful life. Maybe he has a family he deserted, too, or they deserted him. It's possible he felt like he had no choice, either.

"How are you, dear?" Mrs. Stewart asks. "Any plans for the summer?"

If only she could tell her. *Yes, as a matter of fact I want to find out who I am and where I belong.* "I'm good. No. No plans. Just staying home. My mom has to work." She looks over towards the dark screens of the three computers lined up along the wall. "I have to do a project for school."

"Ah." She nods. "Let me know if you need any help, okay? Maybe you could even use an actual book. What's your project about?"

"I'm not sure yet. I mean it can be anything about my family. Thanks anyway, though."

"Well let me know." Mrs. Stewart goes back to her book and Margaret sits at one of the computers, ready to start searching. It's so strange to be looking for herself.

She takes a deep breath and types *Adeline Jenkins*. The name means nothing at all to her. Only news sites come up, the t.v. station that did the report last night. The pictures she already saw are on the screen. Then and now.

If Mrs. Stewart were to see her looking at this, would she know? Would she recognize her? Margaret is pretty sure she would. And what would she do? She clicks on another site, then another, all with the same information and the same bad things to say about the people who should have been watching out for the kids and how broken DCF is. It's like her birth parents never existed.

She deletes Adeline Jenkins and types in *foster children New Hampshire*, clicks on a few web sites that say just what her mother said, that most children in foster care are there because they were abused or neglected at home. Physical or emotional abuse. Neglect. Just like her mother said.

It says that some of them are able to reunite with their birth families after the parents get help, but everyone works together to make this happen. Obviously her birth parents didn't want to do this. Or maybe they did and just never got the chance because she was taken.

What if her birth parents are looking for her? What if they just needed a chance to learn how to be better parents? They could have been really young and didn't know how to take care of a baby. They could have just needed help. Or they could have been really horrible people who didn't want her and didn't take care of her. And the foster home they put her in obviously wasn't much better. But still, she can't help but wonder if someone is looking for her.

Margaret searches for sites that help people find who their birth parents are, but they all want so much information, information she doesn't have. One site says you have to be 21 or older, another one needs adoption records. They all assume you were adopted, not kidnapped and not in foster care.

Her mother's words come back to her, that if anyone found out the truth she would end up being arrested and Margaret would be put in a foster home. *The system,* she calls it. And as angry as she is at her mother right now, there's no way she could get her in trouble like that. Of course they would arrest her. She may be crazy but she has taken care of her since she was three and she is the only mother she has ever known.

Still, she can't get the idea out of her head that her birth mother might be out there somewhere and she might believe her daughter is dead. She might not recognize her if she gave her up when she was just a baby like her mother did with Margaret's baby brother. Or maybe she didn't want her and doesn't even care if she is dead or alive.

According to one web site there are about 50,000 children abducted every year, and now she knows she is one of them, and because of that she may never be one of those children who get reunited with her birth parents.

For more than an hour Margaret searches, finding nothing that even remotely helps her find the truth of who she is. As frustrating as it is, she also feels a connection to a lot of people now that she never even met, children who have been abandoned or are missing, even the children who have been abused. She finally feels part of a group, and not nearly as bad off as so many of those children.

The library has been quiet until a mother comes in with her two small children asking about Story Time. When Mrs. Stewart explains it is cancelled because of school summer vacation, the woman is upset, says the program is supposed to be for children who aren't even in school yet. The two little boys look about a year apart, definitely under five, and keep pulling at their mother, tugging at her shirt and saying they are hungry. Mrs. Stewart tells her where the children's section is, but the woman says to never mind and leaves. Margaret looks over at Mrs. Stewart, who rolls her eyes, shakes her head and smiles like she and Margaret are friends.

The man by the window is gone and it's time for Margaret to go, too. There are no answers on the computer, at least not yet. She picks up the notes she took, the hot line number for people with any information, phone numbers of agencies she will probably never call.

On her way home, Margaret finds herself glancing into the back seats of each car parked along the street, wondering what she would do if she saw a child alone. She crosses the street to the small parking lot in front of the bank and walks by the line of cars.

When she sees the top of a car seat in a red minivan she looks around, and when she doesn't see anyone she walks to the side of the car just to check, and is startled for a minute by the sight of a baby, then realizes it is just a doll. For that split second, though, her heart starts racing.

She turns as a woman and a little girl walk out of the bank, towards the minivan, holding hands. The girl has a lollipop in her mouth and the mother is telling her they have just one more errand then they will go home for lunch.

When the woman looks at her, Margaret smiles and walks away, her heart still beating fast. What was she going to do if that was a real baby? Was she going to take her? She doesn't really know, but for just a few seconds she could understand what her mother must have felt when she saw her in the back seat of that car all those years ago.

It is hard to imagine having the courage to do something like that, even if it felt right at the time. The courage to save a child even if it meant you would get in trouble.

When she comes to the Quik-Mart, she goes in to get something to drink. She takes her time choosing from the rows of soda and water and energy drinks, finally choosing a can of root beer.

There is a woman with a little girl ahead of her. She looks about five, a chubby little girl with black curls.

"Mommy can I have this?" She grabs a candy bar and holds it up.

The woman is choosing scratch tickets from the rolls behind the counter and barely looks at the girl. "Put it back."

"But mommy, can I please have it?"

The woman grabs the candy out of the girl's hand and puts it back. "You need to listen."

"But I want it." Now the girl starts crying, a whining, high-pitched cry. More like a scream.

Margaret is amazed how the woman is able to completely ignore the little girl as she buys forty dollars' worth of scratch tickets, two packs of cigarettes and two Red Bulls. She takes her change and drops it into her purse, grabs the girl's hand and pulls her out of the store, the little girl still crying and screaming *I want it.*

People like that should not have kids. At least she didn't hit her, but she is probably yelling at her now, maybe threatening what she will do if she doesn't stop crying. Or maybe she is just ignoring her some more, scratching her tickets and drinking her Red Bull. Whatever she is doing, it is child abuse. Neglect. Would that girl be better off in foster care, or would foster care be worse?

As Margaret walks home she thinks about children who are wanted and children who aren't, and she isn't quite sure which one she is. She's not sure about anything anymore, like if she had the chance to help a child, would she do it? And what's worse? Someone leaving her alone in a hot car or someone stealing her and lying to her all her life?

Chapter 18

"I told you what happened," Jenny says. "That's it. That's all there is." It's just after nine and she is not even close to being awake yet. Her head is pounding and right away Margaret starts in on her again about that day, as if she should remember every detail, as if she even wants to.

It has been almost a week since she told Margaret the truth. She has been so quiet Jenny thought she had accepted it, put it behind her. What else can she do? But she must have used every minute of that time to think up questions to torture her with. Jenny isn't in the mood for questions. It was a lifetime ago and she just wants to leave it in the past. If it wasn't for that goddamn so-called news show she wouldn't have told her in the first place.

"But didn't anyone even look for me? What about my parents? Not my foster parents, but the ones who gave me up? Do you know who they were?"

It's that whiny kid's voice Jenny hates. She doesn't need this, not today. Not any day, but especially not today. Yesterday was one of the worst days of her life and that's saying something considering all the shitty days she has had. Just one more in a long line of many. All she's been trying to do is make a life for herself and Margaret, and just when things were finally going her way it's all shot to hell.

If she had known Mike was married she probably wouldn't have bothered trying to start something with him. She rubs her face, pushes her hair back. How could she be so stupid?

"Jesus. Will you leave me alone about it? Let me at least have some coffee and wake up." Jenny takes her cup from the strainer, fills it halfway from the pot Margaret has made, looks in the cabinet for something. A little brandy or whiskey she knows isn't there. She slams the cabinet door, fills the rest of the cup with milk and three spoons of sugar and sits at the table. Margaret knows she's not a morning person, but she keeps it up anyway.

"Did you ever hear anything about my birth parents? I just want to know who they were and how I ended up in foster care."

"I have no idea, but it must have been pretty bad because they never said anything about whoever gave birth to you except they were unfit, which probably means you were taken away from them. They only talked about the foster parents who were supposed to be taking care of you and the social worker who was supposed to be checking on you. No one did what they were supposed to do and that was all they cared about on the news, who to point fingers at."

Jenny takes a sip of coffee, lights a cigarette. "Why? What difference does it make? You want to know where you come from? From a lousy foster home, that's where." She takes another sip of coffee, gets up and opens the cabinets again, as if something will magically appear. She pushes aside the saltines, the cans of soup. Tomato, cream of mushroom. Gene was always good for pulling out a bottle just when she needed it, but that's not going to happen.

She slams the cabinet door again, sits back down and picks up her cigarette. It was probably stupid to tell Margaret the truth, but there's no going back. She's a big girl and she just has to deal with it. She should be thanking her instead of harassing her.

Margaret sits across from her with a glass of orange juice. "Please. I just want to know where I came from. You'd want to know if you were me."

Sunlight pours into the kitchen. Way too bright. She should just go back to bed. It's not like she has a job to go to anymore.

How did he put it yesterday? *I think it would be better for everyone if you found another job. You understand.* No she doesn't goddamn understand. He's the one screwing around on his wife and she's the one who gets fired.

She looks at Margaret, this way-too sensitive girl, and for some reason Jenny's eyes fill with tears she has no control over. Everyone leaves her. So many years gone by, so many people gone and she can't get any of them back. It's just her and Margaret and now Margaret wants to leave her, too. It feels like it has always been just her and Margaret.

She wipes her face with her hands and stares at this girl she raised practically from a baby. She did all right. She did the best she could. "You were so tiny. All skin and bones, like a little bird." Margaret sighs and Jenny studies her face, the way her eyes search for answers as if Jenny has any.

"So you really don't know who my parents were or how I ended up in foster care? Do you know why they took me away?" Margaret sounds so tired, so worried, and there's nothing Jenny can do about it.

Jenny shakes her head. "I told you no. But there had to be a good reason, and you're better off than you would have been." She looks up at the clock. The shop opens in ten minutes. She can just hear those jealous bitches talking about her, saying she got just what she deserved. How could she not have known?

"If it was really bad, or if my parents died, they would have said that, right? That I was taken out of a bad home or something? Don't they usually have it on the news if it's really bad?"

"I don't know. How would I know? All they talked about was the foster family and all I know is it was a long time before there was anything on the news. We waited and it seemed crazy that no one reported you missing, until we found out you were a foster kid and the people who had you didn't report it because the checks would have stopped. Didn't I already tell you all this? Jesus."

Margaret stares at her, looking like she doesn't believe her, waiting for more. Always wanting more.

"So you just kept me." She makes it sound like Jenny did a horrible thing. It's so easy for her to judge.

"We waited to see who your family was." She drains her coffee cup. We waited to see if they'd offer a reward to get you back."

"So you only kept me for a reward?"

"Oh for Christ sake." Jenny gets up and refills her cup, opens the refrigerator. She's starving now. "Did you finish the bread?"

"Yesterday. So is that the only reason you kept me? For a reward?"

"I told you there was no reward. I didn't care about a reward anyway. It was all about saving you.

You needed me." She sits back, lights a cigarette and fills her lungs. "You would have died in that car."

"But you still didn't have to keep me. You could have still given me back."

Jenny shakes her head, stares at her, then takes a sip of coffee, a drag of her cigarette. "You need to listen. Then I don't want to talk about it again. There was no one to give you back to. No one looked for you. No one wanted you. The people who were being paid to take care of you didn't care. You were in a foster home with people only in it for the money."

Margaret stares at her like it's the first time she has heard this. Jenny puts her hand on Margaret's. "I'm not telling you this to hurt you but you need to listen. You want the truth? The people you were with didn't even tell anyone you were missing until three or four months later, and only because some social worker finally came by to check on you. By then it was too late for us to do anything but keep you. What else could we do? Who would believe we saved you and took care of you? Even now. If we contacted someone now to try and find out who your original family was they'd throw me in jail for kidnapping."

She can tell by the fear in Margaret's eyes, and what could even be love, that she doesn't want this to happen. Jenny isn't that worried anymore anyway. They have proof of who she is. They have her birth certificate and she has a social security number, all her school records. Jenny keeps all of it as proof. As far as anyone is concerned she is her Meggie and always has been, and every day that goes by the less worried she is.

"I just want to know where I come from." Margaret's voice is close to breaking.

"You come from a car outside a package store. That's where you were born." She gets up and opens the refrigerator, takes out the milk, smells it, then pours the rest of it into her coffee with a little more sugar. When she sits down across from Margaret again she leans forward. She has to make her understand. "I knew that day I was going to name you after my grandmother. She was the best person in my life. That should tell you something."

She is so sick of always having to explain every move she makes, every decision, every mistake. Margaret stares out the window and Jenny wishes she could get into her head. Or maybe not. She's fifteen, all full of drama and crazy thoughts. "Do you have such a bad life you'd rather have died in that car? Or you'd rather stay some foster kid all your life?"

"No." Her voice has always been so small. "I just want to know who I really am." Margaret looks Jenny in the eye now. "What if you call them? You don't have to tell them who you are or anything. Just say you saw the show and you can ask, *How did she end up in foster care, anyway? Who were her parents?* Maybe they'll tell you."

"Who?"

"That news lady."

Jenny shakes her head, drinks down the rest of her coffee and pushes her chair back. "I'm going to take a shower."

In the bathroom Jenny swallows three aspirin and two Xanax, cups water in her hand to wash them down, then steps into the steaming shower. At least this is taking her mind off Mike. Bastard.

She thinks of Margaret so tiny in the back of the van, Gene driving around, all three of them not sure what the hell was happening, like it was all happening to someone else and they were watching. Poor little thing, so scared at first. Using Gene's flag as a blanket. Whatever happened to that flag?

It's unbelievable that she actually pulled it off, took a kid, just picked her up and walked away with her, and after all these years no one has looked for her. Even that show wasn't about finding her or any of those kids and it wasn't about caring. It's all about ratings and it's all bullshit.

She's been caught for lifting makeup and candy bars and steak, but not for taking a person. Talk about a screwed-up world.

The air feels cool when she walks out of the bathroom, drying her hair with a hand towel and feeling almost human. Just get some food in her, then maybe a couple drinks. She deserves it after what she's been through.

Her stomach rumbles and Jenny tries to remember the last time she ate. Lunch yesterday. In the break room at work, eating a yogurt and looking through a magazine when Mike walked in and closed the door, sat in the chair next to her. She thought he was going to kiss her, put his hand up her dress, but instead of leaning into her he sat up straight and with a serious face he told her his wife had found out about them and he had to let her go, just like that. He said he had no choice. He didn't even seem all that upset. He expected her to just disappear like a mistake he could erase. She stared at the side of his face. He wouldn't even look at her. He sure liked to look at her before. But yesterday he was just anxious for her to leave.

She told him everyone had choices and walked out, her head high as she walked by all those bitches who must have known all along what was going on. It has to be one of them who told his wife.

She pulls the crackers out of the cabinet, thinks of heating up some soup but it's not what she wants. Margaret is in her room with the door open just a crack.

Jenny stands outside Margaret's room for a minute before she pushes the door open. "You want to go out and get a burger or something? Are you hungry?"

Margaret doesn't even look up from her book. "Aren't you going to work?"

"Not today."

Margaret stares at her now, waiting. She doesn't owe her an explanation, but it pours out of her anyway. "I got fired, okay? Apparently the boss's wife thought I was too pretty to be around her husband. He couldn't control himself."

Margaret shakes her head, always judging, as if she has a right.

"You want to go out for a burger or not?"

"I thought we were supposed to be hiding."

"Oh, so you're gonna pout now? You wanted to know what happened and I told you. Let's just drop it."

"You didn't tell me everything."

Jenny sighs. "I told you everything I know. I'm going to get dressed. We'll go get a burger. I don't know what else I can tell you. I don't know anything else." She walks away and Margaret calls after her.

"Can you just start at the very beginning and tell me all of it, like every single thing you remember from that day?"

Jenny sighs. "We'll go to Nick's." She is comfortable there. It's cheap and the beer is cold and everyone minds their own business.

It isn't until she is on her second beer that Margaret starts in again. "Can you start at the beginning and tell me the whole thing? Please?"

"I'll tell you everything I remember. But I swear this is the last time. If I tell you every single thing I remember, will you drop it?"

"I guess."

"Okay." She takes a long swallow of beer. "We had been up all night partying. We had breakfast in this diner and afterwards we were walking down the street minding our own business. I remember it was really, really hot." She takes a long swallow of beer. "We were having a great time, not a care in the world."

"But wait. Where were you?"

"We were living in Mass. A little town called Shirley. We had a really nice apartment, too."

"Did you see any street signs or anything when you found me?"

"Do you want me to tell you this or not?"

Margaret sighs and stares at her.

"We were just walking down the street minding our own business. Gene went in the store and I saw you in the car. I couldn't believe it. You were sound asleep, all alone in that car with all the windows up. Your face was all red and you were sweating. I don't know how long you were in there but I knew I had to get you out. Luckily the door was unlocked, and when I looked around there was no one, so I opened it and unbuckled you and you put your arms around my neck and I just started walking. I needed to get you away from there, so I just walked and walked with you in my arms. I remember you opened your eyes for just a second and smiled at me, not a bit scared. Then Gene was there and you didn't even wake up until we put you in the van." She can't believe she remembers all these details so clearly. She takes another swallow of beer, catches the eye of the waitress and nods. She really likes this place.

"I put my arms around your neck in my sleep? And smiled at you? What did I do when I woke up? Did I say anything?"

The waitress comes and sets down Jenny's mug, glances at Margaret's full glass of ginger ale and tells them their burgers will be right out.

Jenny smiles and thanks her, takes a sip of beer. Screw Mike. She doesn't need him. "When you woke up you were not happy. Gene wasn't so happy either when you started screaming. I guess you were scared. And you were really mad at me at first, like I had done something awful to you. I went back there and held you and tried to calm you down but you were screaming and you wanted someone. I remember being surprised you didn't want mommy or daddy. You were saying *me want Tommy.* I think it was Tommy.

Margaret's face lights up. "Tommy? Do you think he's my father?"

"I have no idea. Maybe you said Tony. Tommy or Tony, something like that. I know it was a guy's name. Or I guess Tony could be a girl's name now that I think about it. But I got the feeling you were talking about a man. Maybe it was the guy who left you alone in the car. Why you would want him I have no idea."

The waitress is there with their hamburgers and Jenny asks for another beer and another ginger ale for Margaret. "I remember how you didn't talk very good." She smiles at the memory. Maybe it is good to talk about this. "You know what you used to say? *My hungry* and *My want this, my want that.* We taught you to talk right."

Jenny squirts ketchup all over her fries, picks up her burger and takes a big bite. She watches Margaret stare at her burger, then up at her.

"So if there was a reward you would have given me back? For the money?"

Jenny shakes her head and swallows most of her food before she answers. "Maybe at first. When we first had you, I guess we might have. We figured you must belong to someone, that you must have a family. I was thinking whoever left you in that car would never do it again if they almost lost you and had to pay to get you back."

"But when you found out I didn't have a family, you guys wanted to keep me?"

"I did." She takes another bite of her burger, a small one. "Not Gene. He would have given you back in a heartbeat." It feels good to finally tell someone all this truth.

Margaret looks so sad now. "I really thought he loved me. It always felt like he did."

Jenny bites into a French fry. "Why? Because he brought you little presents? Jelly donuts and dolls and coloring books?"

"When he came home he always seemed really glad to see me."

"Well he's not coming home now." It's time she stops being so stupid and sentimental. She needs to grow up and face the truth. Margaret looks away and says something Jenny can't understand. "What?"

Margaret turns towards her now, so serious and sad. "I know he's not. When he left? That last time? I asked him if he was coming back. He said not to count on it."

"Well finally he was honest."

She thought Mike loved her, too. Even though he never said it. The way he looked at her, touched her hair or her hand when no one was looking. What a fool.

"We almost gave you back. Gene said we weren't ready for a family. I was, though. We were going to leave you at a church. What was the name of that church? Saint something. I liked that church. It was simple. We told you to stay there, but you followed us out and just as we were going to drive away there you were, running to me. I can still see you running out of that church, right into my arms."

Jenny smiles. It's a good memory, the way Margaret ran to her then picking her up and getting into the van, slamming the door shut so Gene would know she was serious without her saying anything, sitting there with Margaret on her lap, staring straight ahead and not saying anything even when he asked her what the hell she was doing. Finally he got it and drove away from the church to start their life together as a family.

Margaret stares at her like she isn't sure whether to believe her or not. She is trying to look inside her head, but only Gene could do that. She can stare all she wants and she can think whatever she wants. Same for Mike and his wife and those bitches at work.

Jenny stares right back at her. "So that's it. That's all I got. You know what? You might not believe this, but I have always felt like you were a gift from God. I know it seems crazy to you right now, but that's it. Life is crazy." She picks up the check, takes some crumpled bills from the side pocket of her purse and leaves a twenty and two fives. "Ready?"

On the way home they stop at the corner market and pick up milk, bread, juice, and a six-pack. Margaret is finally, thankfully, silent. She'll be okay.

She goes into her room as soon as they get home, and Jenny sits on the couch with a cold beer, flips though the channels. Baseball, golf, car racing, commercials, shopping. Jesus. She drinks down her beer, shuts off the television, and in a few minutes she is under a cool sheet in her bed.

As tired as she is, as drained and worn out as she feels, she doesn't go to sleep right away. She pictures Mike trying to explain to his wife that he is leaving her because he loves Jenny. She can't quite put a face on the wife yet but she knows she is fat and plain. He'll call. He'll call tomorrow and apologize, tell her he is sorry he hurt her and he is leaving his wife and wants her back.

She turns onto her side, facing the wall, and after a while she dozes in and out of a light sleep, a late afternoon sleep she has always liked, a sleep that doesn't completely take over but enough to take her out of herself for a while. Then she hears Margaret's voice.

"Mama?" It is so soft Jenny isn't sure if it's real or part of her sleep, then she hears it again. "Mama?"

Jenny lifts her head and turns around. "I'm awake. You okay?"

"Just tell me one thing. The truth. Did you want me? It's all I want to know."

Jenny turns onto her back, holds out her hand. Margaret isn't crying yet, but is right on the verge. Her fragile girl. "Come lay down with me, Meggie."

Margaret steps over to the bed and Jenny longs for that little girl, the five-year-old or the eight-year-old. The girl who knows her only as her mother. What is she now? She turns to face the wall again while Margaret lays down in back of her, her hand light on Jenny's shoulder.

"Did you hear what I said?" Margaret's voice is soft and afraid.

"Did I want you?"

"Did you?"

Jenny strokes her arm, her white skin, feels the heat from her body, the warm breath on her neck and the fear. "I didn't know what I wanted at first. It's not like I planned to become a mother like that. But when you ran to me from that church I knew for sure I wanted you more than anything and I knew it was the right thing. I think it was the first time someone really needed me. It was like you came straight from Jesus. Someday I'll tell you about seeing the face of Jesus the night before I found you."

Margaret slides her arm down to Jenny's waist, holds her tight, and they both fall into a sound sleep.

Chapter 19

Before she opens her eyes, before she is completely awake, Margaret knows she is not in her own room. She rubs her eyes and half sits, turns to look at her mother, lying on her back, her mouth open, snoring a little. It looks like she is in pain or having a bad dream; it's not a peaceful sleep. Even when she is sleeping she looks upset. Maybe she is thinking about the day she took her from that car.

All the details of their conversation rush in at once, the things her mother told her. She isn't sure if everything is true but she is sure of two things – that her mother isn't really her mother, and that she needs to know who she is, where she came from. It's not enough to know she was a foster child; she needs to know why and how. And it's not enough to know this woman might have saved her life and that she wanted her when no one else did. She needs to know who she really is. Right now she is nobody, just a girl pretending to be someone else. Pretending to be someone else's daughter.

She slides carefully off her mother's bed, walks over to her own room and shuts the door gently. Her bed is just the way she left it, she was in such a hurry to get answers.

She lies down on top of the messy cool sheets, closes her eyes and tries to remember something from her childhood, tries to go back as far as she can and remember some detail from before this life, but there isn't much.

There is really nothing before living in the trailer, country music on the radio, her mother and Gene fighting, Gene leaving. Then he would show up with food and money and promises. Big plans. Over and over again. Mostly she remembers always being afraid, but she's not sure exactly what she was afraid of. Everything. She remembers her mother being unhappy most of the time, and she remembers her mother being pregnant and happy, then quiet. She remembers her mother not talking for days and days, not one word.

And she remembers staying with Darlene when she went to have the baby, eating and waiting for them to come back. It wasn't as bad as she thought it would be, then they came back with no baby. That's something she will always remember, how sad she felt, how disappointed and devastated she was when she thought he had died. There has always been an ache inside for her little brother. Even though she knows now he wouldn't really be her brother, not by blood anyway but definitely by circumstances. They would have been so close. She isn't sure how, but she will find out who she is. If she could do that, maybe she could find her brother, too.

It's a few minutes after eight when Margaret walks into the empty kitchen. Her backpack is all set behind her door and when the bank opens at nine she will be there. She will start at the trailer park, the only place she has ever known as home. It is as good a place as any. If Darlene is still there she might know something, something her mother told her. It's amazing how few people she knows.

She makes a pot of coffee, pours some orange juice for herself and sits at the table reading the bus schedule she got at the library. It seemed like a sign that it was right there at the desk when she returned her books. She knows it by heart but studies it anyway.

At 8:30 her mother still isn't up and Margaret gets her notebook and a pen. This will be easier than telling her. She keeps it simple and signs *it Love, Meggie* so she will know she's not mad. It's hard to blame her too much.

"You're up early." Her mother has lines etched into the side of her face from sleeping on her side and her hair is tangled and dirty. She doesn't ask Margaret what she's doing or how she's doing, but just shuffles over to the counter as if she's an old lady, pulls down a cup and fills it halfway, then looks at Margaret who hasn't said anything. "You okay?"

"I couldn't sleep. I was trying to remember anything from when I was little, but all I really remember is when we lived in the trailer. I remember it was called The Pondview Trailer Park. Was that the first place we lived?"

"The first place that was ours. God how I hated that place."

"I didn't think it was that bad. Except I always wondered where the pond was."

Her mother lights a cigarette, picks something off her tongue, then takes a sip of coffee. "I guess I didn't mind it at first. At least it was our own place. We didn't own it, but still, it was better than an apartment with people over you and under you and walls like paper, smelling other people's cooking and having to be quiet all the time."

"It seems like the only person we knew was Darlene. Do you think Darlene still lives there?"

She laughs. "Darlene. Poor Darlene. I wouldn't doubt it."

"Did you ever keep in touch with her?"

Her mother shakes her head. "Burned that bridge a long time ago." She sits across from her with her coffee, reaches over and picks up Margaret's toast and takes a bite. "What are you doing today?"

It is amazing that she can just pretend to forget all about what happened, as if it doesn't make a bit of difference. Amazing she doesn't know how huge this is to Margaret, or maybe she does but she just wants to put it away and not deal with it.

Margaret folds the note, puts it on her lap. "I might go to the library later."

"Well I guess I need to look for another job. Some people have to work. Unless he calls and begs me to come back. I should sue him. I could sue him for sexual harassment, couldn't I? That would serve him right. He used me. Maybe I'll look into that. Do you think I should?"

Margaret shrugs. She doesn't even know what she's talking about, but it's always about her. Whatever is going on with her is always the most important thing. She stares at Margaret for a few seconds, smiles a sad smile and walks to the bathroom.

Margaret waits until she hears the shower before she takes out four pieces of bread, puts two of them into the toaster and makes a peanut butter sandwich with the other two. She will get a couple of bottles of water on her way to the bus. The trailer park isn't that far away, maybe an hour on the bus and then about a mile or so from there.

She has a memory of sitting in a diner with her mother and Gene when they left the trailer to start a new life. Their adventure.

She butters the toast and cuts it in half, puts it on a plate and tucks the note under the side. She won't come back until she knows who she is.

The bus is practically empty and Margaret takes a seat three rows from the back. She already feels like a runaway or a fugitive. Between her mother and that show that was on, she feels like she has to hide. She has no idea what her mother will do when she finds the note, what she will do when she doesn't come home. She is pretty sure she won't call the police, but she can never be sure what her mother will do. She will probably just wait. She's good at that, all those times they waited for Gene. And he never left a note.

Please don't look for me or call the police, she had written. *Please don't worry. I need to find out who I am.* She wanted to say more, thank her for everything, thank her for being her mother for so long, thank her for saving her, but thanking her just didn't seem right, or maybe it would sound too final and formal, like she was saying goodbye.

Margaret stares out the window for the whole ride, past houses with yards and decks, grills and swing sets and porches, plastic pools and flags and gardens. Will she have any of these things some day? People living their lives knowing who they are, how to act and exactly where they are meant to be. When she knows who she is, no matter what, it will change her life, fill in that part of her that has been missing all this time.

Even though she already printed directions from the internet, Margaret asks the man behind the counter how to get to the Pondview Trailer Park. It sounds so nice.

He looks closely at her then past her and Margaret realizes he is looking for an adult. She is so stupid.

"It's about a mile and a quarter down this road on the left. There's a big sign. You alone, miss?" he asks.

"My mom's in the bathroom. Thanks." Margaret looks around and heads for the restrooms until the woman behind her steps up to the counter asking how much it costs to Concord and Margaret walks out the door. It's overcast, threatening to rain, and Margaret just keeps going. With each step she tries not to think too much. Just go. And though she is scared, she also feels stronger the closer she gets.

"Help you?" The man sitting on a white plastic chair at the gate looks up from his magazine but doesn't stand when Margaret starts walking right past him. She doesn't remember a gate and she doesn't recognize the man.

"I'm just looking around." She hadn't expected anyone to stop her from going in.

"Sorry. This is private property. Tenants and guests only."

"I, um, oh. I thought. Do people still live here?"

He stands up now, smiles a suspicious smile and studies her. "You looking for someone?"

"Does Darlene still live here?" She doesn't even know her last name. *Please let her be here.*

He stares at her a minute, then he must decide she's harmless. "You a relative?"

"No." She almost tells him she used to live there, but stops herself. "I'm an old friend."

He laughs. "You don't look old enough to be too old a friend. You know where her place is then?"

"I haven't been here for a long time."

He looks suspicious again, then points to a path past a small cabin she doesn't remember either, but it looks like it has been there forever. "Down this way, right at the fork. Last one."

"Thank you." Margaret smiles and starts walking. She can't believe Darlene is still living there. Luck is with her. Or Jesus and Mary.

Once she turns at the fork she slows down and makes herself notice everything, tries to make herself remember. She thought she would know which one was theirs but now she's not sure. She stops and stares at a trailer with two folding chairs facing each other with a blue and white cooler between them. Everything looks so dirty and sad. She walks a little further to the last trailer.

There is a small ramp made of plywood leading to her door and Margaret wonders if she is in a wheelchair. She remembers Darlene leaning on her cane and how big she was.

The wood creaks when she steps up to the door and knocks. No answer. She waits, then knocks again and hears someone inside. Then the curtain on the door is pushed aside and there is Darlene staring out at her. At least she thinks it's Darlene. Her face isn't fat anymore, just loose skin and wrinkles, but the same dark eyes that look like marbles.

She looks annoyed, then recognizes Margaret and the door opens and Margaret can't believe how glad she is to see her.

"Hi Darlene."

"Margaret? Is it really you? Come on in here. Oh my God. What in the world are you doing here?

Come in. Close the door before the bugs come in. Did something happen? Is your mum okay?"

"I just came to visit. I wanted to talk to you." As soon as the door is closed and locked Darlene gives Margaret a hug and Margaret can't believe how much smaller she seems, how thin she feels. Margaret wouldn't have recognized Darlene if she had seen her on the street somewhere. She must have lost about a hundred pounds. Same frizzy hair, though, and they could be the same pink slippers. Instead of a cane she has a walker now. "Are you doing okay?"

Darlene waves her hand. "Fine." She turns the walker towards the couch and Margaret follows her. The television is on, a diaper commercial.

As Darlene settles in her chair, Margaret looks around. Everything seems pretty much the same but smaller. The same fan in the window, same couch, even the same afghan over the back. And the same metal cabinet in the space between the kitchen and living room. If she opened it, would it have the exact same food? The cupcakes and chips and donuts? All that food.

She sits on the couch and looks at Darlene, feels a little guilty she has never thought about visiting her before. She feels like she is eight years old again.

Darlene turns to her, raises her eyebrows and then just stares at her. "All right, let's have it. What really brings you here after all this time? It's not just a visit, right?"

Margaret smiles when she remembers how afraid of Darlene he was when she was a kid. "It is a visit. Kind of. I wasn't sure if you were still even here. I wanted to talk to you about something but I also wanted to visit you." She hadn't realized this until she said it.

Darlene shuts off the television. "That's just what your daddy said when he came to visit about a week ago. *Just visiting an old friend,* he said. As if we were ever friends. He never gave me the time of day except when he wanted me to watch you that time. He wanted to know if I knew where you were. He said he's been looking for you and your mum for about a year. Then he got down to why he really came; he needed money."

Margaret can't believe he is looking for them, that he has been looking for them for a long time. She thought by now he would have made another life somewhere. She always pictures him with other people – another wife, another family. A real family. She doesn't know why it makes her so happy to hear about him, to hear he was actually looking for them, but it does. "Was he okay? How did he look? What did he say?" *Did he ask about me?*

"He looked pretty rough. Ragged and desperate and messed up is how he looked. He had some story about how he had been trying to find work and finally found a good job. I think he said it was plumbing or drywall or something. Anyway, he said it didn't start for a week and asked could I lend him some money. He said he had no one else to turn to. Big sad story about someone stealing his wallet. Swore he would pay me back right away with his first pay check. He had the nerve to ask for three hundred dollars." She laughs, and her laugh turns into coughing.

Margaret fills a glass with water and hands it to her. "Did you give it to him?" What a stupid question.

Darlene sips her water, shakes her head. "No way. I told him I was a poor widow on welfare and food stamps. Where would he get the idea I had that kind of money?" He said anything I had would help. That's when I noticed how crazy and desperate his eyes were. I told him I had no money and then he asked me if I had any pain meds. He said he had hurt his back working on a roof and didn't have insurance, was in a lot of pain. Finally. he asked if I had a bottle." She takes another swallow of water, a deep breath. "He was looking around at everything but me and then he was starting to scare me. And I don't scare easy. I told him my physical therapist was coming any minute, an ex-marine, and that he probably wouldn't want to meet him." She finishes her water and smiles.

"So he left? Did he say anything else? Did he ask about me?"

"He said he was going to find you and your mum and make everything right." She takes another sip of water, takes a deep breath and stares at Margaret. "Wait a minute. Did he find you? He didn't send you here, did he?"

Margaret laughs. "I haven't seen him for seven years. And anyway, he's not my father."

"Says who?"

"My mother. Well, she's not actually my mother either, not my real mother." She takes the empty glass from Darlene and sets it on the counter, then returns to the couch and leans towards Darlene. "She told me everything."

She had practiced those words in her mind, hoping it would get Darlene to tell her whatever she knew, but as she looks in her eyes to see if she knows the truth, Darlene's face is blank and she waits for

Margaret to say more. "Did she ever tell you about me? About how she got me?"

"What do you mean 'got you'? You were adopted?" She sits back in her chair taking it in. She has the same small dark eyes that scared Margaret when she was little. "Pumpkin. You found out you're adopted and now you're upset about it?" Now Darlene laughs. "So that's why you're here. I can't believe she never told me. Let me tell you something. Your mum did the best she could and no one could be more of a real mother than her."

Margaret looks at her hands. "I know, but." She thinks about telling her; part of her wants so bad to tell her the whole story, but she's afraid. She realizes now just how afraid she is of anyone finding out, of even saying it out loud.

"There's no buts. You're lucky no matter what. Hey, I know this isn't the Ritz, but you could've had it a lot worse growing up. Lots of kids never get adopted, end up in foster care, bouncing from one place to another. Now I'm not saying foster care is as bad as people say; I know for a fact there's lots of good foster parents out there."

"I know I was in foster care before she and Gene got me. It's just." No one understands.

"Just what? She never seemed like anything but your real mother. That Gene, though. I was never crazy about him, tell you the truth. The way he treated you and your mum. The way he'd leave for weeks at a time, show up whenever he felt like it. He was a shit. Sorry to say, but he was."

"It's just that I need to know who I am, who my real parents were and why they gave me up. Wouldn't you want to know if you were me?" She hates to think of herself as a foster kid. That can't be all she is.

Darlene pulls herself up out of her chair, holds onto her walker and turns it towards the tiny kitchen, takes a few steps as she talks. "You want to know who you are? You are who you say you are. You think finding out who gave birth to you is going to make a difference?"

She stops and turns to Margaret. "Pumpkin, listen to me. Kids are in foster care for a reason, and it's not usually a good one. If I were you I'd leave it and be thankful you had a normal life."

Margaret picks at the green fabric of the couch and doesn't look up at Darlene. No one understands. "It isn't that I want to be someone else. I just want to know who my biological parents were and why they gave me up. I just want to know what happened, if maybe they had problems and had to give me up and now they could be looking for me. Maybe they want to meet me, too."

"I don't understand why people can't just accept what they have. People are always looking for more, always wanting what they don't have." She shakes her head. "You think long and hard about what I said before you go looking for answers you're better off not knowing. Hey, how would you like to make us a bite to eat, pumpkin? Like old times."

As Margaret cooks up a package of macaroni and cheese. she starts to relax. Being away from home, away from everything, helps her to think about what her mother told her and about what Darlene said. She asks Darlene questions about when she and her mother and Gene lived there, asked her again if there was anything she could remember her mother saying, and after a while she realizes Darlene doesn't know anything. No mention of where Margaret came from, no mention at all of Margaret being anyone but Jenny's daughter. *You are who you say you are.*

"She was always bragging about you, how smart you were. *My Meggie brought home all A's on her report card. My Meggie is such a good kid. It was always "my Meggie."* Hey, what about your little brother? You know, I never got to see him. He must be what? Eight? Nine?"

"Seven." Margaret puts two hot dogs in with the boiling macaroni, takes out two plates, forks and mustard, sets a slice of soft white bread on each plate. She shakes each hot dog before she places them in the middle of the bread, drains the pasta and adds the cheese powder, milk and butter, stirs it.

"I never got to see him, either. They gave him away. Actually, they sold him. To some rich family. They said it was a nice family with money who could give him a good life. The money was supposed to be for us to have a new start, but it didn't exactly work out." She spoons pasta on each plate. "You want to eat in there or out here?"

"Bring it out here, pumpkin. We'll watch the news. I'm sorry about your little brother. I'm sorry you never got to know him, but sometimes people have to make hard decisions. It must've about killed your mum."

Margaret nods. She will never forget how sad her mother was, how she seemed to get older overnight, and how Gene went through the money. "Me, too. Even though I was little it killed me, too."

"Well you gotta remember your mum did it out of love. You have to give her a lot of credit for that."

Margaret nods again, takes a bite of macaroni and focuses her attention on the television. "Can I stay with you for a couple of days?"

"Does your mum know where you are?"

Margaret hoped she wouldn't ask. "I didn't have anywhere else to go so I asked her if you were still here. She wasn't sure but I told her I was going to see. She knew I needed some time. Some space." It's not a total lie.

"As long as she knows where you are I'd be glad of the company. How old are you now?"

"Sixteen." She could be sixteen.

Darlene narrows her eyes, nods. "Okay."

They eat in front of the television, and when the news comes on, the top story is about a little boy who was a year old when he was taken from his foster home. It was his father who took him and now the boy is 13. A store clerk called it in and they found him. He took him from Florida to a little town in Kansas. The neighbors are stunned; they say he was a perfect father and neighbor who kept to himself. The father was arrested and the boy was taken into custody. Margaret puts her fork down and just stares at the screen. "What will happen to the boy?"

"Probably right back in the system til he's eighteen. Okay, now that's a perfect example. You think he's better off now that he knows who he is?" She turns the sound down when a car commercial comes on. "They should have just let him be."

Margaret sits silently, staring at the screen. Her mother was right. Everything her mother said was true. If she ever told anyone she would end up right back in the system, and the system sounds like a horrible place she doesn't want to be. Her mother might be crazy sometimes but she really did save her, and at least she has a home.

Darlene turns off the television. "Some kids never have a chance. You're damn lucky to have a mother who cares about you so much, whether you're her flesh and blood or not."

She wants so bad to tell Darlene the whole story, but she can't. And she wants to tell her mother something, too, but isn't sure what.

Margaret realizes how little she knows about Darlene, her family, or if she even has one. She doesn't remember anyone ever visiting Darlene, but today was the first time she said anything about being a widow. "Do you have any kids?"

"I had a son. Killed in Afghanistan, only 24. Stupid senseless war. Not even a war, but kids getting killed over there. Don't get me started on that. How about mixing me a cocktail? You remember how?"

Margaret makes Darlene a gin and tonic and they watch television without much conversation. A repeat of when she was seven or eight, a little girl who wanted her doll.

After Darlene shuffles off to bed, Margaret lies on the couch and closes her eyes. She doesn't know what she will do tomorrow. Her mother is probably going crazy by now, but she still can't just go home and forget about everything. She can't forget Jenny isn't her real mother or that there could be someone out there looking for her.

What Darlene told her made her feel a little better, but not enough to just forget everything and pretend she is someone she's not. If her parents are really horrible people, drug dealers or worse, or even if they are dead, at least she will know.

In the morning while Darlene is in the shower Margaret decides she has to do something. She can't just sit around and feel sorry for herself, and if she just goes home this will all be for nothing. She takes her notebook from her backpack and looks at the list of agencies and phone numbers. Department of Children and Families, Registry of Missing and Exploited Children, Child Protection Services, Child and Family Services, all the agencies that are supposed to keep children safe.

The last number is the hotline from the news story. It's an 800 number so it won't show up on Darlene's phone bill. Her hands are shaking as she picks up the phone, punches in the numbers and hears the ringing. It's a woman who answers and her voice sounds young.

"I saw that story, about the missing foster kids?"

"Could you tell me your name, please?"

She takes a deep breath. "I think I'm Adeline Jenkins"

After a pause, the woman says, "Okay, Adeline, can you tell me where you are? Is someone with you, honey? Are you okay?"

It's too strange being called Adeline. It's not who she is. "I'm fine. I just want to know who my biological parents are and why I was in foster care. Can you tell me that?" Margaret hears voices in the background, maybe tracing the call?

"Okay, honey. Do you know where you are?"

Margaret sighs. "I know where I am, and I'm fine. Can you please just tell me about my parents? That's all I want to know." She wonders how long it takes to trace a call.

There is silence for a few seconds. "Where are you, Adeline? Can you tell me where you are?"

Margaret hears the other voice in the background again and hangs up. Her hands are sweating and her heart is pounding so hard. She flinches when she hears Darlene's voice.

"Who were you talking to, pumpkin? Was that your mum?"

Margaret bursts into tears. They just explode out of her like they have been building up all her life.

What if they trace the call and find her and make her tell the truth and take her away? She pictures a huge room full of girls, beds lined up along the walls. And she pictures her mother behind bars.

"Hey now. What happened? Was that your mum? Come here." Darlene folds her arms around her and holds her and lets her cry.

After a minute Margaret takes a deep breath and pulls away. She did something stupid. Again. "I called someone to see if they could tell me who my biological parents were and why they gave me away. They wouldn't tell me anything but kept asking who I was and where I was and I hung up. Do you think they traced the call? I'm so stupid."

"You're not stupid. Who did you call? Why would they trace the call?" They sit on the couch facing each other. "Okay, now. Tell me the truth. What's going on?" She pulls two tissues from the box by the side of the couch and hands them to Margaret. "Something happen to your mum? Is that it?"

Margaret stares at her hands. "She told me something the other day. She said she took me from a car when I was little. She said I was left alone and that I would have died in that car if she didn't save me. She showed me stories of kids who died in hot cars." She looks up and Darlene's eyes are on her, full of concern and pity. Maybe she will understand.

They sit on the couch and Margaret tells her everything, thankful to have someone listen. "She kept me all this time and made me think I was someone else."

Darlene nods, then frowns. "She gave you a life, that's what she did."

"I know, but it just seems wrong to take someone like that, you know?" Margaret's tears are gone. Now that she has said it out loud, told someone, it doesn't feel so heavy anymore.

"I know how it seems. But I also learned a long time ago not to judge people. It's not up to me, or you, to say what's right or wrong. Sometimes people do things that seem wrong but it sounds to me your mum had good intentions. Who's to say where you'd be right now if she hadn't done what she did?"

"I know." She has thought of this over and over and there is nothing there but that huge room full of girls and all the beds. "I can't help it, though. I really want to know about my biological parents."

"Okay. I understand that. Do you think you would be able to wait until you're eighteen? What's that, two years?"

"Three actually. I think."

Darlene smiles. "Okay, three. In three years you'll be officially an adult and can find out whatever you want, and they'll have no say over you."

"Wait three years?"

"The other option is to go to them now and tell them who you are. They still probably wouldn't tell you anything, and you'll be taken away from your mum. Is that what you want? Is it worth it?"

Three years. She was three when her mother took her. What were those first three years like?

"Where's your mum now?"

"Home I guess." She pictures her with a beer and a cigarette in the chair by the window, waiting, angry and upset and alone.

"She's probably worried sick pumpkin. Don't you think?"

The tears are back now, just quietly leaking out of her eyes. She walks over to her backpack and pulls the bus schedule out of the front pocket.

Chapter 20

All Jenny needs are three things: cigarettes, aspirin and coffee. She keeps it in her head and she will be in and out of the store and home again, waiting for Margaret. Stay focused. She only drank five beers from the twelve-pack and feels fine.

The store is way too huge, too open. But it is close and it sells everything. She walks quickly down the wide aisle, avoiding eye contact with other customers, mostly women who don't care what they look like. A group of teenage boys walk towards her, laughing about something. She feels their eyes on her and walks a little more quickly, turns down the cosmetics aisle and pretends to study the lipstick.

A few aisles further she sees the sign for pain relievers. Right. She picks up the store brand of aspirin. Okay, cigarettes and coffee. In and out and she will pay for everything and go home and wait for Meggie. She will come home, or at least she will call. She won't find any answers out there, not any answers she is looking for anyway. If she wants to know who she really is all she has to do is come home and look in the mirror.

Any other person whose daughter ran away would call the police, but Jenny can't. She hears

Gene's voice from a lifetime ago. *Since when do we call the cops on people?* What would he do? Nothing, that's what. He would wait. Just like they waited for a reward for Margaret. Just like he waited for her to give birth to their son so he could sell him. And just like she and Margaret waited over and over again for him to come home. They were all so good at waiting. *She'll come back.* That's what he would say. *She'll come back.*

At least she left a note, as if telling Jenny not to worry would make everything okay. She is only fifteen and she is so naïve and where in the world would she go? She asked about Darlene, but there's no way she would go there. She never liked Darlene.

As she turns down one of the food aisles in search of coffee, she feels a tap on her shoulder. "Excuse me, ma'am?"

Jenny turns and looks up into the man's face but doesn't answer. He has bad skin and bad breath and is standing way too close.

"I need you to come with me." Jenny blinks and for just a half second she feels like she is in a dream. She hates those words. They never come from anyone she actually wants to go anywhere with.

He reaches for her elbow, but Jenny pulls back her arm and steps away before he can touch her. He thinks he has a right to touch her, to tell her what to do? She has the bottle of aspirin in her hand, and when she looks around she sees the coffee right there and pulls a jar from the shelf, holds it tight. All she needs now is cigarettes. She turns and walks towards the so-called courtesy booth for cigarettes and then she will be out of there.

"Ma'am. Stop. Security." His voice is loud now. He wants to make sure everyone in the store hears him.

Jenny stops and looks at his ugly face. "You're not serious. You think I'm going somewhere with you? Dream on. Jesus. You can't go anywhere without someone hitting on you." She looks around to see if anyone heard her, makes eye contact with an old man who quickly looks away.

"Security, ma'am. I need you to come with me." He taps his plastic badge that says *Tony, Security.* She takes a deep breath. He goes for her elbow again and Jenny jerks it away. What's with guys grabbing elbows?

"Stop calling me ma'am. What do you want?" There is a woman wearing pajama bottoms and a sweatshirt staring at them now and Jenny lowers her voice and tries to sound calm, reasonable. In control. "I'm walking up front right now to pay for these. And get cigarettes. Did you think I was stealing them? What's wrong with you?" Why does everything have to be so hard for her? Why does everyone think the worst? At least she's not out in her pajamas. She needs to get out of there but not without her stuff. Aspirin, coffee, cigarettes. That's all.

She turns again and walks towards the front and he puts his goddamn hand on her shoulder and stops her. A couple of teenagers in tight jeans stare at her from the end of the aisle, and a fat girl pushing a fat baby in a cart loaded with diapers and junk food turns the corner and just stands there staring at them.

"You stole a lipstick. I saw you put it in your pocket." Tony looks at her face, then down at her pocket with his beady eyes, so full of himself. "We take shoplifting very seriously here and we prosecute to the full extent of the law." He sounds like he's making a speech, trying to scare her and whoever else is listening, trying to humiliate her. Little shit.

Jenny is more angry than scared. This guy is a moron. Tony. Why is that name so familiar? She reaches into her pocket to show him it is empty and wraps her fingers around a lipstick. Shit.

She pulls it out, looks at it. "This? Is this what you're talking about? I don't know how it got there, okay? It must have fallen in when I was getting the aspirin. Here. Take it." She holds it out to him but he just looks at it and smiles.

"You need to come with me. I've already called the police. They'll be here any minute." There are more people watching now, just standing there staring at them like they have a right to judge her. Tony looks around and is starting to look more uncomfortable than Jenny, probably wondering what this will do to business, but still holding his ground as he grabs her arm.

When she tries to pull it away she drops the jar of coffee and it smashes on the ground and why does everything have to be so hard? He still grips her arm and something about the sound of the shattered glass makes her want to cry.

"I think it would be better if we handled this in the back. We can wait there for the police." He tries to pull her but she pulls back.

"You called the police for a goddamn two-dollar lipstick? I told you I don't know how it got there, and I'm trying to give it back to you. Take it." She looks around at the people, hoping someone will take her side but they all just stare. She holds out the lipstick but again Tony doesn't take it. He looks around at their audience like he wants to apologize for what's happening but still be the big man. Jenny opens her purse and pulls out three dollars, throws them in his face. "Here, okay? And you can keep your lousy lipstick, too."

She throws the lipstick and hits him in the forehead. "Let go of me!" She throws the aspirin but he ducks and it hits the sunscreen on the shelf behind him, knocking some of them over.

A policewoman appears out of nowhere and now even more people are watching. Where did they all come from? The fat girl with the fat baby takes out her cell phone and holds it up as if she has a right to record Jenny's private business. Jenny turns her back on all of them.

"Okay," the policewoman says. "What's going on?"

"Arrest her," Tony says, pointing at Jenny as if she is some dangerous criminal.

"Look, people, there's nothing to see here," the policewoman says. "Go on about your business. And put that phone away." She has a strong voice, a tough voice, a smoker's voice. She looks at Tony. "Why aren't we doing this in back?"

"Just arrest her. I told her to come in back but she refused." Tony voice is getting higher the more excited he gets. "I have her on video shoplifting. This is exactly why we put in more security cameras. I saw it as it happened."

He sounds so happy, so proud of himself. The highlight of his day, maybe his career. It makes Jenny think of Gene and cameras. Big Brother always watching. He would have scoped out exactly where the cameras were and stayed clear.

Jenny turns to the policewoman and tries to look as innocent as she can. She glances at her badge. Riley. Is that her first name or last? There are all kinds of things hanging from her belt – a police radio, handcuffs, a gun. Riley looks from her to Tony, clearly annoyed. "Let's go," she says. Tony leads the way, then Jenny follows. She feels all the eyes on her as they walk to the back of the store, where Tony opens a door that says *Employees Only*. Screw them. She can get out of this. She looks at the back of Tony's head, the greasy hair. What an asshole.

The three of them stand there and Tony is finally quiet. Riley turns to Jenny. "Okay. Let me see some i.d."

Jenny fishes her license out of her purse and hands it to her.

Riley studies it, looks at Jenny, back at the license, then hands it back to her. "Okay, what happened?"

Tony can't wait to tell her. "I told you she stole a lipstick. It's all on video. She took it right off the shelf and put it in her pocket with no intention of paying for it. When I confronted her she denied it at first, then she took it out of her pocket. She needs to be arrested." He stares at Jenny, narrows his eyes like he is trying hard to remember her. "It's probably not her first time, either. I've seen her in here before. And she also assaulted me. You saw it." Tony folds his arms in front of him and glares at Jenny like he has won something.

"You want to talk assault?" Jenny says. "Look at my arm where he grabbed me." She holds out her arm, the red marks still there from his grip. "He had no right to touch me." With any luck it will turn black and blue.

"She was trying to get away." Tony glances at her arm, then his eyes go back to Riley. He doesn't sound so sure of himself anymore. "I have every right to detain her, don't I?"

Riley turns to Jenny. "And what's your side?"

Before Jenny can say a word, Tony is whining again. "What do you mean, *her side*? I told you exactly what happened. She doesn't have a side. She stole something and now she needs to be arrested."

"Tony, you had your say and now you need to shut up." Riley's voice is calm enough, but she is clearly out of patience. "One more word and you're the one I arrest. Got it?"

Tony opens his mouth but doesn't say anything else. He and Riley both stare at Jenny, waiting for a good explanation.

Jenny wants to tell Riley about Margaret leaving, how she is only fifteen and has been gone for two days. She wants to tell her how everyone leaves her and she doesn't know why, how alone she is and that sometimes she does things like this when she is upset but she doesn't mean to and all she wanted were cigarettes, aspirin and coffee. What comes out is, "I'm sorry. I didn't mean to take it. I honestly don't know how it got in my pocket and when I found it there I tried to give it back to him. I even tried to pay for it but he wouldn't take it. Can I go, please? My daughter is waiting for me. I promise I'll never come back here again." This usually works. There are so many stores now she can never go in again.

Riley studies her, sighs. She wants to be done with this as much as Jenny. "Tony, did she return the merchandise?"

"She threw it at me and hit me in the head. That's assault, right? And she also threw a bottle of aspirin and a jar of coffee on the floor. She should pay for those, too."

"I tried to hand it to him but he wouldn't take it." Jenny keeps her voice calm, in control. It's almost over. "And I didn't throw the coffee; he made me drop it when he pulled my arm."

"Did she try to return the lipstick before she threw it at you?"

"Only after she got caught. She refused to come to the back room and she caused a huge scene, probably lost us customers. And who knows what else she took. If you take her to the police station they can search her, right? Let's go."

Riley sighs again, then turns back to Jenny. "Would you object to letting me look through your purse and emptying your pockets?"

Jenny hands over her purse, hoping there is nothing in there, pulls a used tissue out of her sweatshirt pocket and holds it up in front of Tony.

Riley seems satisfied as she hands Jenny's purse back to her. "Okay."

"But you're still going to take her in, right?" Tony glares at Jenny as he says this, then turns to Riley. "She's clearly intoxicated. Can't you take her in for that?"

"No, Tony. I don't take her in. What I can do is file a warrant and have her turn herself in. I don't have to do that, though. She has admitted she had a lipstick she didn't pay for. She has said she is sorry. We can have her fill out a form banning her from ever coming back here and that can be the end of the matter." She turns to Jenny now. "If you get caught on this property again it will be criminal trespassing. Do you understand?"

"Yes. Thank you." Tony glares at Riley, then at Jenny and back to Riley. His prisoner is slipping away and he isn't sure what he should do.

"Tony? You okay with this? I know you have those forms here. We'll have her fill one out and sign it and let that be the end of it."

They both look at Tony, the jerk who started all this, making her wait and sweat it out, making them both wait. Jenny isn't afraid anymore. "Come on, Tony, don't be such an asshole."

Tony's face changes from hurt little boy to angry man and he lifts himself up a little straighter. He stares at Jenny now and his thin lips make a little smile. "Actually, I do want to press charges. I want to file a complaint for shoplifting and also for assault. She needs to know there are consequences."

Riley sighs and nods and Jenny can tell she still doesn't want to file a warrant, doesn't want to make this into such a big deal. She probably has no choice now.

Tony walks over to a metal file cabinet and pulls out a form, slaps it down on the desk. "And you need to sign this, too."

Jenny turns to Riley "Do I have to?" She doesn't want to give Tony the satisfaction, but Riley just nods, tells her to read it and sign it and she can go.

"You're just going to let her leave?"

Riley ignores him, keeps her eyes on Jenny. "I'll be filing a warrant, and will call you and tell you when you need to turn yourself in. Let's go. I'll walk you out."

Jenny can't believe this is happening. Just when she thought things couldn't get any worse. They won't possibly put her in jail for a goddamn lipstick. But what a hassle it will be, going to court, and who knows what they will do. Probably make her pay a fine. All he had to do was take the money and she could be on her way home now with her cigarettes for tonight and coffee and aspirin for the morning.

When they are outside Riley stops, puts her hand on Jenny's arm, but gently.

"You didn't drive, did you?"

"I don't have a car. I'm not far from here."

"You want some advice? Stay put for the night. You've obviously had quite a bit to drink and you seem like you're looking for trouble. You want a ride?"

"I'm not far. And I'm not looking for trouble. Why does everyone blame me for everything? I'm stopping for cigarettes and then I'm going home. It's all I wanted to do in the first place."

"Do you have anyone at home?"

"No."

"Didn't you say you had a daughter?"

"I do have a daughter." After all the lies it feels good to say something so true.

"How old is she? Is she home?"

"Fifteen. But she's not home." She shouldn't be talking about Margaret to the police, shouldn't have told her Margaret's real age.

"Let's call her."

"She doesn't have a phone. Anyway, she's with her father for a few days and I wouldn't call her there."

Riley stares at her for a minute and seems to understand. "Okay, listen, I don't know if you've ever tried AA, but there's a meeting at St. Pat's, in the basement, at midnight." She turns to her left and looks down the street and Jenny can just make out the white steeple. "And there's another one at six tomorrow morning. It might be good to check it out. It's totally up to you, but it will look good when you go before the judge. I've seen it make a huge difference. The judge could order you to get counseling, but if he sees you're already seeking help the charges could be dropped. No guarantees, but I've seen it happen, depending who you get. I know how hard it can be to be a single mom, raising a kid on your own. But you're more in control than you think. You have choices, and one of them is to get some help."

Jenny hates when people say they know how you feel and what you should do, as if they have any idea what your life is like. "Thanks. I'll think about it." She has never felt so out of control in her life. Her fifteen-year-old daughter is gone and she is doing nothing about it and Riley is dead wrong. She has no choices.

Chapter 21

By ten-thirty the cigarettes are gone, the beer long gone, and Jenny is nowhere near sleep. What if Margaret is with the police right now, telling them what happened, trying to find answers? She wants all these goddamn answers but she is too fragile to handle them. You would think she'd be glad there are no secrets between them. She's the one who hates lies and everything is out there now. She could at least show a little gratitude. No one thanks her for anything.

She slips on her black sweatshirt, brushes her hair and teeth and puts on her darkest lipstick. When she steps outside she puts her hood up and starts walking. The night is cool and quiet; no traffic. Everyone home with their families and their nice cozy lives on this Sunday night. Her footsteps sound so lonely, and a little creepy. She walks quickly with her head down.

Riley said she was looking for trouble, but she doesn't have to look; it finds her easy enough. She just doesn't want to feel so damn alone.

A car speeds down the street, guitar filling her ears for a couple of seconds. Kids getting home late, reasons and excuses all ready if they need them, if anyone is waiting up. Her parents stopped waiting up when she was about fourteen.

She turns the corner and pulls open the door to Nick's.

There aren't many people there, not one familiar face, not even the guy behind the bar. He looks around forty, tired and quiet like he has had a long day and when he glances at her his eyes don't stay on her for long. Jenny pushes her hood back, runs her fingers through her hair

He walks over when she takes a seat at the bar, asks what he can get her and she orders a tall IPA. She feels a little better already.

As she sips her beer, Jenny glances at the other faces sitting around the bar. All men, probably here for the same reason, to not be alone. When her beer is almost gone she buys a pack of cigarettes from the machine by the door and steps outside. She stands there smoking and thinking about Margaret and prays to no one in particular anymore, hopes there is someone listening. *Please keep her safe and don't let her do anything stupid.*

After she finishes her cigarette she stays outside for a few minutes more, takes deep breaths. The fresh night air feels good, different than daytime, not pressing in so much.

When Jenny takes her seat at the bar again she has a fresh beer and a shot waiting for her. She looks around and sees it's from the guy furthest away at the other end of the bar, his back to the wall. He looks up and smiles, raises his shot glass. He has dark hair and a half-assed beard. "Cheers," he says. She raises her shot and when she says "cheers" it sounds sad and phony but it's the best she can do. Then of course the guy picks up his beer and cigarettes and takes a seat next to her. That didn't take long. Goddamn men think they buy you a drink and you owe them. A little company would be good, though, take her mind off things.

He puts his hand out and looks her in the eye. At least he doesn't look too drunk. "I'm John."

Sure you are. She gives him a smile she doesn't feel or want to give. "Meg."

"Meg," he repeats. "I like that. Well Meg, if you don't mind my saying, you look a little sad tonight."

Guys used to tell her she looked beautiful. She stares into his blue eyes and realizes she has nothing to say to him, nothing she wants to share with this stranger in a bar who thinks she is desperate because she is by herself. She shrugs and looks away, drinks some of her fresh beer. She will go home after this one, get some sleep. She tries a smile. "I'm fine. Thanks for the drinks."

He nods, then leans in closer, his beer breath warm on her cheek. "If you need a little something to get you through the night, let me know."

She looks at him, moves away a little and frowns like she doesn't know what he's talking about and says nothing. Does she look like a druggie? She hasn't done any of that shit for years. Mostly because she lost her source when they moved from the trailer. Her doctor.

She wouldn't mind something to take the edge off, though, depending on what he has. Just tonight she deserves something. She would have to use some of the rent money, but that would be like admitting Margaret isn't coming back. She is coming back and when she does Jenny has to be here and everything will be the same except it won't because Margaret knows the truth now. It could mean she lost her forever or it could make them closer. She has to realize she is who she is, who she has been for most of her life, her daughter, named after her grandmother. She is who she was meant to be all along.

"Another shot?" he says.

"I'm all set."

He waits just a few seconds to see if she changes her mind, then he shrugs and smiles, picks up his beer and goes back to where he was sitting. That was all he wanted? To sell her drugs? The bartender says something to him and they both laugh. Jenny drinks down her beer, leaves a five and walks out without looking at anyone. Fuck them.

She jams her hands into her pockets and walks with her head up, filling her lungs with the night air. She takes in as much as she can and lets it out slowly, then turns as she sees a car coming up the street from behind her. Hopefully it's just someone coming home from a late shift, not someone looking for trouble.

The car slows down now and she wishes she had put her hood up so it wouldn't be so obvious she is a woman out alone. Just keep going. She picks up her pace, nearly running as the car pulls over close to the curb and keeps up with her. Her apartment isn't far now. Then she hears her name.

"Jenny? Is that you? Jenny girl?" She stops and turns to see Gene in the driver's seat, the window down and his arm out the window. He has a big high grin on his face and the way he looks at her is like they are meeting for the first time.

How could she be so excited to see him? After all the things he did. Her heart is pounding and she stands there, hands in her pockets. She doesn't smile back.

She needs a few minutes to think, but then he is out of the car and his arms are around her. She can't be imagining this. Even as they hold each other, as Jenny takes in the smell of grease and sweat, it can't be real. God she hasn't been held like this in such a long time.

Then she pushes away and stares at his face, so thin. He has a patchy beard and deep wrinkles around his eyes and mouth. He looks about fifty. His eyes are glassy as always but those eyes could always see right into her brain. She thought she would never see him again. "How did you find me?"

He laughs. "I've been looking for you. I knew you wouldn't go far from where we landed when the car broke down. You never did want to go far." He stares at her and she is frozen. "Thanks for leaving at least some forwarding addresses. You live around here now, huh?"

He looks around at the darkness, then his eyes are on her face and he puts one hand gently on her cheek as if he has any right to touch her. "I knew I'd find you. God you are so beautiful. How's Margaret?"

Jenny stares at him and listens to his drunk voice, pulls his hands from her face. He is a stranger now. "Why? You've been gone seven years and now all of a sudden you care? You didn't care about us all this time. So why now?"

Her eyes are watery but she won't cry. She wants him to say something that will make everything okay, make her believe in him again. "I don't have any money if that's what you came for." Money is all he ever wanted.

"I came for you. You know I always loved you. You and Margaret. You know that. I'm sorry I was gone so long, but now I'm back to take care of you. I have a line on a good job, a permanent job not far from here." His eyes look in every direction but hers. "So where is she?"

Jenny hears the desperation in his voice and takes a small step back. "What do you really want?"

Gene takes a step closer, touches her face again, the way she used to love. "I missed you." He leans in to kiss her. "I love you. You know that."

At the last second Jenny turns her face away. No way she's getting sucked in again. "Liar." She turns and starts walking.

"Wait. What?" He catches up to her, grabs her arm. "It's true. I missed my girls."

"You don't know what true is, and we're not your girls."

His laugh catches her by surprise. He doesn't seem so desperate when he laughs. "You haven't changed a bit, Jenny girl."

"You know what? Neither have you. Now go back to wherever you were all this time. I don't want anything to do with you."

"You don't mean that."

"Don't tell me what I mean. Go away and leave me alone." She pulls her arm free.

Come on, Jenny girl. Don't be mad. I missed you. I missed my girls. Have a drink with me." He leans in close just like the guy in the bar. I have some weed and a little coke. C'mon. Let's talk. C'mon," He has his arm around her shoulders now and is steering her towards his car.

"There's nothing to talk about." She shrugs away from him. "Just leave me alone."

She turns away again and starts walking, wanting so much for him to stop her, for him to be a different person, but it is silent, just her footsteps again. She slows down a little and turns to see him just standing there, leaning against his car with his head down like a lost little kid. She stops and he must feel her eyes on him because he looks up, looks so sad. She wonders how long he has been looking for her. They stare at each other for a couple seconds, then he straightens up and puts his hand out, whispers *Jenny Girl.*

She swallows and walks slowly back to him, takes his hand.

"That's my girl." He walks her over to the passenger side and pulls open the door. She hesitates for just a second before she slides in.

They both know there is nowhere open now to get a drink and he wants to go to her place of course, but Jenny feels the huge distance between them, all the time that has gone by, all the hurt and disappointment. It's all right there in the car with them.

"I don't have anything to drink at home and I don't want to go there. Why do you think I'm out now?"

"So tell me about Margaret. Where is she, anyway? She must be all grown up now. How's she doing?"

She stares at him, tries to see past his empty words to what his angle is. She surprises them both by laughing. He thinks she is the same stupid girl. "Didn't you say you had some coke?"

As he pulls the packet from his shirt pocket, takes a mirror and a little straw out of the glove compartment and sets it on the console between them, he tries to sound casual, like it's no big deal, tries to catch her off guard. "So I saw her on this news show a couple weeks ago. They're looking for her. Finally." He taps white powder on the mirror, cuts four lines with a credit card and snorts two of them.

"Who?"

"You know. The people who screwed up back then, the people in charge of foster kids." He hands her the straw and she snorts her lines while he keeps talking. This is why he wants Margaret, the only reason he ever wanted her.

"You didn't see it? You love watching stuff like that. Remember how she was in foster care and no one even looked for her? While we took care of her? Remember waiting to hear about a reward? And then we kept her. Do you ever think how messed up that was?"

She thinks of that day, getting into the van with Margaret holding her so tight, her arms wrapped around her neck, holding on to each other for dear life. It was just the two of them. The only two people in the world right then. She expected Gene to fight her on it, and back then he always got his way, but he just drove away and Margaret was theirs.

Gene turns and pulls a pint of rum from somewhere in the back, takes a swallow and hands it to Jenny. Good old Gene. This is one of the things she missed most about him. It was his way of taking care of her, the only way he was good at. It used to make her feel special and loved, how he always knew what she needed, but now she realizes it was nothing. Not love. Or caring. It was nothing, and it's still all he has to offer.

"I knew how much you wanted her. I knew you needed the company. I know it wasn't easy with me being gone looking for work all the time or on a job. I knew it would be good for you to have someone to take care of."

What a guy. It feels good to laugh at him for a change. Jenny takes another sip of rum, a small one, and hands him the bottle. "How about another line?" The coke is waking her up, helping her to think more clearly.

Gene smiles that smile she used to love so much, the smile that seemed to have so much behind it, but right now it makes him look phony and full of himself. For the first time ever she feels like she is using him for a change, if only for a little coke, a little rum.

He spills out a little more coke and his hands shake as he cuts it, so she reaches for the card and he lets her take it. She cuts herself one small line, snorts it while he talks.

"So anyway, that show. I'm surprised you didn't see it. There she was, just like that day we saw her on the news after waiting so long. Remember we couldn't figure out why no one was looking for her? They did this computer image of what she would look like now and even though I haven't seen her for a while I knew it was her. So I'm thinking, maybe there's some kind of reward now. Finally. We waited a long time for this. You sure you didn't see it?"

"I don't have a television."

"Where did you say she is, anyway?"

Jenny looks away, out the passenger window to a building in darkness, then turns back to him. "I don't have her anymore."

"What do you mean? Where is she?"

"Out in California I think, or Texas. I'm not sure. She's been gone three years now, living with a nice family."

He takes her face in his hands, not so gently this time, looks her in the eye. "No way. No way you'd let her go like that. Now you're the one who's a liar."

Jenny pulls his hands off her. "I'm telling you I don't have her anymore. I went through a really rough time and had no money. We were practically on the street, not that you care. I wanted her to have a better life, a life I could never give her. I did the best I could for as long as I could. I just couldn't do it anymore."

"Damn. So you just, what? Put her up for adoption?"

"Something like that."

"So you got money for her."

"It wasn't like that."

He slumps back in his seat, shakes his head. "I can't believe you got rid of her like that. I can't see you doing it."

"I couldn't see me selling my own baby, either, but I did, didn't I?"

"So how much did you get?"

"I got the satisfaction of giving her a better life."

"Right."

"You think people are going to pay for a teenager?" She laughs.

"If you could find out where she is we could get a reward. Can you find out? We can get the reward and then we can finally have a life. You and me. We can get set up somewhere just like we always talked about."

Jenny looks him in the eye and shakes her head, wonders how she ever loved him, believed in him. "I can't find out where she is, and even if I could, which I can't, I wouldn't. You want them to put her back in foster care? You actually think I would do that to my own child?"

He laughs, takes a swig of rum. "She's not *your child*. She's a kid you took from the back of a car."

She won't get into an argument with him and his twisted words, his twisted mind. She needs to get away from him. As she turns away and opens her door she says, "Have a nice life." It sounds like a line from a movie and it feels good to say it.

She gets out and he calls after her as she walks the opposite way from her apartment. The last thing she needs is him following her, finding out where she lives. When she looks up, there is the white steeple of St. Pat's, and she heads towards it.

He catches up to her and she sees the desperation in his eyes again as he grabs her arm. She is so sick of people grabbing her arm. "We can finally do the right thing, Jen. We can get her back to where she belongs and we can have our life back. Together. You and me. That's what you want, right?"

Jenny looks at his face, looks into those eyes she used to believe. For so long a life with him was all she wanted. She is so better off without him and without Mike and without her father, and all the men she thought she needed to make her whole, make her feel like she mattered. "Wrong."

Gene laughs again. It is a desperate laugh and she is done. He lets go of her arm and she walks away. He won't follow her into a church. When she turns for just a second, he is standing by his car, his arms crossed and his head down, but this time Jenny keeps walking, walking and remembering and remembering walking with Margaret in her arms. That was maybe the only other time she felt sure about what she was doing. Then and now. Keep going.

She slows down when she sees four women standing outside the door of the church, smoking and talking in low voices. Their backs are to her and when she is almost there they all turn around and one of them is Riley. She nods and smiles at Jenny. Before Jenny can say anything the women put out their cigarettes in a bucket full of sand and she follows them inside.

Acknowledgements

Thank you to my sons, Jason and Matthew, for all your technical and creative assistance with the cover. And to my daughters-in-law, Donna and Kerry, and my brothers, Dan, Joe and Rick, for all your support. Special thanks to Ruthanne McCarthy, Pat Egan, K.A. Lamond and Donna McMahon, for taking the time to read this story and for your thoughtful comments.

I am especially and forever grateful to my husband, Garry, for always believing in me, for understanding how special Margaret and Jenny became and for welcoming them into our life. And thank you for encouraging me so often to get up to the lake and write.

About the Author

Norma Murphy was born and raised in Lowell, Massachusetts, where she lives with her husband. They also have a home in Newbury, New Hampshire, where she does much of her writing. She was an educator for 18 years, the last eight of which included teaching the power and joy of writing to middle school students. This is her first novel.

Contact Information:

Email: normamurphywriter@gmail.com

Blog: norma-murphy.com

47959429R00176

Made in the USA
Middletown, DE
11 June 2019